CONTEMPORARY AMERICAN FICTION

REUBEN

With this new work, John Edgar Wideman further confirms his position as one of America's most important novelists. He is the author of six other books of highly acclaimed fiction including The Homewood Trilogy: *Damballah, Hiding Place,* and *Sent for You Yesterday,* the last of which won the PEN/Faulkner Award in 1984. His nonfiction work, *Brothers and Keepers* (available from Penguin), was nominated for the National Book Critics Circle Award. Mr. Wideman was professor of English at the University of Wyoming and is now at the University of Massachusetts in Amherst.

Reuben

JOHN EDGAR WIDEMAN

Penguin Books

To my sister, Tish,
and my brothers, Gene, Dave, Rob.
The circle is unbroken.

PENGUIN BOOKS
Published by the Penguin Group
Viking Penguin Inc., 40 West 23rd Street,
New York, New York 10010, U.S.A.
Penguin Books Ltd, 27 Wrights Lane,
London W8 5TZ, England
Penguin Books Australia Ltd, Ringwood,
Victoria, Australia
Penguin Books Canada Ltd, 2801 John Street,
Markham, Ontario, Canada L3R 1B4
Penguin Books (N.Z.) Ltd, 182–190 Wairau Road,
Auckland 10, New Zealand

Penguin Books Ltd, Registered Offices:
Harmondsworth, Middlesex, England

First published in the United States of America by
Henry Holt and Company, Inc., 1987
Reprinted by arrangement with Henry Holt and Company, Inc.
Published in Penguin Books 1988

1 3 5 7 9 10 8 6 4 2

Grateful acknowledgment is made for permission
to reprint portions of the following:
"Chain of Fools," written by Don Covay.
Copyright © 1966 by Pronto Music and Fourteenth Hour Music.
Used by permission. All rights reserved.
"Sent for You Yesterday," by Count Basie,
Jimmy Rushing, and Ed Durham.
Copyright © 1939 by WB Music Corp. (Renewed).
All rights reserved. Used by permission.

LIBRARY OF CONGRESS CATALOGING IN PUBLICATION DATA
Wideman, John Edgar.
Reuben/John Edgar Wideman.
p. cm. — (Contemporary American fiction)
ISBN 0 14 01.0595 6
I. Title. II. Series.
[PS3573.I26R4 1988]
813'.54—dc19   88–17457

Printed in the United States of America by
R. R. Donnelley & Sons Company, Harrisonburg, Virginia
Set in Sabon

Acknowledgments

Thanks to Robert Farris Thompson for Flash of Spirit *and its exposition of Kongo cosmology.*

Reuben

1
KWANSA

Reuben was a small man. His face was long and his hands long, but Reuben never grew taller than the average twelve-year-old boy. That long head atop a puny body, the way he carried one shoulder higher than the other, reminded people how close Reuben had come to being a hunchbacked dwarf. He wasn't built funny enough to be pitiable, but he wasn't put together quite right either. So you were careful when you spoke to him. Certain words you didn't want to say, certain lines you didn't want to cross. The pitiful thing Reuben wasn't was also what he almost was. Which made you careful. Made it hard to talk to him without your mind straying.

And if your mind did stray as you spoke to the little man you were liable not only to think of crippled-up hunchbacked dwarfs. Reuben's long bony face tapered to a point. From the splotched gray hair on his head to the splotched gray of his Vandyke beard, the face narrowed drastically, coming to a sharp point at his chin, a point, some said, sharp enough to bust balloons or prick your finger and that's why he wore a beard. To camouflage the deformity. And that's why it was a pointy beard, because the truth will out, no matter how hard you try to hide it. So you were liable to think about rats when you looked at Reuben's beady-eyed ratty face, just like you were subject to be reminded of a dwarf when you went to see Reuben.

Hard as it was to keep your mind on your business, if it came down to needing to see him, you would. Reuben helped people in trouble. People with pesky problems, people in big, bad trouble with the law. Nobody else in Homewood would do what Reuben would do for the little bit of money he charged. Reuben would take your troubles downtown. Peace bond, bail bond, divorce, drunk and disorderly, something somebody stole from you, somebody catching you stealing from them, child support, a will, a birth certificate, driver's license suspended or applied for, permits to tear down or build, papers to put people away or free them—for as long as anybody could remember Reuben had been performing these tricks for the poor and worse than poor in Homewood.

Kwansa had been seeing him her whole life. The small neat man in his three-piece suit with a gold chain draped from one vest pocket to another, a white handkerchief folded so it sprouted like a flower from the breast pocket of his suitcoat. Always decked out like that. Part of Homewood Avenue like the A&P's big window, the pillars of the bank, the music pounding from Dorsey's record store, the sweet burnt grease smell floating half a block on either side of Hot Sauce William's rib joint. Since she'd moved down off Bruston Hill to Kelly Street, she'd find herself walking Homewood Avenue much more often. It was like being a little girl again. Shopping again with her mother in the mysterious aisles of the grocery store, staring in the busy windows of Murphy's 5 & 10. Even though everything had changed, except the massive stone front of the bank, which had never belonged on Homewood Avenue anyway. For years she had managed not to acknowledge its presence. She can distinctly recall discovering the bank building one day, a little girl stepping into the shadow it spread across the pavement, a sudden chill as her eyes traveled up the stone columns to the tangle of naked figures carved in a triangular frame. Barred windows of an upper story trapped her gaze until she craned her neck further back and there was blue sky and scudding popcorn clouds above the somber gray mass. For a second the bank, darkly printed against the sky, seemed to be racing sideways, then as she slowly lowered her eyes from the roof line, the wall tilted toward her as if the whole crushing weight was about to come tumbling down.

Kwansa tried to keep her mind on her business. Unless Reuben could help her, they were going to take away her baby. She needed Reuben. This man whose enormous hands squeezed and pulled at each other on top of the table at which he sat. Hands that looked naked because the rest of him, even his face with its pencil-line moustache and pointy beard, was so dressed. Hands as bare and worried as she felt standing there, stooped over in the musty shell of the trailer she'd known all her life was Reuben's office.

She couldn't start to say what she needed to say because she didn't know his name. Reuben. That's Reuben sitting there in all this heat with a tie and jacket on. *Booker, you better get your behind over to see Reuben. Hey, I heard Hazel's in a trick even Reuben can't fix. Reuben's a dog. Least Reuben do for you when none the others will. Reuben got piles of money. Just too crazy to spend it. Reuben's crazy like a fox. Like a rat, you mean.*

All these years seeing Reuben, but she didn't know whether he was Mr. Reuben or Reuben something else. Whether his first or last name was Reuben because all she ever heard anybody say was the Reuben part. Maybe it was Reuben Reuben like in that nursery rhyme or song, whatever it was they used to sing in school.

Bad enough not knowing his name. The other thing she didn't know was how to address a lawyer. If she was coming to get the pain pulled out of her back, he'd be a doctor. Doctor whatever. She could say Doctor Reuben or just say Doctor and she could get on with telling him the part that was worse than not knowing his name. Worse than anything she could name.

3

Her dream of sweet little Cudjoe crying all night for his mama. The dream she couldn't shake. So real she keeps popping up from her bed and checking on him. And soon as she's sleep again the sound of him crying and coughing and choking on his tears. So she's up again. Checking again. Cudjoe pining away all night and not a damned thing she could do.

May I help you, young lady?

Yes . . . Yes, sir.

Please sit down.

Mr. Reuben . . . Mr. Sir, they trying to take my baby. They gon take him less I find a way to stop it. You got to help me, mister.

Reuben's tired eyes shut. Like he's turned her off. Or like he just clicked a shutter and snapped her picture. Beady eyes settled deep back, a million wrinkles away from the gaunt bones of his cheeks. Old-man eyes, gray she thinks, like the beard, or brown, brown like the hands that have forgotten about each other and rest at either end of the table, splay-fingered with knuckles like somebody tied sloppy knots in the finger bones. Or black like the blood rushing to her heart, the top of her head. She thinks the eyes must have changed colors while she watched, in the split second from shut to open, all the colors eyes could be, or ever were. Wet now, glistening and opaque, no color, just something wet swimming in red. She thinks he's spread his hands so he can lean on them and rise up from his seat. So he can holler at her and chase her away for calling him out his name.

Take your baby?

My little boy, Cudjoe. My son. . . .

The welfare people?

They ain't the ones start the whole mess. But they in it now. Now everybody lying. Talking bout I ain't fit. That rotten Waddell and the rest of em. Ain't doing nothing but trying to hurt me. Take my Cudjoe away.

I'll help you if I can. That's why I'm here. What's your name, miss?

Kwansa Parker. It's Lily Parker, really. But everybody know me call me Kwansa. That's the name I took. You know how

4

people be taking names these days. I took Kwansa cause it mean something good.

A celebration. A holiday.

Yeah, that's it. How you know that?

Hundred years on this corner. I should know a few things, don't you think, Miss Kwansa?

Yes, sir. I mean I'm sorry, Mr. Reuben. Mostly be young folks and kids into the African thing. And most them don't know the meaning behind nothing. Be doing it cause they see somebody else do it.

We've had African names before.

That's just why I called my son Cudjoe. He ain't never had no slave name.

Ironies abound, my child. Many a slave wore the name Cudjoe because that's what the slave master chose to call him. But that's neither here nor there, is it? Please sit down. Tell me your story.

Kwansa almost turns her head to find the person Reuben is talking to. It can't be her. She has no story. Her life is now. The pain sitting on her lap is her life. There's no room in the trailer for her head to turn around, let alone space for another person behind her. The walls, the low ceiling, squeeze her. The trailer is somebody else's rummage-sale clothes she must wear. Unwashed, funky. The little man hides his dirty socks in here. His nasty underwear and dirty shirts somewhere in heaps. Rusty slits for windows. Places where the wall coming apart, losing its stuffing like Cudjoe's old, split teddy bear. Kind of room you get in and don't want to put your hand on nothing, rub up against nothing. Piles of boxes. Yellow papers everywhere. A ratty kinda couch nobody would sit on less they's close to death.

From the outside, when you walk up Hamilton toward Homewood School, the raggedy trailer been there so long and weeds growing all around it you pay it no mind. Like tires and broken bottles and garbage people dump round there where the trailer sits. You could pass it for years but if somebody asked you what color is that old wreck of a trailer, what shape is it,

5

you'd shake your head. Don't ax me. Been sitting in that lot all these years but I'll be damned if I know. Then you think, Well what's it matter anyway. And who needs to know stuff like that about color or shape. It's just Reuben's place of business. Little and humpbacked like him. They say he used to draw it round behind his Buick. It go wherever he go. You need Reuben and here he come like a turtle or some damned something his whole house dragging behind him. On Saturdays he'd have that contraption parked up on Homewood Avenue. And people be in and out all day like ants after honey. Used to be a sign above the door. ATTORNEY-AT-LAW. Used to be a sight you could figure on seeing any Saturday you go up on the Avenue, but that been a while ago now. A good whiles. To see Reuben now you got to go to him. Trailer sits in that vacant lot behind Hamilton over near the school. Wonder is nobody run him away from there. I mean, you can't just plop no trailer anywheres you wants to now. Guess it's too old to bother with. Guess it look like it's just growing out the ground like the rest of the weeds over there. Naw, I ain't never heard nothing bout no color. Think it was blue last time I looked. Kinda sickish, peeling, light blue. They say one time under the moon it was blood red. They say it shivered like silver or gold when it stood Saturday afternoons up on Homewood Avenue. Course no police gon bother it. Reuben's the law, ain't he?

If Kwansa were on her feet, she'd shuffle her weight from one hip to the other. She'd sway back and forth and start her rhythm going and use her hands and that's how she'd tell her story. Dance it, sing it. Sitting on the funeral-parlor folding chair, the hard wood slats pinch her back, squeaking every time she thinks about drawing a breath. She presses her knees together and tries to hold herself still as stone. A calendar on one wall is soot-stained, faded, and she can barely read the year. Almost as old as she is. That paper been hanging there almost long as she been breathing. The thought makes her sigh. Inside the purple toreador pants her thighs are damp. Reuben is tilting back in his chair. Like he can hear her thinking and decides he'll also give a little thought to the idea passing through her mind.

He pulls that pointy beard, runs his fingers through the gray hairs, and strokes the pointy chin she cannot see. How old is anything? How long has she been sitting in this hard chair, squeezing herself tighter and tighter, like if she squeezed hard enough what needed to come out just might?

Her story. Her once-upon-a-time. Reuben asked her to tell it, didn't he? He wasn't laughing at her. He understood her name and tried to smile so she'd feel welcome.

Well, see. It ain't nothing to be shamed of, really. Waddell. He was nice. Started coming round to see me, you know. The first one, really. Like my grandmama, she always warned me. You know. Boys and what they after. So like, I knew. But I had to find out for myself. And Waddell seemed nice. Different. Wasn't always pestering me or nothing. Just coming round and being nice. Grandma didn't like nobody, but she didn't get way-out ugly with Waddell. Least he the only one she let sit around awhile before she chased him away. Kept on like that maybe six months or so, then one day his aunt ain't home, you know. Tipped over to where she live in the projects. What everybody else doing, so that was it. Waddell said he'd marry me and take care me. Maybe he did mean it, too. Maybe he believed that lie when he told it but ain't no take care of nothing in that dog.

By the time I finds out Cudjoe on the way, Waddell long gone. Then what I'm spozed to do? I'm keeping my baby, don't care what else happen. Gon have him and give em all the love I got. That's what I did, Mr. Reuben.

And now somebody's trying to take your child away.

Waddell think he something now. He was a sure enough nothing before. Dogging everybody around him. Come creeping back to me and Cudjoe cause nobody else want him around. On that dope, you know. Got hisself straightened out now. A new yellow wife. It's her and them sisters of his put Waddell up to this mess. Sisters never did like me. Said I was lowlife. Pulled Waddell down. They ain't the ones nursed that nigger. They ain't the one rocking his baby and stepping on the roaches and sick in the heart with worry. Is your daddy alive? Is he gon come in off the street alive tonight? Or tomorrow? Or next week? No.

7

They was high and mighty then and still high and mighty now. Didn't raise a finger to help they brother or me or Cudjoe. Now Waddell got something going, they done talked him into coming after Cudjoe. Yellow bitch of a wife probably too high and mighty to have one her ownself so they coming after mine. Trying to take mine.

How old is the child?

Four going on five in February.

And he's been with you the whole time?

That's right. I raised him my ownself. Ain't had a dime from Waddell or none the rest his family.

Then they don't have much of a case. You're the child's mother.

The chair has no arms but she needs to grab something. Her fingers clutch the raw wood frame beneath the slatted seat. The chair's flying through space and she can't let go. Tight as she holds herself, all her strength going now. She bites the skin inside her bottom lip trying to hold everything in, hold it tight. Warm blood seeps into her mouth. Holding everything in like she must with a man sometimes, a stranger when he eases over next to her stool and buys her a round, then even stranger as his stink and wetness and noise collide with hers. Sometimes as she feels her flesh slipping off with this man she doesn't know and couldn't care less about, she wants to strangle that foolish part of herself going on about its business as if nothing but its pleasure mattered, as if the man belonged right where he was. As her body sneaked away to do its thing she'd cry out *Stop . . . come back,* and pummel the stranger's back with her fists. Wanting herself back again. Fighting him for control. Losing as she twisted and punched and made him feel like God.

Yeah. Yeah. Yeah. He'd be whispering in her ear. It's good. Tell Papa it's good.

The strength would go out of her. She'd let it happen again. No longer caring where her body had gone. Wondering who was talking at her in the darkness. Who was all up in her face breathing his bad breath on her, who she'd be ignoring when

8

she turned her back and sat on the side of the bed and covered herself and felt the cold wetness, sticky between her thighs.

As long as she gritted her teeth, as long as she yelled stop and then said good-bye to her body when there was no stop to it, then she was not a whore. She did what she had to do. Nothing to be shamed of really cause that's what she had to do. Those few pennies don't make no difference. No better or worse than what other women got to do for they money. She wasn't selling pussy. It was hers. Always. Couldn't nobody take it and she couldn't give it away if she tried. Might get sick and have it sewed up, but what she did with men and what they gave to her was nobody's business. You lay down and do what you have to do. He rolls up off you and if he ain't no fool he know you can't live on air, your baby can't live on air, so if he be a decent man he leave something.

The dark ships move. The dark ships move.

At the Homewood branch of Carnegie Public Library they were saying poems. One about slavery days and slaves carried cross the ocean in sailing ships. Sharks eating the poor Africans they throwed overboard. Negro History Week. A celebration. But that poem was sad, sad. A boy in sunglasses saying it by heart. She'd been amazed he could remember all the words. Somebody said later he was blind. Blind as a bat behind those black glasses. Could have had seven books in front of him and wouldn't do him no good if he forgot the words. The dark ships move. The dark ships move. The strong backs of the men, their hunched shoulders as they covered her, driving their selves into her. They were dark ships. Dark ships and she was the storm, the wind beneath their wings, the sea rocking them, the shore they'd never reach.

Ms. Parker . . .

Kwansa grips the wood. The chair is not soaring through space any longer. Waves lift it, then cushion each slow descent. She is breathing again. Addressing the half a man behind the card table. She recognizes the table as the kind with legs that fold up. Her grandmama spread the Ouija board on a table just

like it. The old women would touch the board with their fingertips. Some had arms like toothpicks. Some had quivering meat,
drooping like loose brown hams off the bone. Only fingertips on
the edges of the board. With the power of their minds they'd
start the token sliding. When the chip danced answers to their
questions they'd get happy like in church. Squeal and holler and
shout. In their shapeless dresses and funny hats. Miss Clara
never took her hat off indoors or out. In winter they'd wobble in
like bears in their ancient fur coats, flip up the tails of their long
dresses, and toast their buns over the furnace grates.

What would a man like this dressed-up Mr. Reuben think of
those crazy old ladies and their magic Ouija board. One day
when she finally asks him he will say: It's as old as Egypt. Ouija
is our way of remembering the "Wedget," an eye, an all-seeing,
sacred eye of the god Horus, and old women in a circle with
their eyes closed are summoning its power. Giving up normal
vision for the Wedget's second sight. But she does not ask now.
She watches the board tremble, the chip spell out her son's
name.

Ms. Parker. Kwansa . . . how do they intend to prove you
unfit?

Lies. Nothing but barefaced lies. I'ma tell you up front, Mr.
Reuben. I ain't nobody's angel. Been out there in the street. And
guess who turned me out? Guess who learned me bout shooting
dope? Guess who took my money so's he could stay high? That
dog, Waddell. And now he's after my baby.

You're clean now?

Clean as a whistle, Mr. Reuben. Got Cudjoe to look after.
Got to stay straight for him. Still ain't no angel. But I ain't no
dope fiend nor no whore neither.

Then I believe I can help you.

Please, Mr. Reuben. I ain't got nothing but I'll do whatever
it takes to get you behind me. Ten dollars all I got now but I can
pay you something every week. Don't care what it cost. I'm
good for the money.

We'll talk about that later. We'll work out a mutually satis-
factory arrangement. First I need to know exactly what's going

on. Have any papers been served? Have you been contacted by anybody from welfare or downtown?

Yes, sir. Got the paper right here. Man from the sheriff's office came to my door. That's when I knew they was serious. Didn't pay no attention long as it was just them niggers talking, but this paper scared me. They can walk in your house anytime night or day. They can take what you got if they don't think you should have it. If Waddell and them got the man on their side, if the man believing their lies, I know I ain't got a chance.

You leave me those papers, please. And bring me anything else you've received pertaining to this matter. I'll check downtown. We'll get this straightened out.

You sure?

I promise to do my best. You are the child's mother. That still counts for a lot in these cases. Come back in a week. I should know how things stand by then.

They ain't gon come get Cudjoe?

No. They can't. Certain steps must be taken. Papers filed, judgments rendered, hearings. There's a process. A routine. There's always a procedure. One thing must be done after another in a certain order, a certain sequence. That's the law. The way it works. So we have time.

Kwansa . . . You can help by staying on your best behavior. Stick as close to home as you're able. Someone may be watching you, taking notes. And sooner or later you'll be getting a visit from a social worker. One morning when you're just rising out of bed and your hair's not combed and yesterday's dishes still in the sink and you'll have to say, Good morning. How nice to see you this morning and invite her in. Or at night. And maybe you're not alone or maybe you're undressed in your slippers and robe ready for bed. When you least expect it. So beware. Be ready.

His eyes are shut again. He has long lashes like she'd always wished for. They flutter as he talks. Girl lashes. You'd think he was far away dreaming his own dream, or listening to music like they do now with earphones on and you can't hear what they be listening to but they steady grooving on it and you talking to

11

them or a car blowing for them to get the fuck out the way but they in another world. You'd think he was sleep except the lashes fluttering and his long knobby-knuckled fingers make a steeple and wiggle like he's making the people inside the church. She strains to hear him. He whispers low like he don't want to wake his ownself up. When she stands and the chair squeals one last time like she's stepped on its tail and killed it, she misses part of what he's saying, leans closer to hear the rest. She's standing. Pauses another moment, unsure whether he's still talking or if he's humming now, a riff from one the old gospel songs like her grandmama used to murmur washing dishes or combing hair. Word or note, it doesn't matter because the old man is mumbling to himself or humming to himself and the droopy lids shut again like curtains.

Reuben's fingertips drum lightly, tap, tapping each other. The song's the one about the garden they sang at Miss Clara's funeral. Miss Clara looked like somebody else, like anybody but her ownself, her bald head on a silk pillow and no hat.

Kwansa blinked once in the aching light. Reuben's trailer was like being inside an old tin can. With the lid sealed and whatever's been packed in the can before still stinking it up. She blinked once as the lid opened and thought she'd walked into winter, into the snow-blind whiteness of that winter five years before when scared, sorry for herself, having no idea what to do about the child growing in her belly, she'd watched the bag lady Etta Thompson lay down in Susquehanna Street and cry till she was blue, blue and frozen as the walleyed cod on piles of ice in the fish store on Homewood Avenue. The same blink now as then because it was the same moment of surprise and almost laughter then as now, something twisting round Kwansa like a storm, but she is in the eye, untouched, seeing everything, not able to make sense of any of it—not fat blue-black Etta Thompson like a whale caterwauling in the public street nor the lump in her belly, nor five years later, the frozen streets, the light cutting through her like a razor when she steps down from Reuben's trailer.

She'd seen better. She sure to God had seen worse and in her heart of hearts no more room for surprise or pity or being kicked in the ass unexpectedly because she always expected the kick, her ass was a hump of scar tissue so tough now somebody'd need to tell her she'd been kicked before she'd holler. No, it was no big thing then, watching that trampy ragpicker finally lose her mind on the pavement, or now coming out Reuben's in summer and finding snow covering everything. No. What struck her was the littleness. What chilled her was the stinginess of her reaction, the little so-what blink, her eye falling like a guillotine on the neck of the world, her shameful little nod to her ownself like the nod she'd sneak to Toodles when one the niggers at the bar acting cute and think he's cute, God's gift to women, a secret, nasty nod because after all everything stayed the way it's always been.

But the baby, her Cudjoe, made a difference, didn't he? That's why she was here. Why she'd begged Reuben to help. Her son had saved her. He was her mirror, she could find herself in his eyes, laugh because he laughed, cry when he cried. Touching him, touch lived again. When he slept, she could dream.

She let one foot follow the other down the pavement. Spots of mica blazed. Where was the ice, the sleet, the snow? You never knew what was coming next. Even if you'd seen it all before. Even if it had hurt you a million times before.

Reuben studied the document, committing names and dates to memory. On a sheet of lined, yellow paper, below his client's name, the date, he copied other names and dates from the official paper. For his records such as they were. For the time he'd need to recall the facts, the time when, more likely than not, he wouldn't remember the names and dates staring back at him now. Not that he'd forget. The prodigious well into which he dropped everything he needed to know was still unmuddied. He could still hear the little splash when some new piece of information entered the cold, clear pool in the shaft's gut. He could feel the subtle disturbance, the ripples expanding outward, the illusion of light as deep in the well a black shimmer cut across the blacker surface. Everything was down there. But he was losing his ability to get at what he wanted, when he wanted it. He dreaded those instants when the immense reservoir of all he'd absorbed twisted in the air, a mirage teasing a man dying of thirst. Then suddenly, unexpectedly, the flood gates would open. He'd be swept up, lost. A day twenty years before would reveal itself to him, demand all his attention. He'd walk down Homewood Avenue talking to ghosts, oblivious to the folks he passed, the client at his desk waiting for a simple answer to a simple question. He wondered if people saw him when he was gone. If the blindness ever works both ways. Did he escape, could the circle be broken?

Reuben had once thought of his memory as a voice, a voice like God's, sure of itself, alone, unimpeachable. It spoke to him and he listened. Then for a time, as he examined his past, trying to capture and understand its meaning, the form of memory was conversation. Two, at most three or four earnest, compatible souls in compassionate dialogue. Lately, his memory had become more like those all-night, call-in, radio talk shows, an unpredictable mix of voices coming from everywhere and nowhere, voices with nothing in common but an 800 number that gave them access to a private space within him, the quiet that seemed like it might reign forever, till some prearranged signal opened the lines and the phones began to jingle. Crazy people howling at the moon, thoughtful shy ones who choose words carefully, smart alecks, mental defectives, know-it-alls, neurotics, bullshit artists—voices unspeakably lonely, voices full of themselves or full of that profound emptiness apparent only when people come together in numbers to quell it. From every nook and cranny of the country. Mountain people, ocean people, the slow drawl of plains people scrubbed clean of affect by ceaseless winds. Like the talk shows, if he paid attention night after night, his memories contained recurrent themes, characters who reappeared, suggesting continuity, narrative momentum, a haphazard semblance of plot. Yet no one was in charge. No host, no writer, no master of ceremonies. No shared notion of style or propriety among the callers. No censor at a control

14

panel quick enough to cut off obscenities, non sequiturs, death threats. Each voice was supreme, aggressive, irreconcilable. Reuben's memory of his past was just this bizarre, urgent competition for air time, disembodied souls calling in from the four corners of the universe.

Beneath the precisely inscribed names and dates he scribbled in a looser, sprawling hand the signature of Eadweard Muybridge. He'd never seen Muybridge's signature, but he knew it had to be ornate, full of flourishes, curlicues, a work of art not finished the first time through, but one of those patterns to which the writer returns, after lifting his pen from the page, compulsively adding a few more dots and lines to complete the design. An egomaniac if there ever was one. Eadweard Muybridge. Complicating his name with extra *e*'s and *a*'s because that's how he guessed Anglo-Saxon kings had spelled Edward. The egomania transferring to monomania in Muybridge's quest to capture motion in still photographs. "The great panorama of life is interesting because it moves." Muybridge hadn't written those words. Someone else did, and someone else had decided to use them as an epigraph in a brief biography of the photographer's life prefixed to a new edition of the 1887 text of *Animal Motion,* and the words fit Muybridge perfectly. Reuben could hear him saying them as Muybridge climbed stairs in a strip of twelve photos, each picture freezing a stage in the progress from bottom to top. In each frame a frizzy cloud of white hair, a full white beard, incongruously dark pubic hair and dangling member. The lean old man contributed these shots of his body to his monumental study of animal motion. Humility or exhibitionism? An "ex-athlete, aged about sixty" mounting stairs, sawing wood, lifting dumbbells for the camera, naked as the day he was born.

Reuben envied the man's sleek, vigorous physique. Maybe you got that way carting around the cumbersome baggage required to take pictures in those days. Climbing mountains, trekking across prairies and deserts with cameras and developing paraphernalia strapped to your back, loaded down like native bearers in jungle movies. You never knew whom you'd meet

15

next in Muybridge's folio. Black athletes posed for *Animal Motion*. One reminded Reuben of Jack Johnson with his shaved head and brutal muscularity. The last volume of *Animal Motion* contains "clinical" studies, patients from the Philadelphia Hospital whose various pathological gaits—locomotor ataxic, lateral sclerotic, spastic, epileptic, rachitic, hydrocephalic, stuporous melancholic, etc.—are preserved for posterity. In addition to these firsts, Muybridge also managed to capture on film a convulsive subject in the midst of her convulsions, standing, sitting, and lying down. With the threat and consolation of "there but for fortune" stewing in his inner ear, Reuben is simultaneously attracted and repulsed by nude portraits of victims of these disorders. All pictures in the book are black-and-white, since they predate the technology of color photography. Reuben wonders what shade of gray his brown body would have registered, what he'd look like without clothes climbing stairs with a Greek water jar balanced on the hump of his right shoulder. What caption would fit him. Would he exemplify a disease? Would Muybridge have recruited him? Would he have answered Muybridge's knock?

All motion a series of stills, succeeding one another fast enough to create the illusion of motion. The law was a series of steps. Each step depends on the one before it, as he'd assured the young woman in his office. The law created its particular fiction of motion, its metaphysical passage from disorder to equilibrium, unfair to fair, chaos to order, by establishing a series of steps—a due process. If those steps are followed, so the fiction goes, there is motion, progress, results can be reached, the world made a better place for litigants, for all of us.

Reuben knew he'd been on the job too long because he was having trouble extricating himself from individual frames. Each step would trap him. It took all the energy he possessed to rise from his chair, leave the interview with Ms. Parker, get on with her business and his. He was losing the knack of suspending his disbelief. Since he doubted he'd ever reach somewhere else, he preferred staying where he was.

So much to do. So much work in just a simple interview. He

16

should rush out into the street and call the young woman back. Admit his incompetence. His fear. They needed to start again. Go over familiar territory until it wasn't familiar anymore, till it was a starting place unlike anyplace either of them had been before. Unless they started fresh they'd be caught up in one fiction or another, and that fiction would carry them wherever it was going. And its destination would have nothing to do with where they needed to go. He should be out on Hamilton Avenue hollering her name, begging her to come back. Then they should sit and listen, learn the first words of the story they need to tell.

Reuben fingered the knot of the striped rag circling his neck. The space between each step in the sequence of steps required to lawfully kidnap this woman's child would give him time to subvert the intended motion. He must study each link of the chain. Like Muybridge with his stop-time frames of animal loco-motion, he must break down the process into discrete, manage-able units. Then he could prevent it, stop it from happening by creating a counterillusion. Law was detail work. Freezing things into unnatural frames. Forestalling an inevitable conclusion by the logic of another conclusion, just as inevitable if the dice are given a slightly different spin. A spin imperceptibly different, unless you get down to the level of minute detail, of shutter speeds calibrated in ten-thousandths of a second. Yes. Muybridge had proved his point about a galloping horse. All four hooves are airborne simultaneously. You move faster, you traverse the hard earth more efficiently by touching it not at all. You leave it behind you, beneath you, but you don't tell anyone, and no one knows unless they're willing to get down, down, down, stoop to the black-magic tricks you conjure to win the race.

There was a place once . . . and a time when the sun rose and night fell and not a soul alive to see any of it. No witnesses. No dreams to color it or sing it or mount it like you'd mount a winged horse and fly away home. The land was black and the sea blackly lapped it and the sky pressed a weary black breast

17

against the earth. Into this emptiness where there was no tree storing testimony, no road crossing, cracking the mirror, up through the infinite waters beneath it, from the invisible island of Guinee, the first and last breath rose from the dead.

This single finger of mist contained all life in itself as it shivered and twisted in the cold, the darkness; as it shrunk back into itself, wavering, guttering, the single strand became two, then three, then seven and finally was like the raffia skirts swaying on women's hips when they whip past, hurrying to the fields in planting season, tightly woven raffia baskets wrapped in both arms, full of seed.

Reuben had chosen the old Dogon sage Ogotemmeli's story as the best one. He'd start things that way. The mist, then women, then the word. The rustling of women's skirts gives a voice to the mist. The first cry, as it issued from beneath the raffia skirts, would recall the original sliver of mist, the terrible loneliness and fear of that first moment of life so close to death. The waters that brought us here. Waters to which we must return dance in the strands of raffia hanging down the women's hips. The journey home beginning and ending with the first word.

Chain, chain, chain . . .
Chain of fools.

Aretha's song danced from nowhere into his daydream. Up-tempo, electronic funk, tambourines ringing, sounding brass. Into the quiet of that old African's story shaped by hands and breath and eyes. The creation must be followed by something, by whatever's needed to produce this. *This* being, for starters, a tired old Uncle Remus man with knobby, wrinkled hands, half asleep at his desk in a trailer like a second skin he'd just as soon be buried in if someone kind was prepared to dig a hole big enough. To arrive at this bad dream of Homewood and lost children and mothers grieving you needed a chain of events, one after another, didn't you? But why did Aretha's big loud song jump on him?

Chain of fools.

Was it coincidence? The airwaves busy with signals overlapping, bleeding into each other, wandering, lost. Two people bump into each other because they just happen to wind up on the same crowded corner at the same instant. Or was it spozed to be? Always, everything, all of it, spozed to be. Was he always learning more of the same story?

Mind chains and body chains. The need to wear them or drape them over someone else. If you begin with loose strands of raffia, revealing, animating, perfect metaphors for speech, for breath, how did you end up in chains. Confinement, crushing weight, the cross and crisscross of iron branding, bloodying soft flesh.

Chains had to be what people wanted or they would not have happened everywhere, always.

Reuben wondered if coincidence was just another link in the chain or could it be the chain snapping, light breaking through, a gate opening into another, better world, a world chains could not bind. When X and Y turn up on the same street corner at the same moment when there's every reason for them not to and no ostensible reason why they should, especially after twenty years of living separate in the same city and never catching a glimpse of one another's face, and this coincidental meeting occurs five seconds after X thinks of Y for the first time in the twenty years since X has last thought of or seen Y, then . . . you think, why not, anything can happen, maybe the thought's what brought them together. Anything's possible . . . or is it? Possibility just a name for another chain, one of the most perverse because it allows you to play on your tether, fools you by expanding your range so you mistake possibility for freedom. Reuben thinks of the big ugly dog guarding the junkyard. Stupid thing fights his collar and leash. Snarls and snaps and leaps and rages all day as if the leash is his problem, as if biting through it would tear down the barbed-wire-topped, heavy-duty chain link fence that would keep him penned no matter how many steel leashes he chews through.

Maybe nobody ever escapes. Maybe it's boxes within boxes within boxes cutting off your air. But you smile anyway when you hear of crazy coincidences or when they happen to you.

Coincidence was not like your number hitting or your lottery ticket winning. Those kinds of things pie-in-the-sky. Rip-offs. Somebody getting rich because somebody else is down so low, so desperate, the best they can hope for, the only games they can play, are ten thousand to one or ten million to one. Coincidence wasn't accident. Coincidence proved something. Maybe. Maybe no one was in charge. Maybe there was a plan you couldn't count on, but nobody else could either. The deck stacked in some peculiar, perverse, funny fashion so it caused you to smile or be amazed, even when the plan wasn't acting nice. A deck stacked so bizarrely, a plan so simpleminded, ignorant, and absurd that sometimes it just rocked back on its heels and had to laugh at its ownself. Something happens and you say, No way. The more you think on it, the harder it is to believe. But you also get the funny feeling that whatever happened had to happen, was supposed to happen because it turned out so neat, so impossibly right or wrong in spite of all the reasons it shouldn't.

Reuben liked books of photographs, so he'd hefted the oversize Muybridge folios off a shelf of the public library. He was immediately fascinated by the pictures and the life of the man who took them. Then eerie correspondences abounding. Two men unawares, moving toward the same corner in the same city. One says a name he's never said before, and in an instant he's staring into a face that couldn't have shocked him more if it had been his own. And maybe it is.

Muybridge's project to investigate animal motion had been underwritten by the University of Pennsylvania. For three years the photographer had worked on the university campus, in West Philadelphia, Reuben's stomping grounds when he had studied the law. That coincidence enough to alert Reuben to a strange intertwining of fates. Woman trouble, murder, the law, prison, lives piled on top of lives. The book with its thousands of photos of naked men and naked women, this album of dead faces and dead bodies, was no plaything. Reuben's curiosity deepened. His interest had been *seized*.

Because also there was the matter of Egypt. Egypt a long-standing fascination, and Egypt somehow hooked up with the book of photos. The week before he'd discovered Muybridge, Reuben had been savoring the treasures of Tutankhamen's tomb. An intriguing volume juxtaposed black-and-white photos of the tomb as it was originally discovered with new color plates of its splendors restored. Reuben had pondered the mystery of young King Tut's death, his tangled relationship with a brother who might be his father, a woman who might be the boy king's mother, sister, wife, or all three. For years Reuben had been reading about mummies, about everyday life in ancient Egypt, about Egyptian architecture and art, about the gods and goddesses who presided over the Nile Valley, deities assuming many forms, many names, as changeable and constant as the great river itself with its alternating seasons of flood and contraction, gods who wore the heads of beasts: crocodiles, cobras, hawks, jackals, baboons, lions. Reuben loved their outrageous couplings. Wept with Isis, bellowed with the Apis bulls.

Poring over Muybridge's photos, Reuben had taken a mental note: Reuben to Reuben. Listen and don't forget. This Muybridge joker right at home among the pharaohs. Ego big as a sphinx. His book of pictures a giant honeycomb of a tomb. Photographs accomplishing what the Egyptians attempted when they embalmed their dead. Here I am stirred by the shapely buttocks of this kneeling naked woman dead for half a century. Dead and dust, yet she kneels and her body talks to my body. This old man in a chair rises up like a butterfly and meets her in the air. Fluttery doo-dop. Summer salty and wheely-dealy though she's dead as a doorknob. I'm knocking and she's in, yes she is, twelve views of her lovely butt still in its prime, cracking, cracking the tomb. As long as I can look she's there to see. In the middle of the air. Halfway home.

When he puts you in his camera he does not steal your soul. He opens its window. He builds you a pyramid and spares you the ravages of time. Beetles, worms, gravediggers and grave robbers and all the rest leave you alone and forget. You are young forever. Saved forever. As long as someone remains to look. . . .

The ancient Egyptians were not willing to travel to the land of the dead—the black Land of Spirits with its fields of rushes, the land they pictured lying to the west, beyond the setting sun—without the company of their bodies. Hence the absorption with mummification and preservation, canopic jars, elaborate spells in a Book of the Dead, towering pyramids with their blind guts, labyrinthine chambers within chambers and coffins within coffins within stone sarcophagi. The weak flesh washed in natron, bound in linen, and caparisoned with amulets bearing magic incantations. Bundled like the green itch of life in the innermost eye of a seed. On their great getting-up morning the Egyptians wanted hands and noses and eyes and toes and hearts. Flesh with its senses and appetites. What good was eternal life if you lost your blood and bones and meat. To feast upon, to offer up to another's hunger. Muybridge had stopped time for his subjects. The half-moons of a woman's behind glow white and fine when Reuben turns a page and watches her kneel forever, step by step.

Reuben couldn't say it right yet. Not even to himself. Points to be made about bandages and film, about wrapping and unwrapping, about being born and dying in swaddling clothes, about nakedness and rooms and wombs, parallels, coincidences and contrasts to be pondered, but the note was long enough. He'd lost his place in it. Was this still note or something else? Time later to elaborate, neaten up his thoughts. Besides, he didn't have to make everything fit. Not yet. His sense of things, the notes he'd accumulated over the years, added up to nothing. Incompleteness their main virtue. Connections almost made suggesting other connections unmade, stymied, or possibly connecting or etc. . . . Sometimes Reuben saw stars. Sometimes he saw the strings attaching stars to the ceiling. A million million spider-spun filaments without which the stars would fall. But did stars need strings or were strings what he needed to keep stars visible, possible?

Reuben tugged the gold watch from its nest below his heart. Eleven forty-seven. Coincidence? All numbers had their secrets, but this one didn't even try to be coy about what it was hiding.

Eleven once. Then eleven again as the sum of four and seven. What do you have: eleven twice. Four ones equal four. East, west, north, south are the four points of the compass. The four corners of the world. Four moments of the sun. A circle connects them. Everywhere, everything, perfection.

He smiles at the tired ivory face of the clock cupped in his hand, the trinket, his twin, attached to it. The whole world . . . including the intersection of Homewood and Hamilton, where lunch will be waiting in a tiny, four-table Muslim restaurant eleven steps from the corner.

2

WALLY

The bat felt good in his fists. He squeezed its heft. Wiggled the
end invisible over his shoulder, danced it, the weight, the light-
ness of it teasing his fingers, stirring the big muscles bunched at
his shoulders, the muscles rippling across his back. The terrible
weight, the quick, blink-of-an-eye swiftness hovering, ready to
explode as he waggled the bat, gripping tighter, digging his
spikes in for the swing. The heads were on posts, an endless row
of letter-high posts, spaced just far enough apart so he could
assume his hitter's crouch beside each one and not disturb the
next. The rows of heads stretched as far as he could see, from
life-size just a few feet away to the last one, shrunken small as a
golf ball on a tee where the row slanted down to meet the earth.

No one's face in particular. Features hidden. He would swing
at the back of the heads, the thinning hair, bald crowns, go for the
fat part with the fat of his bat, the bulge of skull bone above the
few inches of neck left to steady the heads on the posts. All male.
A woman's floating hair might distract him. These were like the

24

heads of businessmen who flew with him into the wide blue yonder, over the amber waves of grain. How many times had he found himself stuffed into a jetway, crammed in the aisle of a plane behind a legion of these balding white heads, these ringless collars, dull suits, the stink of motels, rich food in ridiculous restaurants, heads all facing one direction, chattering about weather and connections, getting the world's work done?

He loves them better like this. Quiet, their heads frozen on the ends of sticks. He sights far away, in the green distance where he'll aim with his follow-through, the weight of his over-stuffed, major leaguer's ass and thighs, far far away over the green carpet beyond the fence into the abyss.

A loud, satisfying crack. Nothing gives. The head is as hard as he's always known it would be. Nothing nasty splatters back at him. Instead there is a solid, crisp pain in his wrists as the bat makes contact. Like a stone, a rock, he thinks, as his arms swing through and the sharp tingle in his wrists dissipates instantly, shooting up his arms, lodging in his shoulders where it's pain no longer, where it's transformed to power, lifting, driving, taking the head for a ride. Give me a bat long enough and I'll move the world. It's all happening so fast he can't say the words to himself but feels them surge up his arms as the nerves sing and the muscles release their coiled strength. The crowd rises as one, gasps, holds its breath, fifty-five thousand ready to die if they don't let it out, and when they do, a sonic boom tears across the sky. He can tell by the way they're hollering and screaming he won't have to run. That it's gone. Out of here. Over the wall. Hallelujah.

He is edging sideways and back into position for the next one. Grateful there are more. As many as he can bash in a lifetime. He twists his fists around the wood. Lets it dangle to test its weight. Again. He wants to hit again. . . .

Wally tasted spring in the blood seeping from his head. Like the taste of dried apricots. An astringent tickle and bitterness with the sweet. His skull crackled, the sinuses doing their spring thing, hypersensitive to changes in temperature, pressure, wind velocity. A weather station in his temples, under his eyes, the roots and tunnels of his nose. All rooms full. The overflow hadn't begun to drain, to show up as yellow-green guck when he laughed or blew his nose, yet the parade was beginning. A spring thaw unclogging the bloated passages. A bloody tang when he breathes deeply, when he sniffs and tastes the insides of his swollen head.

Planes made it worse. Landing and taking off, his nose went crazy. Sensory overload. What the fuck is happening to me? I don't need this. His nose fusses while he squeezes it, picks it. Snorts, sniffles, clears his throat. He's rough then gentle, but no way to calm it, soothe it. Plane rides torture this time of year and this time of year he must be on planes, so that was that. He knew. His nose knew. Put me on a plane, I'ma give you pain. So that was that.

Wally had been asleep. Been somewhere far more pleasant than a plane. Though he couldn't put it together yet, not in words or precise images anyway, he knew he'd been dreaming and the dreaming was good. He resented being snatched away. Losing recall. Hadn't been his sun dream, his sea dream, floating in the bluest, calmest, clearest, safest water on a rubber raft with anything else he wanted at his fingertips. All he needed to do was open his eyes, blink away the red spider webs, and anything he wanted at his beck and call. Not that dream exactly. Whatever it was, though, had left the same relaxed tingling satisfaction deep in his chest, his groin. Left that aura of power and completion and the certainty he'd been asleep.

The last thing he'd seen out the window before an endless canopy of cloud was terrain into which someone had gouged huge circles, circles perhaps miles across, given what the altitude of the plane did to the scale of the landscape brownly stretching below. What had happened to the land? Plowed, burned, scoured, planted, scorched. The circles were too perfect to be accidental or natural. Somebody had used a compass. People had drawn them on purpose. He wondered why he'd never noticed the circles before. Couldn't figure them out and damned sure

26

wasn't going to expose his ignorance by asking these crackers on the plane what the circles might be. He'd file the fact. One day he'd discover another piece of the puzzle and see how it fit here, snuggled tight against these mysterious circles scarring the plains.

Clouds, thin at first, thin and white like hair on the backs of their old heads above their white collars, fringing their red necks. Then thicker, layer upon layer, obscuring the ground, wrapping the plane in premature darkness. Rock and roll for a while. The pilot apologized, informing passengers and crew that he'd received permission to cruise at a higher altitude, above the massing clouds. What made the pilot believe trouble was something he could soar above? Why was his voice so sure of itself, so serene? Like a preacher's voice, Wally thought. A preacher who thinks he's God.

Wally had dozed through the miracle. Awakened to sunshine streaming through the ports, sure his head was going to explode, sorry he'd missed something special in the dream he couldn't remember.

Would you like a pillow, sir?

He couldn't help frowning at her smiling face. What the fuck did she want? He was awake now. A pillow would have been fine when he was asleep, but what the hell could he do with a pillow now? Unless she wanted him to slip it up under her skinny ass and hump her right there in the aisle.

Wally grunted *no* as nasty as he could. Her smile never broke stride. Trotted past him and into the next fray as if the surly nigger in 15D didn't exist. Which Wally didn't like. Any more than he appreciated her hovering over him, grinning cause she was paid to grin, even at niggers, even at big black burly surly niggers, waving a pillow she'd smother him with if she could.

Course if I was sleeping, she couldn't very well ask me if I wanted a pillow, could she? But that wasn't his problem, was it? He didn't put pillows on the plane nor pussy on the plane to peddle the pillows, the drinks, the jive food.

They were descending, losing sunlight abruptly. All the sunshine pouring out through the tilted nose of the 737.

Make me love you, bitch, is what he had told her. She sat up naked in the bed. Eyes wide, left breast larger than the right so her body seemed to lean perpetually, tilting to one side so everything ran that way. Lopsided outside and in.

I don't understand. I don't know what you mean. Please, Wally.

What he was telling her was get out. It's over. And they both understood quite well.

Saying make me love you was like saying make me say uncle. He wanted a fight. A chance to kick her ass or her to kick his. Then they could break clean, be done with it.

People can't make people love them.

Yeah. You right, babe. You probably right. So ain't nothing happening. And ain't nothing gon happen.

Hard. Hard. Hard. Down on her case. She'd cry. The tears and sobbing her way of hitting him. He'd have to take all her shit, her blows, till he got tired and hit back the only way he knew how. Tit for tat. Then the bitches always acted like he's the bully, like he's the only one doing damage, the only one putting a hurt on people. Well, let's get it on. Cry . . . cry . . . cry . . .

She had black circles around her nipples. White girls tipped with shades of pink. Funny how most of them curly in the crotch. White or black they could tear you up when you're sore in the morning and they want to go again and you in a hurry to get it over. No time to loosen them up. Get it ready. Briar-patch bitches. Peter Rabbit got tears in his eyes.

She said, Would you like a pillow, sir? Would you fluff it up and ram it behind my pink behind?

It's no longer clouds below. It's dirt and soot, the gray, greasy stuff he spit up in hunks when he played ball outdoors on hot summer afternoons. The city. A gray cemetery junkyard rising to meet them. City grit and city shit. Home.

Hey, traveling man.

You got that right, Sidney.

28

Where you been, champ?

Here, there, and everywhere. West Coast, Midwest, all up and down the East. Where ain't I been is the question.

Well, you home now.

I'm stopped now.

Vodka?

Like always.

You want me to take your case back here?

Thanks, Sid. I'm sure nuff tired hauling this motherfucker around. Tired of looking at it, too.

Do any good?

Never can tell. Young niggers today. Boy. They ain't giving away nothing. Want to know what you got to give them. Like they want a no-cut contract, a guarantee they'll start first year, money up front, money in the bank, a car somebody else be making the payments on. And ain't played one minute of college ball yet. Prima donnas, too. Everybody wining and dining they overgrown asses. Start believing they cute. I'ma smack one one of these days. Be doing the chump a favor, you dig? Bringing his ass back down to earth.

Hey. The man paying you good for your trouble, ain't he? You always sharp as a tack. Flying you all over the country. Good food, high living.

It's a gig, Sid. That's all it is. Put in my time. Walk away with a dime. Just a gig.

A gig a million cats wouldn't mind having.

One day soon they can have it, man. I'm tired.

Traveling man.

Hit me again.

Midnight. Wally lays across his bed, fully clothed. His legs ache. If he falls asleep his legs will run him awake again. Remind him they never stop running. He scared them one day into fleeing from blackness, from having nothing, and now they never stop, don't know how to stop.

He hears the ocean, the dull boom of surf, waves washing

29

over and over again something they'll never scrub clean. But tonight he's not at Bimbo's Castle, not in San Diego or Santa Cruz. No breezy motel by the sea. He's home again. His inland city built on hills so the sound is not ocean sound. He's listening to a pulse that throbs beneath the sidewalk. Power plants, office buildings, factories, row houses, tons and tons of cement pushing down, everything they've buried pushing up. Perpetual creaks and groans as the earth gives a fraction of an inch one way then strains back in the opposite direction, recovering what it's lost. Slow-motion tossing and turning. Millimeters in a decade. But he can feel the rock and roll. His insomnia plays the notes.

After drinks, bullshitting with Sid, scoffing down a huge plate of food Miss Myrtle had served him on the end of the bar, Wally wanted to be alone. The late-night crowd had begun to drift into the Hi Hat. Their quarters, plunked into the jukebox, started to take over. If you weren't wide awake and ready to party hearty, their music was too loud. You couldn't talk over it or hide under it. You swung with it or carried your ass home to bed, because their music was the way things were going to be till last call and somebody's slow blues, the last jam on the box, closed the Hi Hat.

When you were out there in it, you didn't even hear the blast of the music. Like you didn't see shabby walls, dirt on the floor. Like you stopped asking for more than what was there at two A.M. when the Hi Hat started winding down. Yeah. What you see is what you get. Trick was not seeing what you don't want to see. How scabby the bitch was under her paint. How silly her dress would look in daylight. How long the heavy-duty perfume she's wearing would stink up your sheets. Trick was being out in it, letting yourself be fooled for as long as it took to act a fool. Baby, baby, baby with the red dress on. Shake it, don't break it, mama. Looking good till the red dress hanging off the back of a chair and everything that held in her fat ass, held up those floppy titties is on the floor, and you pull out, finished before the tired meat collapses on yours.

With a crust of Italian bread he'd circled the rim of the

dinner plate. Myrtle'd get a kick out of how clean he'd leave it. Heap it higher next time.

The plate was deep and wide with fancy edges like the ones in his grandmother's china cabinet. Only this plate was thick and white and no blue roses boogied across its face. Miss Myrtle too skinny to have grandchildren. Yet she did. Seventeen. She knew each one's birthday, she said. Would have mailed cards if she knew their addresses, their last names. She'd given up trying to keep up. With names, addresses, the men who'd been daddies and granddaddies. Far as she knew, her men still out there live and kicking. She wasn't the kind to cling to a man, squeeze him till he died or she died. No. I always known when to get my hat. Ain't tied to nobody's name, nobody's claim. Myrtle tell you in a minute: You don't like what I fix, don't eat it. I know it's good. Cooked it my ownself, so if you don't like it, leave it. . . . After you lay down your money on the table.

Some people you wondered why they didn't break. Miss Myrtle's arms no bigger round than his finger. She caught him staring at her ankles one day and cracked up. Laughed till she choked. Not bad for a old lady, is they? Mmmm. Mm. There was a time. Not today, mind you, and not yesterday neither, but there was a time. And she laughed some more and winked at Wally, and he had to laugh too. Because all he saw was bone. Little mice bones poking out from under her long crisp white uniform dress and once-upon-a-time white speckle-tailed apron, bibbed, knotted round her scrawny neck. Because she'd caught him trying to undress her. Imagining what was under her clothes. Not because he desired her—wasn't she older than his dead grandmother—but because he was curious. How did somebody that little and skinny hold together? Why didn't she break? How were the anklebones connected to the shinbones, shinbones connected to the knee bones, knee bones connected to thighbones. He didn't care nothing about what was between those chicken-wing thighs. Skipped that, ignored that just like he ignored old ladies sitting gap-legged on their stoops. Hurried past her private parts to the rib bones, to the chest flat as a board. Like a little girl's. Topless. Miss Myrtle shouldn't have to

31

wear a shirt in summer if she didn't want to. He'd been taking inventory from her Minny Mouse feet to her chin, and she caught him dead in the act.

Miss Myrtle got happy behind it. Teasing him for weeks. Extra helpings of whatever was special the days he ordered dinner in the Hi Hat.

Some people all bone. Some lived inside a sea of fat, quivery as his waterbed. Before he'd slept on his waterbed he thought it would be like floating. Maybe even like his dream. Blue sky, blue water. Everything, anything within reach. But the sucker slept hard as sand. Only when he shifted could he hear water slooshing, squishing under him. If you punched, there was no splash. Like hitting sand, meat.

Once he settled down on the bed all motion stopped. Except the constant roar of the city, which sometimes seemed to be outside the walls of his building, and sometimes echoed inside the walls of his skull. He stared down at the bulk of his suitcase resting on the navy surplus trunk at the foot of his bed. When he packed for a trip, each item was a choice about who he would be while the trip lasted. Living out of a bag forced you to decide beforehand the kind of impression you wished to make. Gradually he'd learned to be an efficient packer. He could go for days out of one folding carry-on and a briefcase. In the bag would be an elegant junior exec, a baggy-tweed assistant prof, a hip cookie just this side of pimp and gangster, college-boy jeans, T-shirt and sandals. Disguises in a way. And part of the game was the fun of fooling people. Part of it was a pain in the ass because you had to be ready to dress for situations you couldn't always anticipate. Tension, pressure as each item is packed or left hanging. Part of it was sweet, crazy because you were free. In a city a thousand miles distant you were unknown, you could be anything you wanted to be. Suppose he slipped a dress into his bag. The thought had crossed his mind more than once. Not to be a sissy, but to be free. If you didn't test, if you didn't see how far you could go, then what was the point, would you ever be free?

In Chicago, dressed as a bag lady. Lifting garbage-can lids.

Feeding pigeons and drinking wine in the park. Nobody would know him. Nobody would care. Just another old, broken-down hobo woman most people wouldn't notice when they passed by. But he'd notice them. Be laughing the whole time. A different world. He'd groove in a totally new world just by packing his hanging bag with weird shit.

Wally wondered how many times he'd been fooled by tricksters who'd sneaked out of their normal skins. Somebody else must have had the idea before him. What about businessmen on the planes, their white half-a-heads in rows above orange seat backs? Would they land in cities far from home and be transformed? Hippies, policemen, fags, priests. Did they have one family in LA and another in Cleveland? Had any of them worked it out so that instead of flying from place to place to do somebody else's business, they were flying from life to life, a merry-go-round circus of identities and nobody else knew their names.

Some fool must have thought of it. The kick you'd get changing from old to young, male to female, black to white. He'd check more closely next time. For wigs, makeup, pillows under shirts. Perhaps women infiltrated the planes disguised as businessmen. A foxy lady stands naked in front of a full-length mirror in her bedroom. She picks out a three-piece cord suit, a striped tie, shiny cordovans from her closet. A running bra flattens her breasts, and her suit is tailored to hide curves and bulges. Bald as a cue ball under the luxuriant blond wig she tosses on her bed. Another hairpiece snugs over the emptiness. She sticks on a graying moustache, matching bushy brows, pulls on boxer shorts over her fine, slim ass. For the duration of the flight no one penetrates her disguise. Maybe she sits next to Wally but he never guesses what a nice surprise he'd find if he unzipped her fly.

You just never know. Wally undresses her. Now she's naked again in front of her mirror. She's the prize you cop for guessing her identity.

No one knows. No one cares. Wally packs in order to make impressions. Impressions are what's called for. All anybody wants to know, to deal with. I'll pretend to be the person you are pretending you want to see. As long as nobody breaks the rules, everybody is happy. As happy as knowing nothing and not caring can make you. Which ain't the worse way to live, he thinks, savoring the woman's naked smile as he steps out of the mirror. Wally can go along with the program, but what makes him happier is an edge, a way of getting over. Secrets.

Hey. Listen. Here's something I bet youall don't know about me. He's in a city park, an ancient oversize female ragamuffin on a park bench office workers stroll past, scrupulously avoid. Surprise. Surprise, motherfuckers. Pigeons scatter in a flurry of cooing, soot, and flapping wings when he snatches up his tattered dress, whips out his joint, and pisses all over them.

Night gnaws the city. Rats trafficking inside the walls, roaches scavenging the black guts of ovens. Some nights he paid it no mind, other nights the sound stole his sleep. He'd tried to describe it to Reuben. Like when you hold a seashell up to your ear. People said do it and you'll hear the ocean and you don't really believe that shit but you try anyway and goddamn if the ocean ain't in there. Even if it ain't nothing but you listening for it, you hear yourself listening so it's the same thing as finding what they said you'd find. Something's in there. Even if it ain't nothing but you listening to yourself listening. How you gon fall asleep behind that?

Reuben said your own blood pounding is what you hear. But then he shook his old rat head and said you never know though. Young Bentley Higgins come back from the war. Complained to me about disability payments he wasn't receiving. He carried around this shrunken-up, nasty ear in a sandwich baggie. Claimed he could hear the war in it. You know. Hold that ear to his like you're talking about doing with a seashell and he could hear guns and jungle and helicopters blowing everything away. Said he toted it around because he didn't want to forget. Of course poor Bentley was crazy. Tried to get me to put that ugly thing next to my ear. Not I, I told him. Don't care if the

34

war's in stereo and 3-D in there. I'm not hardly sticking a dead Vietnamese ear on mine.

Boy was crazy, but he swore he could hear war in that ear. Now, maybe he could, maybe he couldn't. You never know, do you? I mean, unless you're Bentley Higgins. Unless you're the ear.

Reuben was like that. He seemed to talk sense. Then he throws in shit that makes no sense at all and just leaves you to deal with it. Come away asking yourself what did Reuben say? Did he really say that?

Whatever it was about Reuben that made him Reuben was something kept people coming back. You'd be halfway there before you realized you were headed toward his humpbacked little trailer.

Hey, Wally. What's happening, my man?

Nothing to it, Ells. You got it, Ells.

You passed somebody on the street and you'd read your destination in their eyes. Like they knew before you did. Ellsworth in his lectric-blue jumpsuit, styling down Homewood Avenue. Gold zippers, gold chains, gleaming gold buckles in his Florsheims. Ells's high five raised on one side the Avenue and you return the greeting from your side. Both black hands invisible, slipping their moorings, floating to a spot in the center of the street where they came together with a pop. *Cool, brother.* The exchange consumes only a few seconds but the air is charged by it, by the million words and gestures that pulsate in the air all along the length of Homewood Avenue. Everyone hiding, yet no one has any secrets when you catch them on the Avenue. Ellsworth didn't wink, but he could have. He was privy to the knowledge even before it settled down as a certainty in Wally's mind. The knowledge, bright as a halo circling Wally's head, that he was on his way to Reuben.

Wally was tall. He had to stoop to enter the little man's trailer. A shaky step up. Bend gingerly so he doesn't agitate that cross of pain in the small of his back. Bending and drawing in his broad shoulders, his breath. Not until that moment, those familiar adjustments, would he admit to himself, Yes, I'm going to Reuben's. Yes, I'm on my way straight as my legs will carry me. That's why I'm up and dressed and out here in the street. No other reason. No other place to go but this place I cannot name even as I tap on the door and pull it open and lean over the threshold.

The needle's eye, Reuben had giggled, one crooked finger aimed at the opening behind Wally's chest.

Getting to be a tight squeeze isn't it, my friend? One of Reuben's habits was laughing when Wally didn't know the joke. Made you want to strangle the little dude. Who else the joke on if it wasn't on you?

Squeezing in not funny. Whether you were too big or the hole too small not the point. What mattered was your flesh and bone squeezed to a pulp, to a mushy kind of oatmeal. You couldn't breathe, couldn't think. If you made it through to the other side, not enough of you left to do business.

You were a ball of nothing. Squeezed in. Then you saw Reuben and you bloated up again. He was smaller than you, so you couldn't be but so tiny. Always smelled like bug spray inside the trailer. Kills-Em-Dead perfuming every nook and cranny. Roaches not dying, though. Getting high on the spray. Nodding away the daylight hours so they can prowl all night. Stink of roach spray and the buzz of them snoring.

W: What's it like, then . . . getting old?
R: Why you ask me that? You think I'm old, Wally?
W: No offense, Reuben. You know. You just happen to be the oldest dude I ever talk to. Just curious . . . you know.
R: Sure you really want me to answer?
W: Asked, didn't I?
R: You don't really want to know, but I'm going to tell you anyway, now you got me started.
W: I'm digging.
R: Well, it's just like being young. Except when you're old,

what you don't know upsets you more. You've been around
long enough to realize that whatever you don't know will (a)
be held against you, and (b) probably make things worse. So
you damned sure ain't in no hurry to find out. But you're
scared to death you might not.

W: Do you think much about dying?

R: All the time. Only it's not exactly thinking about dying. It's
more like being aware anything can be fatal. You see the
wheel. Folks climb on and folks drop off. Sooner or later
everybody falls. Babies make me think of slobbery old men.
I look for beautiful young girls in the faces of their grand-
mothers. Being in the world with your fist wrapped around
a porkchop and grease on your chin don't mean a thing,
Wally. Next bite you take might snatch you away from here.
It's always that quick and after a while, after seeing it happen again and again, you can't forget the lesson. You see
through things. You try to take your pleasure from what's
behind things, inside things, propping all this mess up.

W: You mean your dick don't get hard no more?

R: Speak for yourself, sonnyboy. But that's probably part of
what I mean. Not the biggest part. Not the part makes me
cry, anyway.

W: What's worse?

R: Worse is having no one to tell it to. Takes years to learn the
easiest, simplest things. Like you finally figure out what one
plus one equals. A light bulb goes on inside you and you're
sure, as sure as you've ever been about anything in your life.
You're sure you finally got it figured right. Sure in your
heart, sure in your head. You're like a kid again and you
want to find somebody and play with this new shiny toy you
just discovered, but nobody has the slightest idea what
you're talking about. Either it's a dumb thing everybody
thinks they know already. Or a thing nobody couldn't care
less about knowing. Here you come with your ray of sunshine and it's nothing. Nobody cares. Your whole life spent
finding it, but what's it matter? Wheel still turning. People
dropping off like flies. You're next. Light or no light.

37

W: That's all?

R: Just this one last bit. Since you asked. Sometimes when I try to look back and piece it all together . . . my life . . . the pieces . . . I think about being young and it's like youth, my own youth, is the son I never had.

In the hard cradle of water, waiting for sleep, when voices poke at him and scenes flicker on and off, when his life is these fragments, not *his* really, but *like* him, floating with him, adrift in the same uneasy sea, Wally feels lost. He hates the sea, the countless islands dotting it, the islands he'll never reach because they are caught in the same slippery motion, the ebb and flow and queasy twisting in the pit of his stomach. If the islands were big enough, solid enough, if they weren't so far away, he could hoist himself up on one of them. Save himself. But he can't trust them. Sometimes he drifts closer to one. A talk with Reuben. Reuben's words making sense. Then, just as he's ready to climb on board, doubt slams into his face. Did Reuben ever say these things to me? Are those his words or am I telling myself what I want to hear? Is there a dwarfy little man named Reuben sitting somewhere twisting those crooked hands too big for the rest of his body, playing with the hands intently, seriously, as if he's searching for a way to unhinge them, exchange them for a pair that fit better? Did Reuben ever say anything about getting old? Would I have the nerve to ask? Do I want to know? You never got closer to an island. You only thought you did. And then the same thought breaks the island into a million pieces. Into dust, into wind singeing your ears.

This is what happened in Chicago. I can tell it now. I'm home now in my bed. Safe. Perhaps Reuben is awake. Maybe he'll hear me. Maybe he'll forgive.

I cop a rental car at the airport. Credit cards make me real. I wonder why the women slam down so hard on their machines. Can't be that tough to print numbers on the tissue-paper forms I sign. Chick lays plastic on the track. Bram. Clickety-click. Like she's ironing somebody's pants she hates. A lover's trousers and she knows he wears them when he cheats on her.

Waiting for a shuttle to the rental car lot. Four or five of us in a spoonful of light that spills for a few seconds through the overcast. No one speaks. No one is sure where we are. Across a jumble of traffic the giant glass wall of a motel three blocks long gleams blackly, mirroring the business of the terminal. It could be raining. Rain would make no difference. We're in the middle of nowhere, a group of travelers on our separate ways somewhere else. We're not here, beside this skimpy plastic-roofed shelter. We're not in these clothes, these skins. Arriving at our destination is all that matters. This is a hitch, a temporary slow-down. Pretend you don't see us. We're pretending we're not here.

Shuttle van to a car. Study the pencil line drawn through a maze of highways and streets. Remember what to look for after the interstate. Remember the exit number. A right turn and the boulevard you should find. Map comes with the car. She drew the route for me in green pencil, absent for the minute she took to find her way through interstates and city streets. I thought of a teammate whose ambition was to poke catheters through people's arteries. Would the map bleed if she slipped? Did she know what she was doing or was the woman behind the counter putting me on? Her cheeks are pocked, nuggets of makeup fill the craters. She looks good in spite of bad skin. Sexy flounce to the shingled frieze of dark hair. Full lips. Strong straight nose. Her green eyes pleased with themselves when she finishes marking my map, when she looks up and unfurrows her brow and catches me full in the face. I'm returning the attention of her attention—we both like the exchange. But is her smile part of the sham? Is she putting me on? *Keep this nigger running*. Trick him with a green lie snaking through the map.

Stars, always stars in the sky. But you must wait to see them. Till night falls, till the haze lifts, till the dirty lid blows off. Always heaven up there but you got to wait your turn to see it. Since it was Iowa it must have been a cornfield. Too dark to tell.

39

The rental car askew on the steep shoulder of the interstate, its emergency lights wailing. A million braying crickets doing whatever they do in the fields beyond a fence. Fence silhouetted, catching little sprigs of moonlight on wires stretched between posts. Only night-owl trucks on the interstate, distant ships, plying the black river of highway. He's almost finished emptying his bladder before one roars up on him. Like a train then, hurtling past. Road buckles, noise explodes. He hears a string of passenger cars rattling, whining as they're yanked past him, through him, by the engine. The last silvered car light as a ghost. He listens to it sigh long after it's gone. Above the maul of the crickets, the spray of himself like a zipper opening the weeds. He shakes his rod and lifts his eyes. Stars. More stars than crickets, he thinks. Enough stars to mow down the world if each one took just a little bite. He remembers someone telling him to be good. A hand as soft as water pressing a coin into his. You be a good boy, now, Wallace. And don't you never forget God loves you. Was it a nickel, a dime, a penny? He remembers holding a coin between his fingers and thumb, rolling it, like he rolls the end of his joint to wring the last drops. Writing *star, star, star* on a furry sheet of Big Chief tablet paper. A kid, he did stuff like that when he was a kid. Wrote one word over and over. In columns, in strings. His poems. Scribble-scrabble waste of paper to everybody else. A page full of *star,* full as this Iowa night sky till he turned the word around and *rats* ate it all.

Sometime late tonight, after the drive into the city and checking into a motel and seeing the folks he must see, he'll find his way to a bar where there will be music, silky music, and its tight, nasty sparkle will follow him out the door, hover lightly, a stylish cape draping his shoulders, hover easy as the buzz he slowly stitches together shot by shot leaning on the bar, counting bottles, nodding at shadows in the mirror. He'll be sleepy then, exhausted beyond wanting company, beyond wanting anything besides the quiet darkness of the city streets, the stars rising like a mist off his shoulders, losing themselves again in the night sky.

Reuben. The only reason I'm telling you this . . . He stops

midsentence, midthought because he cannot finish, because he can invent no reason, believe no reason. Anyway, he's talking to himself. The little man is far away. Dead perhaps. And perhaps that's the reason. Why.

I wasn't scared. No reason to be scared. Nothing bad was going to happen to me. I had nothing to worry about so even the first time I did it I was ice cool. The iceman, you dig? Had a job to do and I did it. No sweat. No shaky hands or trembly knees. I used to get the shakes terrible before ball games. Couldn't tie my shoes sometimes I be shaking so bad. Okay once the game started, but I wasn't worth shit the last few minutes or so before we got it on. I'd keep to myself in the locker room. Put on my game face so nobody'd fuck with me. Last minute before a game tough on everybody, but I had more to lose than the white boys. Off in my corner about to bust. Nobody'd know it, though. Have my stone face on. Hard rock. Like you better not get too close. Like I'm ready to blow and you better keep your distance.

None of that. Not even the first time I killed one. Nothing to it really, because what did I have to be scared of? Like stopping the car and pissing beside the highway. My black ass in the black night in the middle of nowhere and who knows, who cares. Pissing beside the road and by morning my piss is gone, I'm long gone, and who gives a fuck? Who knows except me. And you now that I'm telling you? If I tell you.

Reuben is a cloud, small and humped. The joke is you can become anything but you must always wear your fate like a badge. Wally picks out the little man from the flock of clouds gathering on his ceiling, on the blue face of the sky. Wind drives them. He doesn't have much time to tell his story. The hump, the beard work their way out of the white fog. This same wind forming Reuben screams at the lakefront, spattering it with beards of froth, raining down in invisible needles that pit and shatter the lake's skin. The wind remembers all Wally's sins, forgives none of them. When anger gags him, when the veins in his neck bulge, when anger is a high, hot singing in his throat

41

and his eyes burn and his lips tremble, the words he cannot utter ride this skein of wind blowing in from west or north, from whichever direction the winds come to punish Chicago. Because it's Chicago he sees on his ceiling. A panorama unfolding. The broad, gray shoulders huddling together. Sky behind them. Blue as hate, as silence. Then a flock of clouds, one of which, a crippled maverick, has strayed off and shivers, absorbing the brunt of the wind alone, cringing or laughing as wind tears it apart.

This is what happened, old man. Perhaps it was in the zoo, or a museum, an art gallery, an airport maybe. Definitely a public place. In Chicago, in the late afternoon and wind is blowing. Like at the seashore. Sheets of light bellying against the flanks of buildings. Spray tickling my face. White clouds in a panic. Nowhere to run. Milling like cattle in stockyard pens. If white clouds could sweat, they would. And stink.

You would feel those things probably if you'd been there in my place. They're what I felt, what I remember. And since it's my story, they'll have to do, Reuben. When you tell it you can jazz it up any way you'd like. Your famous bullshit, old man, smear it over everything if you please. But for now let's have it my way. Clouds. Sky. Wind. A public place. Two or three Bloody Marys for lunch turning into a need to urinate. Piss. Quick. Any port will do.

A public bathroom, but large and clean, immaculate even, the kind that the public seldom uses, in a public place away from the beaten track, an art gallery, the stacks of a library. A cavernous, deserted, regularly cleaned oasis with no graffiti on its walls and toilet paper on the rolls, paper towels in the dispenser, mirrors clean and black as holes.

Into this setting, this almost antiseptic, almost oppressive as a hospital corridor's quiet and chemical chill, this setting that surprises Wally and momentarily confuses, disorients him (Where the fuck am I . . . where is everybody else?), into this setting walks another human being. Male. Caucasian. Middle-aged. Unlucky.

He is dressed more appropriately for this bathroom than Wally. The man's subtle double take lets Wally know. Wally

42

feels for a second like a roach. He wants to scurry away, return to his proper element. The man either decides against pissing in Wally's presence or knows better than to soil this kind of public bathroom with human waste because he proceeds directly to the bank of marble-topped sinks and begins washing his hands. Not much water. Not much finger action. More a willing away of contamination, a ritual immersion in symbolic water of a symbolic sink bowl. Wally wondered if maybe this is what you should do *before* you piss. He'd never tried it or considered it, of course. But that's why blacks and whites were different, wasn't it? Lots of areas of human experience about which they'd profoundly disagree. Rights and privileges and priorities. Even in a bog this large the two of them competed for space when there was space for fifty. Fifty of him or fifty of Wally but no space for one of each.

The man's back was turned to him. Hairs barbered to a precise fringe above stiff, white collar. Twenty years ago this guy might have been a hippie. Wally might have bumped into him down here smoking a joint. Once upon a time a luxuriant ponytail hung from those pitiful clipped locks. In better days they might have shared a toke or two, laughed, lied, scandalized a couple of three-piece-suited dinosaurs who came to scrub their webbed paws and caught them in the act.

So it was almost with regret that he swiftly brought the knife edge of his right hand down, down on the man's neck. An ugly whoomp knocked flesh senseless as a sack of flour. Sharp clicks of bone or teeth cracking on marble edges as the suit crumbles and the body caves to the clean, hard floor.

Wally drags him by the scruff of the neck to a stall. There is very little struggle. Perhaps he snapped the neck. Karate was a passing fancy but he remembered some useful concepts. And his body was basketball hard and willing in spite of the extra pounds he carried.

A splash getting the head in the water. Not very much, actually. The place was neat as a pin. Even the water in the toilet bowl. No sense making a mess. Some people, you just couldn't take them anywhere. But Wally wasn't like that. He remem-

43

bered how delicately the man had washed his hands. Wally patterned himself on that example. Gingerly, slopping very little water out of the bowl, he lowered the face into the spick-and-span fluid. Stepping back he raised his leg and brought his foot down slowly, scrupulously on the white-collared neck. He braced himself for a struggle. Weight back, arms stretched so he was tautly poised between the walls of the stall. Then he pushed down. More water splashed the clean floor. But it was clean water. Didn't even stain his shoe, although one foot was soaked by the end.

Be on the lookout for a nigger wearing one wet foot. Perhaps swollen by now, perhaps faintly stinking of urine, fecal matter, blood, and guts. He is unarmed and dangerous. Approach with caution. Last seen wearing a chessy cat grin, a pink carnation in his lapel. You can hear his heart beating for miles and miles.

Wally washed his hands. Dried his wet foot as best he could with paper towels, crumpled them, neatly disposed of them in the proper receptacle, exited the way he came in.

That's a helluva story, helluva story, Wally. Damn . . . Now do you mind if I ask you a dumb question?

The clouds were eating each other. Big ones swallowing little ones, getting bigger all the time. Little ones leaving nothing behind but holes in the blue, the big ones eating those too.

Help yourself. . . .

Is the story true?

Wally doesn't think he ever really saw the man's face. What entered was a pinkish blur expressing its disapproval of Wally before Wally could register its features. Then a glimpse of a face in the mirror. Wally'd given no warning so it was unlikely that the man's eyes had bloated with panic when he saw in the mirror a dark shape suddenly looming behind him. It all happened too quickly, but for some reason an image of the man's startled face was becoming part of Wally's memory of the scene in the bathroom. A fish face. Popeyed, wide gasping mouth, the raw obscene white of a fish belly yanked from sunless depths of

44

a mirror. The truth was he didn't know now what he'd seen in the glass. His own dark face? The man's white one? An image of dying or guilt or just a flash of light billowing in from the streets as walls collapsed around them and the building disappeared, and the city disappeared and he was here on his bed dreaming the death clash of two puppets on a bare stage. Open to the sky, the wind.

You said it, Reuben. You said it was a dumb question.

Well, if it was nobody, if you can't put any particular body's face in the blank, why don't you make up somebody, give him a face, a name. For the sake of the story. For your sake. For fun.

Okay, but remember. You asked for it, old man.

Who, then?

Your mama.

3

CUDJOE

Reuben watched the woman's behind split again into two even, round lumps, a perfect valentine's heart inverted as she knelt to pick up the amphora. In the jar's shape were buried memories of her curves. Flank and cheek and furrow. Sand in an hourglass shifting its weight in a spiraling *s*. Flow, fissure, cleavage. He traced the neat wave of her buns with his finger. Ran off the page as he repeated the scalloped line forever into the space engulfing his desk. His folding table cluttered and busy as his brain this afternoon. Was it necrophilia? His intense interest in the buttocks of this dead woman caught snap-snap-snap-snap-etc. twelve times by Muybridge's battery of cameras. She's walking, then bending; she kneels daintily, her bare bottom a heavy petaled flower. In the old picture focus is not crisp. No spidery beard of hairs in her crack. A kind of perfect air-gunned fantasy of a naked body in black, grays, white. Reuben's knotty finger still dolloped in the air. Playing a song, leading an orchestra or choir. Soft music of the spheres.

Above and below this "woman kneeling for jar" were similar strips of other naked women in various positions, performing various acts, natural and unnatural. Locked inside them, like the woman's form transposed into the jar's clay, was that elusive secret of motion the photographer sought. And motion was life, wasn't it?

Extraction was the problem. Releasing the genie from the jar, cutting these strips of photos into separate frames, multiplying them infinitely, stacking them and flipping through them fast enough so they ripple into motion, life. Illusion, of course, but one that's slick enough to grab your attention, your belief, for as long as it takes to fly through the stack. Reuben was accommodating. Muybridge's strip of twelve frames enough to trigger his imagination. He fills in the blanks. Pats the dead fannies. Falls in love.

Today was the day he'd promised himself he'd move. Later this morning he'll take Kwansa Parker's problem downtown. She was due in his office tomorrow and he didn't want to disappoint her. For her sake he'd play the game. Trek downtown. Pretend he could change her story.

Toodles was buying so Kwansa was drinking. Toodles's hand played with Kwansa's knee in the darkness under the lip of the bar where nobody could see and nobody cared. Kwansa paid the hand no mind. Toodles had a knee just like she did. And a pussy and titties. Kwansa made no more of Toodles's hand than she would her own hand fingering her own self. She liked Toodles. The heavy black lips, the caterpillar scar on her neck. Toodles's bad mouth that kept everybody in their place. The way-out shoes Toodles and nobody else would put on their feet. Today Toodles's shoes looked like bedroom slippers. The softest, baby-butt purple suede with bootie toes like long string beans curled back toward zippered, floppy tops. Toodles knew who she was, what she was, and wasn't shamed of none of it. Sheeit. Show me one these bullet heads strutting round here got more going for him than Toodles, I'll drop down right there in the street and kiss his behind. And Toodles ain't known for kissing ass. Huhh. Uhhh. Least not they kind of hard-leg runty rooster ass, sugar pie.

Kwansa had never loved with a woman, but the few times the idea crossed her mind, it was with a woman like Toodles. Not mannish. She could have a man for that. Not simpering, cling to anybody-have-them trash like Pearl. No. Had to be somebody got something going for they ownself. Something special you couldn't get nowhere else. Kind of something Toodles kept saying she had. And Kwansa halfway believed her. Never heard nobody say different. Least not to Toodles's face.

Tell the truth, dear, I ain't never give kids that much thought. My sister's got kids. They know they Aunt Toodles give them anything she got. Loves them crawling over me and giving them sugar and all such mess. You know. Being they Aunt Toodles. And they can be sure nuff sweet little devils, too. Make you want to eat them up. Then again they gets to fussing and squabbling. Lips poked out. Whining. Make you want to wring they necks. I guess what it is is I sees them when I wants to. They start being a pain in the ass, Toodles gone, aunt or no aunt. If they yours, you ain't got no choice. They wit you and you wit them. Twenty-four hours a day. Three hundred and sixty-five days a year. Now, that's stone serious. That's hard time. Love them to death and I'd give up my life in a minute to save one of those monkeys, but Toodles ain't ready to be locked up wit nobody, man, woman, or child.

You love em when they yours. Nothing to think about, really. They yours is all.

Well, part of me can dig it. But I gots that other part saying, No way. Uh-uh. Course, I don't have it to worry about no more. Never did have it to worry about when you get right down to it. I mean, my taste never ran that way so I ain't hardly getting knocked up. Alls I know is part of me says yes, but a whole lot of me tired watching women get tore up behind taking care some nigger's baby. Like what they think spozed to happen they steady fucking some hard leg? Ain't no storks in Homewood. Don't these young girls be knowing where babies come from?

48

Sure don't seem like it most the time. Women round here younger than me and they been grandmas for days. How that sound? Grandmas and ain't hardly thirty years old! Women round here having babies fast as they can. All these kids wit kids. How come none the hard legs hustling pussy in here every night ain't got no kids? No kids they taking care of, anyway. They all free and single and disengaged hear them tell it. They quarters ain't going for diapers and shit. They steady buying drinks and playing the jukebox. Hey-babying theyselves to death and ain't none them worrying bout taking care no kids. That's what I see going down round here. Sit right on this stool day in and day out I see it. Everybody in on the fucking. Then it's Mama's baby . . . Daddy's maybe. Seems to me the women ought to figure out how to have they fun then be done. Like the men.

Sometimes you just get caught.

I can understand that. Anybody subject to get put in a trick. What I'm saying is this ain't no new thing. Toodles might get tripped up, but she ain't falling over nothing been in the middle of the road a thousand years and got neon signs and detour and sirens hooked up to it.

Sometimes it's just love.

You getting too far out there now, girl. We talking bout babies. Babies comes from fucking. Love's another thing. This being in love stuff don't make young girls pregnant. It's the fuckin they doing get em knocked up.

You know what I mean. Don't try to tell me you ain't never loved nobody, Toodles. You know how it is. Turns your mind around. You don't be thinking straight all the time.

Trouble is you thinking too much. Thinking about one thing and don't think nothing else. That's when you get foolish. Some Romeo gets your nose open and your legs open. Next thing you know here comes this sweet little cuddly forget-me-not. Then you really got something keep your mind occupied, twenty-four hours a day, sugar. And where's Daddy? Out in the street being lover boy again. You home studying the mailbox. Hope the welfare check come fore the man kick you and baby both out in the street. Somebody ought to write a love song bout all that.

Sing some sense into these empty-head young girls. Sheeit. Old ones too.

I hear you, Toot. Cain't argue with nothing you say. But Cudjoe's mine. Be mine till I die. Long as I got breath in my body, I'ma take care him. He's mine.

Unless they take him away like you say they trying.

Naw. That ain't gon happen. One way or the other I'ma put a stop to it. See Mr. Reuben tomorrow. He's on the case.

Where's Cudjoe now?

Miss Bracey's over on Susquehanna. Old Miss Bracey. You know the Braceys. Leo, Paul, and Isabel. Miss Bracey they grandmama. Raised them, now she raising state kids. Keeps two or three foster kids and she'll watch your kids while you work.

This a pretty good job you got sitting here, Miss Parker.

Go on, girl. My white lady don't need me rest of this week. Thought I'd check out how you good-time folks live.

Well you see, don't you. This here's Heaven, child. Winos and dopeheads and these halfway slick hustling spooks round here sitting up at the bar all day. Yeah. They got it made, don't they? Ain't slaving for nobody. Ain't punching no clocks or standing in no lines. No babies. No old folks to take care of. Got they hustles and they habits. Don't owe nobody nothing. Free as dogshit outside on the sidewalk.

And Toodles laughs and slaps her hand down on the bar and cracks up louder and louder, giggling, choking, points her finger and waves her arms, hollering at this one, motioning another one to get out her face. Nobody knows why she's laughing but everybody knows they're in it so they better laugh too or the joke's on them. Listen at that fool. What's the matter with Toodles? That woman's crazy. Always been. Always will be. Listen at her. Kicking up her heels. Them silly-nosed shoes. Why's she carrying on? Almost fell off the stool. Look at her. Simple bitch. Toodles ain't never had good sense. Mr. Weaver wipes his three-fingered hand across his mouth. He's hiding his bad teeth. The bad ones he has left. It's also a matter of hiding the bad ones long gone. He's taken to laughing with his mouth closed because it's mostly gum when he opens up. Sometimes he can't help himself so he brings up his hand to cover his gappy smile. He's lived with the crippled hand longer than he's lived with the crippled mouth so it doesn't even occur to him to shield himself with his good hand. He smiles at Toodles carrying on and loves both hands the way he can't love his emptied mouth yet.

Toodles still shaking, like the laughter might break out again, but the shakes are like hiccups now and Toodles is trying to ignore them. Her face isn't young anymore, she's staring at the gin in the squat shot glass beside her tall glass of ice water. Mutt and Jeff, Kwansa thinks. She'd look like Mutt standing beside Toodles's long body. It's quiet now, she thinks. More than quiet because something's gone now. Toodles put some- thing in the air and shook it up and now it's gone but you're listening for it so it's more than just quiet, it's you listening for something you lost. Paying attention now. So it's more than quiet now. Toodles is through. She was stirred up but now she's just hiccuping away the little bit that's left. Her hand, the one closest to Kwansa, the one once busy rubbing Kwansa's knee, is on top of the bar now. Two big rings with bright centers. One blue, one yellow with little beads of the same color surrounding the bud in the middle. Make you think of flowers. And Murphy's five-and-dime, where they used to sell little-girl rings like that. Tape wound around the bottom curve because Too- dles got skinny fingers. Some her black rubbed off on the tape. There is a tuck, a pin, because the elastic's gone in the waist of Kwansa's drawers. When she remembers, she's afraid it will stab her. You pinned and taped because nothing fit. Everything lasted too long or didn't last long enough. Kwansa pats the hard flowers, pats the hand in which they're planted.

Be over my dead body. That's the only way they'll take my Cudjoe.

Kwansa starts up the steps of Miss Bracey's front porch. It's a nice porch. Cinder blocks and wrought iron and a freshly painted green roof. An aluminum awning, green and white

51

striped, the kind you used to see on lots the houses up here on Monticello when Monticello was a nice street to live on. She knows something is wrong because as she mounts Miss Bracey's steps she's thinking about taking Cudjoe home to a house nice like the one she's about to enter. Little neat yard out front with sunflowers and a rosebush. Porch steps whitewashed, gleaming like the picket fence guarding the green yard. What she's thinking doesn't make sense so she knows it's wrong, she's never lived in a storybook house, but it's also right for the moment and she keeps thinking it. Lets herself enjoy the picture of a clean, neat, private place where she'll take Cudjoe when they leave Miss Bracey's. Then Cudjoe comes out the screen door a grown man. She knows it's him because he still has his little-boy pouting lips behind the thick moustache. He's wearing Waddell's clothes. He has something nasty in his hand, but the man is her Cudjoe. Six or seven feet tall. His shadow glides to her first. Starts eating her. She can't figure out how she'll gather all this big man into her arms and carry him home. She realizes it's not going to be easy. She could get hurt. Hurt him. But none of it makes sense. He's too big, too old. She'll have to think whatever she's thinking all over again because it's not happening that way. She's been drinking gin all afternoon and Toodles is in the ladies'. It's time to go pick up her child.

His daddy come by and got him just a lil while ago.

What you say?

I say his daddy took him. Your Cudjoe a sweet little boy. He minds so nice. Not like some these wild Indins. Sitting right there on the couch minding his business, looking out the window. There's my daddy. Here come my daddy. That's what he said in his little, sweet crickety voice. My daddy. My daddy. They ain't been gone a half hour. No more than that.

Kwansa stares at Miss Bracey, who keeps a mob of children like the old lady in the shoe. Miss Bracey is the tallest child. Her smile, soft housecoat, her white hair, bosom broad enough for a whole nest of woolly heads, the pleats in her face, do not make her different. She's just one of the children, and Kwansa's urge to scream at her, kill her, passes as quickly as the rapid-fire sputter of words from Miss Bracey's mouth. She speaks fast so her voice carries above the children's chattering, so you'll know this wrinkled one, this one a smidgen taller than the rest is in charge.

Shit. Shit. Shit. God damn his soul. Kwansa turns away abruptly. Wraps her hands around the throat that isn't in the crowded room. Chokes Waddell because she can't choke Miss Bracey. She's down the steps into the street before Miss Bracey remembers to ask for her dollar.

That's when it starts to rain. A sudden, slashing downpour. And Kwansa caught out in it, soaked before she can decide to wait out the cloudburst inside somewhere or ignore it and comb the streets for her boy. She knows that fool Waddell ain't got no better sense than to keep Cudjoe outdoors in the rain. Cudjoe can't take it. Half his life he carries a little snot worm on his upper lip. Kissing him good-night after she turns out the light, if he bounces up and bumps against her lips because there's still all that wiggle in him even at bedtime, even when she's tired as a rag and tucks him in and ready for the day to be over, if he leans up to meet her kiss in the darkness, she'll get salty worm on her cheek, her lips. Sometimes it's like a scab on the back of his hand, the hand he uses all day to wipe the snot off his lip. Flaky scar-looking trails, dried to a darker brown on the back of his hand. Like blood. Like tracks of tears. Cudjoe's dusty fist. The scabby seams she scrubs clean every night because every day, that drippy nose, that cough, then his ears plugged up and the cough turns hacky and you see the fold in the center of his chest when he wheezes and the tiny bones shudder and his heart beats like a bird's wings. So easy. A draft could get him going, a day starting sunny and he doesn't wear his sweater to Miss Bracey's and it cools off in the afternoon and Cudjoe gets a chill. His lungs, chest, nose, eyes—all droop and leak. Prone to respiratory illnesses, the lady doctor at the clinic said. Because he was born early. Before his lungs matured. He'll catch up. Don't worry. He'll be a fine healthy young man before you know it.

But the worm dogs him. Eats at his lip. Raw sometimes from rubbing, from wiping. She smears on Vaseline. A shiny clown's mouth. Rastus the clown. Her Cudjoe getting bad sick because Waddell has him out in the rain. No sweater, no jacket, nothing but his thin, brown skin and sneakers on his feet won't keep water out a minute.

She's soaked before she realizes she's standing in one place, not searching, not seeking shelter, just standing in the pouring rain calling his name. Cudjoe, Cudjoe. Like a crazy person. Like Etta Thompson on her back, a big fat black whale beached and screaming for Jesus. The gin cloud long gone. The sky black and heavy now. She looks up to find the peephole, the window up there somebody's emptying buckets through. She's the only fool out in the street. If she moves, they'll move the hole, move all the damn buckets, to keep it raining on her nappy head.

Look at you, sugar. A drowned rat. Didn't your mama teach you come in out the rain?

She wants to tell Toodles the whole story. Remember it all for Toodles so Toodles will understand. How *yes* her mother told her things all the time. How her mother's voice and words and face have faded, blended, a soft, warm blanket kind of something when they come and wrap round her and take her back. Because her mother loved her so much, held her in her arms and whispered secrets, fed her the world in easy, soft pieces. It comes and wraps round her. Feathers, wool, tickly almost, Toodles, when I remember my mama I can hear her, touch her. Funny how you forget. Even Mama's face, even those things she whispered over and over to me when I sat in her lap or held a corner of her dress while she's cooking or ironing. My thumb's in it, too. Like I used to hold a corner of a rag and rub my nose and suck my thumb. That comes back, too. The taste of it. But I don't remember how she looked. Couldn't draw a picture for a million dollars, but I smell her and feel a kind of cuddly warm thing wrap round me and it's her sure nuff from those years before she died and I can't remember hardly nothing about her now except she loved me and talked in a soft, sweet voice to me and now you ask me did she say this or say that, I swear I don't know.

You shaking like a leaf, girl. Come on here and sit down next to me. You gon catch the walking pneumonia.

Kwansa ached to tell Toodles the whole story of her mama dying, and if she could die, anybody could die. Cudjoe melting in the rain. Coughing, spitting blood. People storming the house with food. Got to beat back the flies buzzing over the potato salad, cakes, mounds of fried chicken. Cudjoe's lungs like tiny wings of baby birds fall from the nest. Bubble-eyed. Yellow and wet as snot smeared on the sidewalk. They tumble down because wings ain't ready. Little broken toothpicks on their backs. Her baby's lungs need time to grow. She thinks the doctor means she should pull them out Cudjoe's chest. Little snotty wings. Lay them in the palm of her hand and gently carry them to a window where sun comes in. Like she thinks she remembers the sun used to lean into her mama's kitchen. There on a shelf under the window in a little glass dish half filled with clear warm water she'll set his lungs and they'll grow like onions. Long, tough green roots spreading in the water. Stronger and bigger every day till they're ready and she can tuck them back again next to his heart, one on either side like wings. Like two strong gates to seal away evil and hurt and watery tears.

Double down two times, Mr. Chandler. Don't you see this child's drowning? Wipe your eyes, sugar. Dry your face. Put some this heat in your belly.

The gin makes Kwansa stagger. A fireball tearing her up as it zigzags and pops through her insides. It zaps the last of her strength. A fizz, spiff sound like two fingers snuffing out a candle and there's nothing left, no thought to think, no word to say, no way to hold back tears. She's crying like a baby at this bar, next to this busy-fingered dyke. She's a pitiful thing low as low can be.

Go on, finish your drink. Chandler got more where that came from. Let it all hang out, sugar. Whatever got you, got you good. Let it all come down.

When Cudjoe coughs, his whole feverish body rises off her chest. She clutches him tighter, snuggles him deeper in her bosom, afraid he might fly away.

God damn his soul. Damn . . . damn him.

Who, baby?

Waddell took him. Waddell took my Cudjoe. My Cudjoe's gone.

Hey . . . hey now. Give it to me slower now. What's Waddell done? Where's your boy?

Took em. Stole him away from Miss Bracey's. I ought to known better. Ought to told her Waddell ain't his daddy. Waddell ain't nothing to him but a thorn. A hurting thorn. And I just know he let Cudjoe get soaking wet. I know Cudjoe's coughing and that fool don't know the first thing to do. Cudjoe be real sick in the morning. Worse if he ain't took care of.

Slow down, girl. You jumping way head of me. Nobody be outside in rain like this. Even Waddell got better sense than that. Even you had to come in out it. Wherever he is, your little boy ain't outside in this storm. He probably somewhere all toasty, playing, eating sweets. Stuffing his little self with sweets. The men do em like that. You know they do. Stuff em wit cookies and candy cause they don't know what else to do. Every time I used to see my daddy, or the fool call hisself my daddy, he got a piece of candy waving it in my face. Jelly beans. And I hated them sticky things. But that was him. Ain't seen him in years, I'm grown as he is and here he come with a bag of jelly beans. Nigger always good for a jelly bean. If he's in hell today he got that bag down there with him. Be grinning and poking one in my face when I show up.

You think he took Cudjoe home?

Where else? Listen at that rain, child. You been out in it. You know they under somebody's roof, somewhere.

I don't even know where Waddell lives now.

Somebody in here bound to know where he stay. If Chandler don't know, he'll know who knows. . . . Mr. Chandler, bring over that bottle and your own brown-eyed handsome big-behind self a minute. Got something to ax you, baby.

Now is a time, Kwansa thinks, I need to be better than I am. Smarter, prettier. So somebody will listen. Somebody help. She wished away the blackness of her skin. The dumbness that let her believe too many of the lies people told her. She is on Toodles's itchy couch, shivering. If it's still raining outside, it's rain quiet as a cat. The street was out there, blacker than the darkness folded in these thin walls of Toodles's place, but she couldn't hear a thing. Listening for hours it seemed and she'd heard nothing moving outside. Hours or minutes that seemed like hours. She couldn't really say. She's been listening since she was a nappy-head, ashy-legged little girl. Listening in the stillness after rain for someone to come touch her, tell her everything was going to be all right.

She starts to call Toodles. Not call and wake her up. Not call her to do something or say something. Just *Toodles*. Speak her name like you turn on the radio in the morning because the house is empty. Or snap on a light in a room you're leaving so it'll be on when you come back.

When you were prettier, smarter, they had to treat you better to get what they wanted. Take a little time with you. Give you little things. There'd be a song maybe they sing at you. A favorite place they'd take you to sneak away from everybody else. If you had that special look, the bright skin, the good hair they liked, you could have things your own way sometimes.

She is shivering. Cudjoe might be sitting somewhere just as cold, just as damp. Coughing his life away. Blanket from the back of the couch was balled round her feet. She kicks it loose, picks it off the floor, and stretches it over her legs. Turning on her side again she draws her knees up closer to her chest. Her feet are wet and her shoulders. The rest dry enough. Shivers keep walking back and forth anyway, from her toes to her neck. She tries to get situated better in some old robe or something Toodles had tucked around her before she had turned out the light and spread the blanket over Kwansa's legs.

You sleep now. Your baby ain't hardly out in the street this time of night. In all this rain.

But how did Toodles know? Couldn't anything happen?

Couldn't anything be true? If you loved somebody, couldn't the worst thing happen just because you loved them and needed them?

Lay down on the couch here. I'll pull something over you keep the chill off. Ain't nothing we can do tonight. This over your shoulders . . . and here . . . this blanket. Toodles had tucked her in like she should be tucking in her Cudjoe. . . . *Now I lay me down . . . Now I lay me down . . . pray the Lord . . . pray the Lord . . . my soul to keep . . . my soul to keep.* When she taught him the first time to say his prayers and his voice echoed hers, a phrase at a time lined out like hymns in church, learning the words as they're sung, one strong voice, then the stronger swell of all the voices together, when she said the words of the prayer she hadn't said for years and hadn't intended to say that night till the words came and said themselves, and he repeated them, recited the music in them, she was remembering, learning the prayer again herself as she hovered over Cudjoe, swaying to the cadence, amazed at how serious he was, kneeling with his little popcorn head bowed, and she realized she wasn't sure who was speaking the words first, realized that she was following as much as leading.

She thinks now of climbing a mountain. Of the mountain climbing her. She lived at the bottom of its steep, rocky sides. She could never see the top. She knew another mountain, just as high and cruel, grew down in the chalky shadows at her feet. Twins. Like a tall, pointy scoop of chocolate almond atop a buttery cone. The ice cream cone always clutched in somebody else's grimy fist. Why didn't they go head and lick it? Bite it. Why they got to keep looking at it and licking they chops so she got to look too? Always some other kid with something good like ice cream. But she owned this evil mountain. Her long trip up. Her fall and plunge and sinking forever if she lost her grip.

Eat your damn ice cream cone and leave me alone. They are out there in the dark, gathering round, waiting. She can hear them whispering as they bump and jostle and settle in. They have the faces she's been seeing all her life. Homewood faces. She had learned to smile at them, speak to them, turn up her nose or cut

58

her eyes. Their names are like flashes of light, gone as quick as they come, never lifting the darkness yet tickling it, teasing a corner of her eye, gone before she can speak to them. They are gathering round to listen to her story, and when she has nothing to tell them they'll start talking nasty about her. How she lost herself and lost Cudjoe and her whole life she's been good for nothing but losing things. Boys, then men, then anybody got one and got the price sixty-twice stick it in her. Spilling what they don't want in her. Dirtying her with what they got no use for. What they care nothing about. Shake it, rub it, wipe it on her. All the washrags, all the hot water in the world can't clean up what they dump on her. What they lose. And she couldn't even keep Cudjoe. She couldn't even be better for him. *Now I lay me down* . . . She'd patted his spongy hair. Never let the barber touch it. Cudjoe's hip little fro. His natural African wool growing free in this strange land. He rubs his sleepy eyes. Bedroom eyes. Grown women would say that and giggle. Better watch him, girl. He got them bedroom eyes. He'll be a heartbreaker.

The silence from the street fills her chest. She sits up and the room empties. The party's over. She doesn't want to hear what the voices have to say. Same ole. Same ole. She's heard it all a thousand times before. She believes it. She ain't shit. Never will be. Cudjoe's gone because he's spozed to be gone. Gone before whatever brings her down so low brings him down too.

Sometime that night after the downpour, the gin, the darkness of a strange room, after she gives up on the couch where she'd twisted and turned trying to hug herself to sleep, Toodles says to her: I thought you'd come. Didn't want to push it but I wanted you to come so bad I could taste it. Left the door open. Turned back the covers your side the bed.

Then it was like the ache of morning. Too bright, too hot to handle all at once. You cover your face. Fight it. Like it might do something hurtful. Till slowly warmth and sweet light find you where you're hiding, open parts of you that have been dreaming through the long night of sunrise.

4

THOTH

Two knocks. Knock. Knock. The sound of someone at the door represented as it is in novels, cartoons. Knock. Knock. A rapping at the door expressed by the word *knock,* printed twice upon the stillness as if Reuben's life were being written, not lived. An afterimage floats where the words had disappeared. His old eyes playing tricks. His ears being silly. People hear sounds, not words. Words are bred in books and newspapers. Chunks of alphabet with arbitrary meanings attached. Sounds were like birds or rain. Part of the world that went about its business ignoring words because words didn't matter, didn't care. Wind, sunset and sunrise, roaches, fire—no matter what words claimed, no matter how hard they tried to fool themselves and take the world to hell with them, Reuben believed certain things would persist, would find new colors and mate in new combinations, push up through the rot and charred rock, bloom again, ache again as his stubborn hands ached snapping and popping and pinching each other to life each morning. Plans were fermenting deep in green sap even now as words faltered on their last legs, *knock, knock,* desperate to keep their power, to be seen as well as heard, seen as real by weak creatures like himself who pretended they were authors of the universe.

I agree. I agree, said Eadweard Muybridge, doubling his words just as he'd doubled his knock before pushing through Reuben's door. In a rush, he always seemed in a rush, driven by the god of motion he chased.

I believe you're quite correct. Yes. Yes. The spiral of one age is closing, another's about to writhe into being. The word's dead. Long live the deed.

Reuben stared at the ruffle-bearded, breathless white man who'd thrust himself into his trailer. He saw the whorled length of a steel drill shaft tapering to a point, a chicken's scrawny neck being wrung. . . .

Nothing changes, but every thousand years or so we all take a bath, a great plunge. . . .

Into what, Mr. Muybridge?

A medium, an element, a bunghole. Doesn't matter what you call it. A great plunge into . . . stuff. Yes. One kind of stuff or another which washes away the dust of the past. Not all the dust, mind you. Not all the past. Only those scales the latest epoch has crusted over our eyes. Cycles. The old concentrated into a single bit of . . . stuff . . . that serves as a pivot, a starting point for the new. All very simple, really. One age, one set of assumptions, wears itself out, but there is simultaneously a concentration of vital force, incandescence, a final focused energy . . . exhaustion, depletion . . . but also a final, life-sustaining flash of spirit.

And a sigh.

Yes. Perhaps a sigh, an incredibly concentrated sigh. Everything ever spoken, ever learned, loved, and lost available for an instant on the end of a pin.

The pin pricks the balloon.

Yes. Yes. A bang and a sigh. Both. Simultaneously. One vision of the world reaches its limits, blows itself to smithereens. The air is clear, rushes away, free to be shaped again according to a new dispensation.

Whimper, not bang. That's how Eliot put it.

Oh, really. And he's not even born yet.

What time is it, then?

Let's call it the Stone Age. We want what we build to last forever. Inventing steel and concrete so we can write our names with them. Pretending such mementos last longer than messages scratched in sand. Which is more permanent, Reuben, a fossil or a hawk's shadow flickering across a rock?

Well . . .

Careful now. Don't answer before you consider this: Which is heavier, a pound of iron or a pound of feathers?

That one's easy.

A conundrum to dupe a schoolboy, aye. Still it does befuddle people because everyone thinks they know iron weighs more than feathers. But that's not the question, is it? As that old uncle of yours used to say, Pound's a pound the world around.

So a pound of fossils and a pound of shadows weigh the same.

Quite. They are equally impermanent measured against the endlessness of time.

Minutes, hours, years, all the same.

Exactamente. Because they are bites out of a pie that can't be eaten.

A pie.

A bottomless bowl of cherries. Or a snake with its tail in its mouth. Or a turtle shell. Or a sacred hoop. Or the round face of a clock, the circle of numbers from one to twelve to one, spinning invisibly over and over again. Still, yet always moving. Perfect representations of time. Everywhere and nowhere at once. Eternally moving, eternally still. The same numbers on the clock face can tell today's time, tomorrow's, yesterday's. A clock's face registers every moment, past, future, present. It expresses our true relation to time. How time mothers us and orphans us. Our immersion in a great sea, drowning, spewed forth endlessly. Each sounding we take connects us to all soundings. Each time different, each time the same. Many in the one; one in the many.

Gods, then.

We bay at the heels of time. Like good Christian soldiers we drive it upward and onward, worshiping duration, progress. We've debased time. It's no longer a playground we share with the gods; it's a commodity we buy and sell, get and spend, save and lose. We're afraid to let go. We forget where we've been is where we're going. We don't enjoy the ride.

But your pictures. Aren't they trying to stop time? Isn't that the whole point of *Animal Motion,* stopping time to unlock the secrets of motion?

At first I believed I could understand motion by halting it, free it of illusion by freezing it. For centuries words had reigned. And words engender stillness; they chill intellect and body. I preached motion, explosion of boundaries, exploration of the acts which precede language, give language its excuse for being. After all, dance was the first speech, wasn't it? We pointed and wagged our heads and hugged our bodies and mimicked shadows flitting in the cave. I wished to prove that nothing is what it seems. That the word is always too late or too soon or nothing at all. I was anatomizing motion to unveil its mysteries and discovered motion is irreducible. No matter how many cameras I banked to capture the stages of a single gesture, motion escaped my net. I learned motion is like time in its invisible, indivisible plunge from one frame to the next. My pictures never caught it. I had been determined to bring forth a new heaven and earth. Drag it kicking and screaming from the sea. Instead I was sucked under. I thought I was cracking the Stone Age but I created rows and rows of cells. Tiny, isolated cubicles with a pitiful little figure marooned in each one. Prisoners who couldn't touch, didn't even know the existence of the twin living next door.

I failed miserably. Wound up in my garden, Reuben, building a scale model of the Great Lakes.

I'm sorry. And I think I have to go now. Work . . . promises . . .

We could still do it, you know. Take the next step. Become like angels. Let go of our stony notions of starts, stops, beginnings, middles, ends. Let the spinning hands take us. Fly us away.

Must go now. But you'll return, won't you?

What goes round . . .

Comes round.

Gimme some skin on that, brother.

Reuben watches the naked old man pass through his trailer's walls. Like a turkey through the corn, he thinks. A hot knife through butter. "Nigger" through a cracker's lips. A sword through stone.

All that heady double-talk about time makes his gold watch heavy this morning. If it's morning. Guiltily he consults the ivoried face of his timepiece. Ten-thirty. Has he been asleep at his desk, in his clothes? And if sleeping, how long? Rip van Winkle years or just a few, sweet nods? An old man's oatmeal head drooping into the pleats of his turtly neck, his skin bunched under his chin like the bib his mother ties round his neck. Here, baby. Take this, baby. Her face is broad and round as an Eskimo's. He can't be remembering that woman born in another century who lay down and spilled him out upon the damp earth. Like a doe in the forest. Not only him. Two of them all spotty like fawns. A dark one and a light one. Twins on a bed of soft earth and leaves and grass. He cannot be remembering because it happened too long ago. Was he ever that young once? The cries, the shivering, light slitting open his eyes. It began when a crowbar pried loose sky from earth and he was just there, where he'd always been, under the rock of darkness waiting. Light. A terrible weight lifted and then levered down again on his shoulders. He thought his heart had been broken in two when his brother was stolen from his side. Always he had heard only one heart, strong, firm, its beat a fire within him, warming, pumping light. Then the sound was halved. Two hearts beating, the slightest syncopation, his brother or himself off by a quarter beat as he discovered he was two, not one.

At the bottom of his watch a brass charm was attached by the thinnest gold wire. Reuben fingered the bullet-shaped object. The wire passed through a hole bored in the bullet's nose, then through a loop on the watch. To see the charm Reuben had to pull his watch from his vest pocket and to check his watch he had to drag out the charm. Since the watch was linked to a chain and the chain pinned inside his vest and his vest fastened around his midsection, the container of his heart, lungs, liver, et cetera, Reuben sometimes thought of the charm wearing him. Conceived of himself as an elaborate headdress flowing from the pointed helmet crowning his brother's skull. Because the charm was an image of his brother. Yes. If you looked closely, you'd see that the object decorating Reuben's watch was not a bullet, not a miniature whistle or pencil but a man, severely stylized, African style, all torso and brow and arching crown. Only the barest suggestion of arms, little amphibian nubs held stiffly at its sides, and stubby, elephant-toed feet. Years of rubbing, of talking to the little statue with his fingertips, had streamlined its features. He'd fashioned a man Muybridge would have approved of. Honed for motion, speed, a charge of bristling energy compressed under the conical cap.

On the idol's chin, below huge frog eyes and triangle of nose, you could still discern a pointed beard. Below the beard a circular pendant bearing a raised scarab covered most of the man's chest. Foreshortened legs bowed outward from the body, suggesting coiled strength or graceful submission. One day the tiny figure would be smooth as a stone. It would become a teardrop, a petal, abstract as grief.

Reuben closed the gold lid of his pocket watch and held the timepiece in the palm of his hand so the little man dangled upright, suspended a few inches above the cluttered desk top. No one had told him his brother's name, so when he spoke to this stern reflection of himself, this twin, this sloe-eyed, long-faced trace of what once had been, of a lost time when he had been more, and the more was better, Reuben called it Reuben. If questioned about the awkwardness, the confusion inherent in brothers bearing the same name, he would have answered: It's not a problem for me. Or him. Conceding at the same time that the other's name was also Reuben II, "Two" for short, a nickname he employed in certain moods.

In a dream or vision or during one of the extra lives he grew more certain he had lived, the longer he lived, Reuben had learned his brother was in prison. In a vast, gray prison in a cell too small for a dog, from which he'd never be released. He mourned his lost brother from that day. Part of the ritual, part of the promise he'd pledged himself from that moment never to break, was keeping the body of his brother always with him. For years when he'd thought of it as a curious but singularly ugly fetish, origin unknown, utility and worth questionable, the teardrop image had languished in the bottom of a file box among exhausted yellow pads, inkless souvenir pens, cuff links that had lost their mates, paper clips, pennies, matchbooks from overpriced, far-flung restaurants. Then the dream or vision or whatever it was. Reuben saw the elongated, straight back of a man sitting on a low stool, his feet, his head, lost in darkness. In a cage whose four solid walls the prisoner could have touched from where he sat. No apparent source of light, yet the incredibly stiff, upright back of the man was silhouetted so that it split the darkness, defining itself, dividing the enclosure in two. Much later Reuben would understand where the threads of light edging the manshape originated. Those heavy-lipped pop eyes averted from him in his first glimpse of the cell were glowing in the dark, backlighting the scene. But Reuben wasn't ready to deal with fiery eyes that first time. He could barely handle what was revealed.

Not the prisoner's voice, but another, strange and familiar at once, a voice Reuben could describe only as coming from "on high." Wherever that was, whatever that meant, was how the voice in the vision sounded when it announced once and for always: This man is your brother.

The million times afterward those same words skewered Reuben, they were never again spoken by any voice but his own. "On high" didn't repeat itself. Once was enough. The point was made. A steel door slammed behind him. Iron clattered against iron, bolts rammed home, keys twisted in locks, tumblers fell. Reuben would need all the days of his life to examine the black cell, become acquainted with the brother sealed there.

So each night Reuben frees the chain and watch and charm from the pockets of his vest, converts watch chain to neck chain, stretches the gold noose round his neck, fastens its circular clasp, then lays back on his bed to sleep. Circles within circles within circles linked over his bony chest, which rises and falls almost in time with his brother's.

Awake or asleep his boon companion. His cut buddy. Reuben dangled him closer to the desk's surface. Walked Reuben to Kwansa Parker's sorry papers.

Oh Thoth, patron of scribes. Full moon springing from the head of Seth, god of darkness. Thoth the "reckoner of days" in his moonship. Time and light and writing overseen by Thoth, and in his spare hours, as protector of Osiris, he aided the dead. Perhaps he'd help with this flood of papers drowning Reuben's desk. Reuben couldn't recall how or why the baboon became Thoth's totem animal. Yet a baboon, brow furrowed in deep thought, middle finger searching his asshole, was a perfect emblem of the writer. Thoth and sloth. A baboon marooned in the moon.

First thing each morning Reuben removes the chain from his neck. His hopeless fingers pick at the clasp. He'd dreamed once of sawing his fingers off, old and bent and useless as they were. Joint by joint down to the nub of his hand. No blood in the dream. Just the certainty he'd be better off without his knotty fingers. Merrily sawing away as if he'd grow new ones or miss the old ones not one iota. He'd pick, pick till the clasp was undone. Entire lifeline—watch, chain, charm—would follow him through his morning routine of shave, bowel movement, bath; then it would be pinned across the front of whichever vest he donned that day. Watch nestled deep in one pocket below his heart, excess chain coiled, pinned in another, a dollop of bright links draping the modest paunch his tailored waistcoats didn't quite conceal.

Had he somehow helped cause his brother's plight? Did years of neglect, careless stowage on the bottom layer of a bottom box, burial under sheaves of yellowing pads, did all that equal turning a lock, throwing away a key? He couldn't know for sure and that vexed him, but he knew he was responsible now, that the image of his brother he'd salvaged depended on him and he depended on it, whatever *it* was. Towing around the little man, touching, talking, sleeping with him on his chest, the frog eyes staring at him over the rolled edge of the tub, impatient on the sink top where he'd gingerly set clock, rope, relic. The two of them joined now. Yet what if his care, his love were too little, too late, beside the point now. Point being he'd forgotten his brother, lost him, killed him deader than a doorknob each day he'd left him languishing in a deadend file.

Perhaps he'd lost a precious part of himself forever. A loss Reuben needed his brother to heal. All those lives he'd lived or imagined he'd lived would not restore the missing part; he needed his brother to complete a Reuben larger than both of them. He needed his brother's eyes to see around corners, just as his brother needed Reuben's oversize, crippled fingers to worry the clasp each morning. His brother's glowing eyes could see through stone, X-ray eyes piercing to the heart of the matter. Reuben's failing parts much less flashy. Yet he taught his arthritic fingers to be doggedly loyal. Doing what had to be done to keep his twin safe, close. Remembering, trying to atone for so much forgetting. Sloth. Fear. For so much missed.

Reuben combs his pointy beard, the itchy skin beneath. He's been napping. Daydreaming again. Have another twenty-four hours passed without him? It's ten-thirty in the morning. A child's being stolen from its mother.

In the old days they used this trick to bind a lover. Perhaps it worked. Perhaps it didn't. Nothing lost by trying the old way.

Reuben straightened in his chair. Shoved aside the clutter. Cleared a threshing ground in the center of his desk.

O Thoth, Mighty Moonglow Maker, Great Inkspotter and Inkblotter, the One who puts the Tick in my Tock, be with me this morning. You and anybody else willing. Do your best. Help me with this child's business. Reuben's watch beats in his vest pocket. Telling time, the job he must do.

68

When Reuben sits on the chair behind the card table that serves as a desk, his feet don't quite reach the floor. A lower chair and he'd be Kilroy to his clients, a half-moon of head, two beady eyes staring at their navels. Reuben is a small man. Which had its compensations. Which also had to be compensated. A telephone book under his butt for certain kinds of visitors. A box under the desk to rest his feet upon when somebody's troubles unravel interminably. He'd nudge his junk box into position when his legs ached. Once large and square and sturdy, the cardboard was molded now, contoured to the weight and shape of his ankles. It was his flower box. He'd plant his feet and feel the tired roots inch down, spreading like the long hair of a woman swimming. Gradually a tingle would saunter up through the blades of his shins. His haunches would sigh. His mouth start working better, his eyes spring alert, his ears turn hungry again. The junk box his briar patch, his pedestal. Mounting it he'd feel the wind in his face. Bright-eyed, bushy-tailed, raring to go.

Sometimes. Other times the box full of miring clay, quicksand. If he gave in, he'd be sucked under. He kicks the box from beneath the table. Unknots the four corners of its flaps, digs down for a strip of cloth.

Reuben was amazed as always by the stuff he'd accumulated. Didn't have any notion where most of it came from. How many lives had been consumed hoarding it. A mess was what it was. Different each time he looked. Junk piling up faster than he used it, discarded it. When had he begun collecting such nonsense? A rag, a bone, a hank of hair. Ancient grains of rice, feathers, stones, a plastic baggie of grave dirt, a string of jingle bells, leaves, dried insects, pebbles of colored glass, seashells, bits of broken mirror, needles and thread, more stones. He'd sift through and discover something he'd never seen before. As if deep down in the bottom of the box a stew percolated, the ingredients churning and turning and propagating new ingredients. He was cautious as he raked his hand through the mix. More than once he'd been stung.

He located the scrap of blue-and-white cloth he'd believed was down in there somewhere. Little more than a foot long, two or three inches wide. It would do. He spread it like a banner across the clear space on his table, smoothed wrinkles, read the staggered accents rhythmed into a pattern on the cotton strip.

A ball of string next. He gnawed it with his pointy teeth so it snapped apart easily into lengths he needed. Then he gathered a little bit of this, a little bit of that from the box, carefully folding each item he harvested into its own compartment in the length of cloth. He hummed as he worked, but didn't pay attention to the music he was making, didn't notice how dexterously, nimbly his fingers folded and tied.

Reuben stops for a moment to consider his handiwork. He hears himself humming, smiles at the words that go with the tune:

> My bonnie lies over the ocean
> My bonnie lies over the sea
> My bonnie lies over the ocean
> Oh bring back my bonnie to me
> Bring back, bring back
> Oh, bring back . . .

Recites them silently while he adds a few finishing touches to the bundle.

Bring back. Bring back . . . the sailor from the sea . . . love from a scented scarf.

They say you can bind a loved one this way. Sew her tight to your bosom. But be careful with them needles, mon. Don't pierce him breast. Don't draw him blood.

Kwansa Parker's son is wrapped in the folds. And Kwansa, all solid, brown bosom, breast and behind of her is in there too. The big, sad eyes. Stiff, hot-combed hair. Her son, as Reuben tries to visualize him, won't stay still. He darts like a fish through indigo and white shadows. He is shy, always seeks places to hide. Reuben braids them together, parent and child. Mother and son together with all they need to survive packed

70

into this closed fist he's manufacturing. Wind, Sea, Earth, Stars. Protect them. Save them.

Oh, my. My, my. Look what I've become. Reuben speaks the words he's thinking. He's ashamed, frightened.

Why do I tamper? Who do I think I am?

He lets the deep blue bundle drop from his hand. Like a hot coal while he held it. He should have squeezed till his flesh sizzled away. Down to the brittle black bones. Down to the foolishness sleeping in the white soup of the bone's marrow.

You are what you are. Mountebank. Charlatan. Fool. Witch doctor. They say it again. He hears again. Nods to the empty trailer. Scans every well-traveled square inch. You are what you are. Their voices taunting him. All of Philadelphia laughing him out of existence again.

5

FLORA

The Philadelphia Transit Commission trolley clatters along Woodland Avenue, inching up the steep grade where the tracks parallel the black iron fence of a cemetery. Reuben's hot in his linen suit. His straw boater squeezes sweat in rivulets down his brow. I'm melting, he thinks, on this hard trolley seat. Wicker printing a checkerboard on my ass. Sweat in all my cracks and creases. A fat cemetery rat wobbles into the middle of the broad avenue, reaches a magic point of no return, and decides to scoot across the path of the trolley rather than slink back to the green shadows it had deserted. Above the rattle of the trolley car Reuben could hear the clumsy rat brain calculating, then skimpy rat legs propelled it over the cobblestones. A skittering, head-long sprint till it disappeared under Reuben's side of the trolley. As far as he could tell, the rat didn't emerge. The trolley chugged on up Woodland. His stop was next.

Why is Schubert playing in the background? Strings. The *notturno*. Pizzicato. A piano strummed so it sounds more harp than keyboard. Go to sleep. Go to sleep. *Schlafe, mein Liebster*. Dear sweet pumpkin. Flora had golden eyes. In the only dream of her he'd allowed himself to dream, once, just once, she'd called him Beastie. Her little wet-nosed puppy. Sniffing and whining on all fours. Ready to mount the olive hills of her buttocks. Down in the valley. The valley so low.

The professor at Flora's house of pleasure, who played mostly ragtime and honky-tonk, knew all kinds of music. While Reuben sat in the parlor waiting for his boys, old Dudley Armstrong would entertain him with snippets from the classics, bits of Chopin, Bach, Schubert. Never a complete piece. Dudley said it hurt too much to play a piece from start to finish. The piano player was reminded of his talents, what he'd dreamed of accomplishing and should be doing now instead of providing musical accompaniment for the humping and grinding going on overhead, up the narrow stairs in the three bedrooms just a few yards from where he sat with Reuben in the parlor while Reuben listened to the last few chords of an interrupted sonata drift away, the adagio richer, fuller, because it mourned notes that would never follow.

On Saturday night, twice a month, the boys from Alpha Omega arrived to take their pleasure. During these visits, Reuben, the boys' leader and mascot, had become acquainted bit by bit with the painful kernels of Dudley Armstrong's story. The professor was not usually a talker. He never spoke to the boys unless spoken to and even then he seldom responded with more than a grunt or nod or sour, glowering frown that let it be known in no uncertain terms any speech addressed to him was a dangerous intrusion on his dignity. Armstrong was a drinker, sullen, aloof, sorry for himself beyond words. When bourbon lubricated his tongue and he sputtered or slurred out facts about his life, the information flowed copiously, yet makeshift, random, as irritating and perverse as the professor's improvisations on the piano. You never knew what was coming next. You became involved in a passage at your risk because it might be brutally foreshortened, segued into something banal and insipid. You'd be left hanging, shortchanged, and the music would

73

shift again. Sweep you right off your feet, trick you into following it, feeling it, believing it could be resolved, completed before the crazy man at the piano lost his way again.

Für Elise. Then *Eine Kleine* . . . then "Old MacDonald Had a Farm." Like life, Reuben would mutter to himself, consoling himself as one unfinished piece clattered into the middle of another.

Conservatory trained. Now tell the truth, man. How many niggers you know ever swept out a conservatory, let alone studied in one? And I was the best . . . no bones about it . . . bop de bop dee dum, the goddamnedest fairest of them all.

Sure I love Flora. Be crazy not to. Best thing ever happened to me. She has her ways. Course she does. But who don't, Reuben? I mean, look at you. Pimping for these white boys. And me. My teacup like a wart on top of this splendid instrument. Whiskey bottle hiding in the shadows at my feet. You know I ain't spozed to be here. Not me. Not Dudley Armstrong. I had a career, a future.

Things happen, Reuben. Not always good. You're a man. You've lived in the world same as me. You *compris* what I'm talking about. No offense. But why'd God have to make you little and bent. Didn't have to be that way, did it? I mean, if He's the boss, He could have fixed you up better. If you gonna make people so's they love to fuck and have it so the fucking makes babies, why not let all the babies come out pretty and healthy. No offense, Reuben. You're as good a man as me. Probably better. But life does funny things to people. Good people and bad. So Flora, my dear heart, she has her ways. You think I don't die a little each time she walks up those steps with one these peckerwoods. It's ugly. *Beaucoup* ugly. You think it don't turn me inside out and rip me to pieces. But that's her, Reuben. Her way. The way she's always been. So if I want Flora, I got to take her like she is.

Make no mistake. I'm not complaining. She's good to me. This a damned fine piano. The biggest and best. You ought to seen them crackers struggling to move it in here. I wear good clothes. Got a roof over my head. Eat good and drink too much

74

and ain't worked a day in five years. Now, that ain't half bad, is it? So see, I'm not complaining. Bitch wouldn't do for me like she does if she didn't love me.

First time I saw her I was playing a party in some rich white folks' house. I knew why I was there. Couldn't figure out why in hell she was. Or just exactly who she was. Something else but I couldn't figure exactly what. Mexican, Indian? A Greek, a gypsy? A fine woman with something colored in her face, her skin. Saying to myself all along she could be a blood. Hadn't seen no niggers besides me, but them folks throwing the party, they the kind of people do what they want to do. All the money in the world. Don't answer to nobody. Uniformed cops parking cars, cop on the door to keep out riffraff. Rich and raunchy and don't give a damn about nobody so she could have been a nigger somebody invited just cause they felt like it. Plenty fine women of all sorts. Kind you know is selling pussy, kind you know you can't touch with a ten-foot pole. Flora seemed standoffish and keeping to herself. Had my eye on her. Piano bench a good place for spying on people. They forget you're there after while. Think the music's playing its ownself. That's what they want you to be anyway. Furniture. A piece of goddamned furniture. But I'm not blind, crippled, or crazy. No, I ain't, Reuben. No offense, Reuben.

Finally she come up to me. Yessiree. She come right up to me ask me do I know "C. C. Rider."

Yes, ma'am. I know it like I know my name.

So she says, pretty as you please, Would you play it for me?

And I say, My pleasure. Very next number, ma'am.

Then she shakes her head. Gives me the goddamnedest man-leveling, dick-grabbing smile I ever seen in my life. Like she was chewing diamonds, man. Chewing diamonds and spitting sparks.

Not now. Not for these fools. Just for me. Just for the two of us.

I think of my rented tuxedo and my clean white drawers. Hope I ain't done nothing nasty in them. Don't know if I should stand still or run or start playing "Dixie." See, cause I still don't know exactly what she is. Then I think, Ain't nobody's business. Don't care if she's Italian or Chinese or the queen of England and Sheba too. Then I think maybe she's one the hookers. Words pop out my mouth before I'm really hearing what I'm saying.

Baby, I don't have one red cent.

You won't ever need one with me.

And it's true to this day. She takes good care of me. Bought me the best piano money can buy. She said just get better and better till you're the very best. All she ever asked me to do. And I'm trying, Reuben. I'm trying, but I don't think I'll make it.

Reuben took pains to learn things because information could be forged into weapons and what he didn't know would always be used against him. When the proper moment arrived he shared with his horny employers what he knew about Flora's. The frat boys insisted he escort them. And so it became a ritual. He was depended upon. A trip to Flora's needed Reuben's connivance to give it the necessary air of mystery, danger, style. Reuben served drinks beforehand in the frat house, summoned the cab, shook hands with the nodding professor, greeted the ladies by name. The Alpha Omega boys assumed he was a habitué, though in fact his first visit to Flora's occurred the first time he chaperoned a group of tipsy students to the house on Osage Street. On that initial foray Reuben had managed, as he usually did, to stay two or three steps ahead of his charges. He appeared knowledgeable because he picked up cues the others missed. His ease in new surroundings was purchased by extreme attentiveness. He didn't always know what was coming next but he worked hard at being ready . . . whatever.

She tells me fucking them's just a job. Easy most of the time. Biff—bam—thank you, ma'am. Nothing given. Nothing lost or changed. Says she's still Flora. Still loves me. Her work keeps food on the table, roof over our heads. They come to her. She don't have to bow and scrape to nobody. Mind our business. Stay clean. Clean, she says. Funny word, clean. Considering the circumstances. I used to be a nut about keeping my hands clean. The piano. Wouldn't touch it less I scrubbed like a surgeon. Maybe that's what I should have been. Started school to be a doctor once. A goddamned people butcher. Think I would have liked that. Gut em like dead rabbits. Plenty come round here I wouldn't mind skinning and slicing. Should have stayed in school. Had the hands for it. The aptitude, they said.

Clean. She maintains her distance, she says. Stays clean in her fashion, she says. Makes the paddyboys wash themselves in front of her before she'll let them touch her. Now, in what other business can you spritz up your customers like that? Make them put their best foot forward. She laughs when she talks like that. Thinks things like that are funny. Because she hates them. For some reasons I'm hep to. But she keeps the worst to herself. She says, You get upset behind them screwing me. You'd fly apart at the seams if I told you the worst.

Reuben has difficulty negotiating the high step of the trolley. He hangs on as long as he can to the silver pole at the end of the aisle before allowing his weight to be drawn after his left foot dangling in the void. He's afraid for his knees, his ankles. The inevitable shock when he hits the ground and always the possibility of a bad landing, something uneven or loose underfoot tripping him up. He pushes the sorry professor with his disjointed music and disjointed story out of his mind. Releases himself down onto the cobbles of Woodland Avenue, the last stop before the tunnel. Impact is minimal. A little skip and he's firmly on his feet. He shakes his arm, the one on fire when he was gripping and leaning and waiting for the trolley to halt. The sun is merciless. He feels dipped in butter.

Reuben's boys had taken up a collection. A special semester's end, Christmas, birthday, Easter, and every other holiday they'd ignored bonus for their indefatigable porter, confidant, and pimp.

Flora for an afternoon, Reuben. Everything's arranged. And it was, that long-ago day in Philadelphia.

A Sunday. An afternoon off for Flora and her girls. Reuben stopped in the parlor as was his custom. Dudley Armstrong, drunk as a newt, greeted him.

Alone for a change.

Yes.

Business.

In a manner of speaking. I must talk to Flora.

You want Flora, huh? Can tell you up front she don't go with niggers or freaks. Even on Sundays.

Not that way. It's complicated. They bought me Flora as a present. I couldn't refuse. They'll check on me. I have no choice.

Flora.

They said it had to be Flora.

Flora don't go with her own kind. Wouldn't be clean, she says.

I don't really expect anything of her. I want to explain, that's all. Want her to understand I didn't ask for this. I'll stay upstairs for a while and they'll get their kicks and that will be that.

Bastards bought her, huh. Bought her and give her away like a . . . piece of furniture.

I couldn't say no. I need to keep my job. The boys think it's all very funny and generous. They're pleased with themselves.

And here you are. Little Mr. Prim and Proper.

May I go upstairs?

Better have a drink first. Couple drinks. Flora might take your head off just for playing along with their shit. I'm ready for another nip . . . you use the cup . . . take it. I'll just snort out the bottle, if you don't mind.

If this—

Drink up, my man. Only one *if* about it. If they paid, you go upstairs.

They'll come here to check. I know them. That's why I thought it best to go up. I'll talk to Flora. Explain . . .

78

No need explaining. Nothing to explain. Business is business. You brought plenty business here. Bout time you took care some your own. You'll dig Flora. Flora's got one them talking pussies, man. I been there, brother. I'm speaking from experience. She's . . .

She's what?

Both men turn toward the bottom of the stairs where Flora stands, one hand on her hip, the other on the carved newel post of the oak banister. She'd floated down the stairs, silent in the constant patter of Armstrong's music. How long had she been listening?

In all his visits Reuben had not allowed himself to look too closely at this woman. Now he understood why. Black hair bobbed in heavy coils to her shoulders. Eyes that could turn you to stone. Her shoulders bare except for thin straps of a lacy, silky something. Peach was the color of the short garment. It draped her nakedness, clearly an afterthought because she had nothing to hide. Reuben realized his mouth was dry, that he was staring at the twin thrusts of her nipples, the patch of shadow at her groin. He'd never looked closely at her before because he'd figured this would happen. This helplessness, this drowning.

Reuben couldn't stop staring, but he got away with his rudeness because she ignored him. Her eyes snarled at the man sitting on the piano bench. Armstrong stopped diddling the keys. Was the professor trembling or was Reuben's wobbly head on his crooked shoulders shaking the whole room.

She's what, Mr. Armstrong? Go on. Tell the man what you know about Flora. Am I goood? Tell him about my nice titties and my soft ass. Do I smell like cloves and cinnamon between my legs? Go on. Tell him about me. About the mole on my thigh. How I purr and like you to whisper nasty in my ear. And I'm limber. Limber as a Japanese. Tickle your ears with my toes while you're kissing me. Is that what you were going to tell him? Before you sent him up for some of this good pussy. My. My. Can you still remember how good it is?

She's grinning now, showing lots of teeth, and Armstrong turns away from her, studies a wall, the one spattered with a storm of cupids, bows and arrows, heart-shaped lyres, pink and rose and white.

Man talk. Little dirty big-britches man talk before you send the customer up. I should have listened. Maybe I'd have learned something. Maybe you can still talk like a man, Mr. Armstrong, even if you can't do like a man.

Leave it, woman. Nobody meant no harm.

Course you didn't, baby. No harm in you. Nothing in you no more. That's precisely why I'm leaving your black tar-baby ass down here stuck to my piano bench and taking this nice little gentleman upstairs with me.

Flora.

You sit right here and tell yourself about me. Maybe you'll get excited. Maybe you'll remember sure enough and be sorry in your good-for-nothing soul.

She shakes her head in disgust and beckons Reuben. The dark ringlets shiver and ting-a-ling round her face like wind chimes.

Damn fool. She speaks first. Reuben hopes she's not referring to him. He's not sure. He thinks he hears Armstrong squeaking up the stairs after them.

What's that?

Don't be nervous, sweetie pie. Just that damn piano. He can't pound it and walk up the stairs at the same time. Relax. Dudley Armstrong's harmless. Can't do right nor wrong anymore. Bastard has the brass balls to tell you about me. As if he knows . . . the bastard. Now what can I do for you, mister?

They said they'd arranged . . . paid you.

They did.

Said you'd be expecting . . .

Oh, I was. Before they said word the first or brought their little blood money here. Sooner or later. One way or another, you'd get here. Like the man said. You can run, but you can't hide. Yes, I've been expecting you for a long time. Her tone softened, her eyes no longer snapped and crackled.

To them it's just a joke. I know the boys think you'll reject me, humiliate me in some fashion. Pairing me, half a man, with a perfect woman like you. A joke on both of us, they hope. But it's strange. In their way they also like me. I'm sure they do. Perhaps it's really no more than the kind of affection people feel for pets. It's something, anyway. A crack in the wall. When one of them comes to me alone. With a problem. Or just to sit and talk. I forget the pleasure they take in running me ragged.

I never forget. I make them crawl. Make them cry and beg and curse their mamas before I wring the necks of those pitiful worms between their legs.

They'll tell me anything. Confide in me.

And I'm your reward for being a good listener.

This gift is what happens when they put their empty heads together. How they act when they're a mob. This gift is a way of laughing at me, giving with one hand, taking away with the other.

You brought those ugly children here. Maybe they're just returning the favor.

I didn't know you then. Except through hearsay.

And now.

I'm learning too much, too quickly. Tell the truth, it's making me a bit dizzy, Miss Flora. May I have a drink of water?

Glasses above the basin are clean. There's iced wine in the cabinet. Help yourself. Part of the hospitality.

Only if I may pour us both some.

You're an odd one. Your tidy suits and manners. When you sit back in a chair, your feet don't touch the floor. I noticed that the first time you brought a batch of those fools here. The cute, perfect, miniature shoes you wear. Not touching the floor.

Don't make fun, please.

Ooh. I'm far from making fun. I'm confessing. You said you're a good listener. Listen to my confession.

I don't understand.

From the first evening, I knew you'd wind up here.

Reuben turns and surveys her over his shoulder. In the mirror built into the elaborate cabinetry framing the sink, as he'd mustered glasses and twisted the top from a decanter and poured wine, he'd studied the woman reclining on her four-poster bed. In the oval mirror she'd been distanced, small, safe. Now as he pauses and lets his eyes play over the contours of her body, her bare legs and shoulders, her hips, delicate bones like wings under her throat anchoring the pull of her breasts, she grows larger than life, an island suddenly looming out of a mist-shrouded lake.

I wanted you. You were cute. Cute is what I thought first. A little boy dressed up like a man. A man's silky ways and a man's voice out of a boy's body. You were cute and maybe at first I wanted to be your mama. Hold you on my lap. Pat your head. Snuggle. Sing a lullaby. That kind of mess. Are you listening?

Go on.

Then. Well. A baby. I daydreamed you with your head resting on my chest. One thing led to another. Like my body suddenly remembers you aren't a baby. My breast is bare and your mouth sucking on it and it's feeling good. And your hands. Your man's fingers and toes. Like monkeys all over me. Before I knew it I'd unbuttoned your pants. There it was. And we definitely weren't dealing with mamas and little boys no more. I wanted you. You were ready for me. So I knew sooner or later it was bound to happen. Since the first time I saw you, I knew.

Then it doesn't bother you that they sent me?

Only if I turn out to be wrong about you. Only if you're here because you're scared.

Scared? No, I'm not afraid of them. For a while longer I need to use them. I'm dependent. Not so much the money as the job. Where it places me. The access it affords me to the university. You see, I want to be a lawyer. The rich boys in the frat, their daddies and uncles and granddaddies are lawyers and most of them intend to enter the law. It's a tradition. That's why I slave at Alpha Omega. I'm learning through keyholes. When they're not around I avail myself of their books, notes, et cetera. I know more law than any ten of them combined. My secret life. You're the first person I've told.

Your wine, madam. He steps closer.

82

Thank you.

She manages to be a lady in the next-to-nothing peachy, transparent chemise as she rights herself to receive the glass Reuben offers. Demurely she adjusts what she's wearing, her posture, her eyes, her voice modulated so that she's not a whore lounging half naked on her bed, but Miss Flora taking tea with her gentleman caller in the parlor.

No, I'm not afraid of them.

Didn't think you were. You're running on your own time. I can tell in a minute whether someone's pulling strings or having their strings pulled. Him downstairs. Would you believe there was a time he wasn't afraid. Dudley Armstrong had plans. He wasn't going to allow anyone to stop him, I wanted him to make it. I'd have given anything to help. But it's out now. Psst. Something, somebody stuck their fingers in his chest and pinched out the fire. He was my lover. But that's over too. For years he hasn't been able to finish anything. Not even love.

Reuben blushes. You're right. I do have plans. Dreams. Bucketsful. Some days I believe I'll make it. Other days . . .

Those other days . . . maybe you'll let me help you get through them.

You're very kind.

Just the opposite. Not a kind word or thought for most people. I'm bitter. Hurt. What I know best is how to use people. Hurt them back. For a long, long time I've understood just what I am. That's my strength. My power. Knowing who I am. This body's loaned to me and I rent it out. I'm sick of it. I don't live in it anymore.

You're beautiful. I'm sorry. I can't stop staring. Your eyes. Your skin. I want to touch you. Hell . . . all the white boys in the world don't scare me, but you . . . you surely do, Miss Flora.

She sips. Holds the glass aloft, curls her bottom lip against the lip of the long-stemmed goblet. Like the glass is a flower she's picked and she's testing its scent. A faint smile. She's listening to him but she's also far away in another world, and Reuben's wondering which is real, the woman smiling at him or the invisible one, the invisible place where she dallies.

83

You'll touch me soon enough. And I'll purr and squirm and be happier than I've been in a long time.

Reuben knows she's right. Remembers that it's all happened before. Yes. Yes. She tongues drops of wine dotting the mouth of the glass. Cleaning it. Grooming. Like it's part of her. Like a cat licking its fur.

She is a sinuous spine of hills rhythming the horizon. He thinks of earth shapes, what lives and dies in spaces those shapes contain. How many times has it happened? With this woman. In cities by the sea, on high, windy plateaus, in Memphis, Timbuktu, New Orleans, Thebes, sand dunes, a field of rushes, seasons whirling so there is a blur, the best of all of them—hot sun and fall colors, the perfume of spring, snow's sparkle and weightless drift—when his lips graze her cheekbones the first time again.

Please. It's time.

He is not in a room in West Philadelphia. He's not anywhere else either. They've slipped from time. He hears her set down her glass on the night table. Her naked feet whispering across silk as she draws her knees up to her chest, making herself a package, a sweet bundle, head to toes, all of her within his reach.

When he touches down his glass beside hers, he hears the absence of music. The piano in the parlor downstairs is quiet. Reuben hadn't heard the music till it stopped. Now he recalls the patchwork of sounds that had backgrounded each word, each move in Flora's room. Is that what it took? Losing something. The music's gone so now he hears it, misses it. Did you only learn by losing? Was he finding her or losing her, this olive woman, this shoulder off which he slides, gently, gently, a thin pale strap? When he eases off the second strap and the lacy peach drifts off her breasts, music starts up again from below.

Tell me you hate them. Tell me you'll do something to hurt them. When you're strong. After I've poured myself into you and I'm gone, promise me you'll hurt them.

Reuben buries his face in titty. He thinks he knows what she's talking about and nods and grunts as he roots in her

84

softness. She's saying yes to him and as he digs and pushes deeper into her, all fingers and nose and blind eyes, he replies yes to whatever it is she's asking, begging. The song downstairs is "Mary Had a Little Lamb." Reuben recognizes the opening chords even though they're off key, dissonant, hears them echoing in the *dee-dum / dee-dum / dum-dum-dum* the professor clanks out to end the song.

When he feels her hands busy undoing his trousers, Reuben realizes he's still wearing all his clothes. When silence barrelhouses up the stairs again, he realizes the music's gone and Dudley Armstrong has played a piece, sorry as it was, quick as it was, beginning to end.

Sweat on his lips. Wine. His. Hers. He frees his mouth a second to say, I think he played a whole song.

The earth shifts under Reuben. He's nearly thrown to the floor. He holds on with one hand, dangling as he did from the mouth of the trolley. A door bursts open and he's flying, lifted bodily into the air. His linen trousers slide down his spindly legs. The room swelters with people. Flora's twisting, bucking, thrashing like a fish on dry land, but they have her feet, her wrists, pinioning her nakedness to the bed's four corners.

Lovebirds. Naughty, naughty lovebirds.

Flora screams once *Dudley*. Reuben nearly tears free when a hooded man cracks her in the mouth. Bright blood beads the lips he was just kissing. Like the rap of a baton, the blow striking Flora's face brought music again up the stairs. Loud, brokenbacked, thundering sounds as if the professor were banging his head on the keys.

Save your breath, bitch. He knows we're here. Gave us the key. Locked the front door behind us so we won't be disturbed.

Just wanted to have a little fun. We were going to toy with you a bit, that's all, Reuben. Let you get all hot and bothered with this cunt here, Miss Flora. Then bust in. Catch you with your drawers down. Do a little kidding around. Threaten to lop off your privates, et cetera. Just a joke. Let you get a good sniff of Miss Ballbuster here, then whisk you away. Pay you handsomely for your trouble. You didn't really think we'd allow you to fuck where we fuck, did you, you randy little ape? Rub your nigger stink where we play. Anyway, Miss Flora doesn't fuck niggers. Don't you know the rules?

Maybe he's not a nigger, Schultzie. Maybe he's a Chinaman or a redskin.

Or a purple-assed baboon.

What are you, little man? And why'd you have to go and spoil our fun?

He hates us, Collins.

The man's knuckle thumps Reuben between the eyes. Pain is sharp and hollow.

Why'd you have to insult us the way you did? You hurt our feelings. Now we must hurt you. Both of you.

Plenty.

A lawyer, huh? Learning through keyholes, huh? Well, we learn through keyholes, too.

Reuben counts eight. Two behind him who had snatched him and slammed him down in the rocker, six huddled round Flora's bed. He grits his teeth against the pain in his crushed arms. Flora's stock-still on the bed, spread-eagled, her four limbs roped to the four posts, her face invisible under the peach gown one of them had draped over her head after another had stoppered her mouth with a gag of silk underwear.

The men stink of whiskey. A rancid wave that overpowers the fruity bouquet of freshly spilled wine from two glasses shattered on the floor.

Bring the bottle over here. Let's see if she can wring its neck.

Wait. Wait. I want a turn first. Don't damage the goodies.

Worms. Didn't she call us worms?

And our buddy, Reuben. He's worse. We trusted him. Arranged a party for him.

Tell us your plan, little man. Why so silent now. The fist is in Reuben's face. Blue hairs curl round the short, blunt fingers. Down, fuzz, the pelt of the beast. Beastie. She'd called him Beastie in the dream.

Four times the thick middle fingers anoint him. His forehead, both cheeks, then once dead in the mouth with a force that splashes his lip. Stinging spots remain, a mask, a tattoo of pain when the hand drops back to the man's side.

Nothing to say, Reuben. Pussy got your tongue?

Sneaking around. Lying. Stealing. A spy in our house. Pretending to obey, to love us. Laughing up your sleeve. Wheedling your way into our affection when all you ever wanted . . .

Was everything.

Our books, our law degrees. Now our whore.

Hot on her, wasn't he? Crawling over her like a spider.

Such a waste. Such a fetching piece of real estate, but when we finish with it and finish with you, no one will want her. You can have her.

Let's fuck her good before we bruise it up. Rub his nigger nose in it when we're finished. Watch how men do it, Reuben. More education through the keyhole.

The evil men do to their fellow men. The unspeakable atrocities. I don't have to go on, do I?

I still have the scars across my back. To put themselves in the proper mood for assaulting Flora, they whipped me. Tanned my hide. Laid on the stripes. Tore up this coon's ass. They gagged me, too, so I couldn't cry out. After the first few strokes, I lost the urge to scream. Didn't want to give them the satisfaction. Five, six strokes and they'd killed the resistance of my body. It believed the strokes, suffered them, cooperated. Curled up in itself and shut out fear and protest, all hope the pain would ever end.

They had just begun playing with Flora, these big kids out looking for fun, these future barristers and judges and bank presidents, these future fathers of families had just started unbuckling and unzipping and stepping out of their boxer shorts when smoke billowed in through the open door and the racket from downstairs was clearly not the professor anymore destroying his baby grand but the hiss and crackle and roar of fire.

Flames were bounding up the stairs. Armstrong must have splashed them with kerosene from the antique lamp in the parlor. Our tormentors quickly lost interest in us. Too late to use the stairwell. Half naked, their eyes bigger than all the hate in Texas, the lynch mob dispersed the only way it could. Crabs scuttling over one another to plunge out Flora's window. I thought one fat one wasn't going to fit through. He must have been closer to the window than his hooded brothers. He'd wedged himself in. It took everybody behind him pushing to stuff his blubbery meat past the frame. All hands abandon ship was the order of the day. And in spite of my eyes screaming, pointing to Flora's body where she lay still tied to the bed, in spite of my arms when they were freed clutching the sides of the window frame, in spite of my heart lunging out of my chest onto the bed beside her, some compassionate soul lifted me from the rocker and I found myself airborne again, my whole life flashing through my mind until I hit the pavement and didn't wake up, they told me, for a week.

Flora.

Burnt to a crisp. Armstrong too. Mixed together into the heap of ashes which was all that remained of Flora's house. In the beginning was the end. Perhaps the professor understood. Ashes to ashes.

Now you're talking like it happened to somebody else, a thousand years ago. Like you weren't in the house. Didn't know the killers, the people who died.

A long time ago, Wally. Longer than a thousand years. I haven't heard much about Philadelphia lately. Is it still there beside the river? The boathouses. The art museum. Gingerbread city hall. The School of Law.

They left her to burn up on the bed.

They were afraid for their lives. One must have attempted to loosen the ropes. Her ankle was free. As far as her savior got. The knots were too tight. If they'd had a knife, they could have cut the knots. But in another light, perhaps it's better they had no knife. No temptation to use it. Because they were a mob. Capable of the worst. As we all are in mobs. An ankle was free and she was struggling with one perfect leg to escape. The last I saw of her. A flash of olive thigh, twisting, climbing.

If you got knocked out, how do you know she didn't tear herself loose somehow?

It was in the papers. The whole sordid story. How a jealous pimp murdered his lady. The demented arsonist caught in his own trap, going up in smoke with his victim. On the back pages because both the deceased were colored. Front page in the Negro weekly. The *Black Dispatch* printed a picture of charred ruins, invented a wealth of lascivious detail.

What happened to you?

Oh. I suppose a good citizen came along and scraped me off the sidewalk. I was mentioned in some accounts as an unidentified visitor to the house. Hospitalized for injuries when he jumped from a second-story window. I didn't read the newspaper articles till much later. The white ones on purpose in the Homewood public library after I'd come across the black version by accident in a barbershop. I began to remember. I had developed a short-run amnesia. Erected a temporary carapace of forgetfulness to protect myself from the horror, I suppose. Till my body healed, till I recovered the strength to deal with what had transpired. For a while I didn't know I'd lost a Sunday afternoon. No recall whatsoever. Gradually it returned. The day, the feelings. They waited patiently for me to claim them. I orphaned the memory, but it's mine again. Entirely, eternally mine again, I'm afraid.

Wally didn't know whether to believe Reuben or not. Reason he'd come to Reuben's trailer was simple. Money missing from the athletic department budget. Wally might be needing ten lawyers after the accountants figured out how much disappeared daily. Phony expense vouchers, unused plane tickets cashed in. A slush fund they all dipped in for sweeteners. Money illegally passed to recruits, unauthorized charge accounts at restaurants, clothing stores. The athletic director, head coaches, assistants, equipment manager, trainer, all of them were in on it. Elaborate hustles with everyone privy, each one profiting. Though of course the ones at the bottom didn't get much after their superiors skimmed lion's shares off the top. Wally's portion a few game tickets to sell. He could pad his mileage, his room and meal bills.

Every now and then cash in a plane ticket for a visit consummated only on paper. The usual stuff anybody who wanted a winning program and a happy staff did. To play by the rules was too restrictive, so nobody did. But if you got caught, all the other cheaters on you like sharks. A feeding frenzy when one of their own leaks a drop of blood. When shit like that came down, it fell heaviest on the heads of the lowest. A conspiracy of silence at the top. Lots of lily-white, holier-than-thou fingers pointing at somebody's chest. The sacrifice . . . the scapegoat trotted out to appease the public, certify the integrity of the ones who didn't get caught.

Wally was on the bottom, and thus a likely target, so he wanted to find out what he could do to protect himself. Reuben might have some thoughts. His advice was free anyway. He might start Wally thinking. Wally'd come to discuss the mess with Reuben, that's all, and somehow the old man had traveled back to Philly. Got Philly mixed up in the deal. Fires and whores. White boys up to their usual shit. Wally didn't know whether or not to believe Reuben's story. Whether Reuben was saying one thing to say another or whether this was just one of those foggy days when you couldn't get through to Reuben. Reuben compulsively rehearsing his own life no matter how hard you tried to tell him about yours. Wally couldn't tell if the little man had heard one word he said. Whether Reuben heard or cared.

Then he found himself tripped up in Reuben's story anyway. The old dude was loony but he told good lies. Like he'd crammed ten or twenty lives into one. The places he'd been, the things he'd done. All that mess coming out in the stories. Just enough fact and detail to trick you into almost believing them.

The white boys got away clean as usual, I suppose.

You suppose correctly. In a way, even if they'd been apprehended and brought to trial, what would they have been charged with? They didn't set the fire. In fact, the inferno nearly trapped them. They would arrive in court sporting their bandages like the Spirit of '76, lamenting the wounds they sustained exiting the cathouse. Armstrong was the perpetrator, wasn't he? Why would

90

anyone wish to add insult to the injury those poor white fellows received? Now granted, the Alpha Omegas were playing a bit rough with a whore and a renegade janitor, but most juries would not have wanted to hear that side of the story, would they? What decent judge would allow that tale to pollute his courtroom? So yes. They escaped cleanly. But plenty of your betters would insist the boys received no more or less than they deserved. Their freedom. Their reputations intact. A measure of revenge upon a traitor. At the cost of a little chastening. A warning not to become too involved with Negroes. A hint of the trouble and danger of race mixing. Important lessons for those destined to inherit the reins of society. Good practical experience for Philadelphia lawyers.

You're lucky you didn't get killed too.

Yes and no. Always yes and no, Wally. I was spared for a little more time on the cross, so to speak. But I suppose I'm grateful. Sure. Surviving, sitting here today, able to tell you the story. That's worth something.

Did you ever go back?

Where?

You know. To the fraternity house.

No. No reason to return. My life there was over. But I did visit Flora's. Many times. You might even say I haunted the ruins. Today. Today I can smell the ashes, the smoke. A small house set off by itself at the end of a row. A vacant lot between it and the drab, gray row houses so the fire didn't spread. Just Flora's yellow clapboard, white-shuttered, neat-as-a-pin pleasure palace burned to the ground. A judgment upon the carrying-ons there. Her neighbors proclaimed it God's will, divine intervention, chickens coming home to roost, et cetera. Cloves and cinnamon. You'd be amazed how long the burnt smell hovers. How silly a grown man could be. Smudging his face with ashes.

Mourning her.

Corking up like a minstrel.

Didn't you want revenge? How could you let them kill her and almost kill you and not do anything about it?

We all have our Philadelphias. Mine's as much about love as it is about hate. So in a sense, I'm lucky. Love complicates the business of revenge. Love exacts its dues, then it's too late. No time for hate.

Shit, Reuben. The woman was dead. They tied her to the bed. That was murder. You owed her. Love or not. Soon as I could walk I'd have been over to that frat house with a torch in my hand. Midnight . . . when the suckers were all asleep.

The frat house was stone. Not a tinderbox like Flora's.

You know what I mean. Stone, bone, steel . . . don't make no nevermind. What I'm saying is they would have paid. Tit for tat. One way or the other.

They paid. I know they paid. I've watched it happen. The house did burn. Years later. A Christmas party. Defective wiring. The blaze started in a Christmas tree. Many perished. Frat boys and their dates. The story was carried by the wire services and network news. It reached me here. Not more than four or five years ago.

Well, if that's your idea of revenge, of evening the score, I'll give you credit for patience. I'd have been on their ass, Reuben. Soon as I could walk.

If things had happened differently. If I hadn't been mercifully knocked asleep and awakened ignorant, with the feeling I was starting a new life . . . if I hadn't been granted that cushion of time, perhaps I would have gone after them. But it wouldn't have brought Flora back, would it? All the days and nights haunting her street, sifting the ashes didn't bring her back. Over the years . . . a great emptiness settling in where she should have been. Like the house collapsing through its own charred timbers. Wood splits and puckers. It flakes. Glistens in the sunlight like a lump of coal. Some of the joists looked gnawed, nibbled, giant bites gouged out of others. Never a trace of her. Nothing I could identify. The city must have carted away the debris. Fire couldn't have disintegrated everything. The brass four-poster bed. After rain the smoke smell was stronger.

Some of the killers must still be alive today. If you are, they could be. Maybe I did you a favor, Reuben, and didn't even know I was doing it. Evening the score. One of them. One of their sons.

I didn't tell it right. If I told it right, you'd understand. Losing Flora, the loss of her was all I could feel. Who or what caused me to lose her was immaterial. I missed her every second then. I miss her now. That's the point of the story. How long I've loved her. How quickly she was gone.

Yeah, well . . . you're right. I guess lots of what you say's beyond me. But that's cool.

All black men have a Philadelphia. Even if you escape it, you leave something behind. Part of you. A brother trapped there forever. Do you know what I mean, Wally? My Philadelphia's strange because for all the horror, more of it's about love. Have you had yours?

I went to school in Philly. Could tell you some cold shit about Philly. Philadelphia . . . Chicago. They're all the same.

Chi-ca-go is three slow syllables, each accented, drawn out so Wally's whole story is there for Reuben to read. Flesh on the bones of the windy city if Reuben catches the hints, fills in the spaces between the signifying beats, *Chi - ca - go,* the lake, the wind, clouds, a bathroom into which you could fit Reuben's trailer, fit each and every house where Wally was raised and still have room to be lost, to be attacked by the light, the gleaming fixtures, the blaze of mirrors.

Old news, isn't it? You didn't come here for old news, did you? What may I do for you today, my boy?

I think I might need a lawyer. Stuff's coming down over at the university. Somebody blew the whistle. Don't know how far it will go. How far anybody wants to take it. See, the hanky-pank stinks right up to the top of the ladder. Costs money to run a basketball program. To compete nationally it costs whole lots of money, money nowhere in the official budget. Money that ain't supposed to be spent the way we spend it, even if we found legit ways to come up with the cash. Anyway, it's a chain of wrongdoing and I'm dirty, Reuben, just like the rest of them. But in this kind of deal it's always the grunts get wasted. Generals got ways of covering their asses. What I got to figure is how to cover mine.

Have charges been filed?

Not yet. Everything's still under wraps. University would prefer to keep the shit quiet. Do its own housekeeping. See, that way the other schools in the conference won't get a chance to stomp on us. If things can be kept quiet, everybody will be much happier. Except the few whose heads roll. You know. Our internal investigation has uncovered evidence of wrongdoing and those responsible for violations have been relieved of their duties. A semipublic semiapology, but then hush-hush. The ranks close. Nobody talks, records sealed and deep-sixed. It never happened, right? Little bit of egg on our chin but we wiped it off good and clean. Business as usual except for one or two chumps shipped off to Siberia. Maybe the suckers get a little payoff, hush money, a jive, going-nowhere job in another town to keep them quiet. I don't want to take the fall, Reuben. I'm going to scream my head off, they so much as look crossways at me. Bring the whole scam down if they try and chop me. So I may be requiring your services.

I'll do what I can. Though it sounds as if what's involved is pretty far afield for me. We're a long ways from the university down here. I must research this matter in more detail. You'll need to keep me posted on developments. We really can't get started now. I have some business to attend for another client today. Can you come back?

Tomorrow or the next day or the next. No hurry yet. The lid's still on.

Fine.

One thing . . . how long did you stay in Philly? I mean after the fire . . . how long did you hang?

I could say—and truth would be in every word—I'm still there. My ashes mixed with hers. Sprinkled into the wind. This may sound like an old man's foolishness, but I repeat, I loved her. Love. Yes. Fell in love and stayed in love even though we only spent a few minutes alone together. And as I've related to you, even those moments weren't private. But they were enough. Flora and I opened to each other in an extraordinary fashion. No stepping back. No taking back once given. I would have gladly laid down beside her. Held her happily, contentedly till the flames

94

consumed us both. I'm not answering your question, am I? And I have work to do for Ms. Parker. I stayed in Philadelphia till I finished learning the law. I stayed till I was prepared to do what I'd promised her.

Promised?

You didn't miss that part of the story, I hope. I promised her I'd hurt them.

That's what I was talking about. Revenge. So you did try to get back at them.

In my fashion. With love and hate . . . yes . . . it's complicated, Wally. And don't bump your head leaving. Either my office is shrinking or you're putting on weight.

Probably both, my man. Probably both.

Reuben retrieves his work, the folder from the edge of the desk where he'd slid it to open space for Wally, the bundle he'd slipped on top of the junk box when his visitor had knocked.

Kwansa watched it breathe, the long, dark body stretched naked beside her. Not much to Toodles. A skinny black snake. Toodles wrapped around you, a soft rope, always moving, twisting, hot where it rubbed your skin. Toodles's bones could cling. Her thighs, her ankles were like hands. Kwansa lay on her side, looking back over her shoulder down into the pouch of raised covers where Toodles's flesh was the darkest shadow except for the hair in the middle of her body, which was even darker. She sleeps on her back with her legs flung open and the arm away from Kwansa outside the covers, stretched toward the head of the bed. She looked flat as a pancake, all splayed out that way, as if she owned the world or as if she were waiting for the sky to fall on top of her.

Kwansa had thought she'd lie still, very very still and let whatever happened when you went to bed with a woman happen. She would be still and quiet and pay attention so she'd know what felt right and what didn't. In control so she could stop if things went wrong. She needed to be sure. To be Kwansa the whole time and not somebody else, not be what people would name her if they knew what she'd done with another woman. She thought she'd keep her hands to herself. Let Toodles do what Toodles did. Toodles didn't have nothing she didn't have. So there'd be nothing Kwansa's hands needed to look for, nothing for them to learn. A narrow boy's behind, next to nothing on Toodles's chest. Kwansa would be quiet as coffee in a cup. Let Toodles stir it around if she wanted to.

Then Kwansa got tangled up in that rope. It was tight, hot. The more it tangled, the tighter it squeezed, the silkier it got. She grabbed at pieces as they slithered by. Mouth, arms, toes, nipples, the tight cakes after Kwansa's finger ripples down the steps of Toodles's spine. Parts like her parts only different, better, because Toodles doubled them, doubled what Kwansa had, and Kwansa could feel both bodies meeting in the mirror, both climbing out. She forgot to do what she thought she'd do. She needed to cry and Toodles's bony shoulder was close so that's where she laid her head first thing. Then her hands on Toodles and Toodles's hands on her. She told the woman her troubles. And the woman kissed away her tears while Kwansa talked about Cudjoe, about wanting to be better than she was. The woman nodded, listened, undressed her gently, like you would a child, not to take anything from it, but giving it what you believe it needs, your hands unbuttoning and loosening and unpinning because it's time. Funny, because turned out to be Toodles doing the watching, the listening, the waiting, keeping her hands to herself. Toodles who was willing to let a tiny bit or nothing at all happen. Kwansa who twined with the long body, took its toes between her teeth and wouldn't let it wiggle away.

Kwansa tried not to wake Toodles as she eased from the bed. She gathered her clothes from the floor where they'd fallen. Dampness still clung. Night had been muggy and short.

Toodles snored. A faint, piping whistle of a snore. Off and on. Soft then loud then gone again for a while. Not so much a sign Toodles was in the room, sleeping behind her back, but that Toodles was far away, in a place that had nothing to do with stepping into underpants, pulling on a bra, a shirt. Kwansa breathed in the familiar odor of her own armpits and crotch.

Something extra this morning made it better. Toodles's snore, how Toodles smelled under her clothes. Kwansa could take those two things with her this morning when she closed the door behind herself and hit the street.

In the bathroom mirror gin showed, tracks of tears showed. The old song gone before it got started good. She wondered where Smokey was this morning. If she blew her breath on it, the glass would turn green. She used to think she could hear Waddell in Smokey's fly voice. Then Waddell's eyes in her son's face and the soft halo of a Smokey song hovering when she kissed Cudjoe's brown forehead. Pulling Toodles's comb through the stiff mess of her hair she remembered old Miss Clara's bald head on a satin pillow in her coffin. Maybe bald wasn't so bad after all. Not a hair on your head to worry about. Toodles's comb was finer than hers. Almost yanked her snaggle-toothed naps out by the roots. She caught her lips moving in the mirror. No song. She was cursing herself out. Mumbling, fuming about something, everything. Then silently she formed Cudjoe's name. The only way she could say it this morning, a wish she was scared to speak aloud.

We'll find him. In the morning. I'll help you . . . don't worry, sugar. Ain't but so many places he can be. We'll find him.

She didn't want to wake Toodles. The scent of Toodles on her skin was enough. She'd let the sound of Toodles's breathing stay distant and safe. While Toodles slept, Kwansa could believe in a place far from this room, this building, these Homewood streets. She had needed Toodles last night when the sky was falling and the sidewalk cracking, the flood rising around her ankles. She was drowning last night and found Toodles to hold. Needed Toodles holding her. Now it was morning. Now Cudjoe must be found. Let Toodles dream on in her safe place. Let her keep it safe.

6

THE RECRUITER

There were moments, days, when Wally treated what he was doing as a memory. He'd be off somewhere watching things happen he couldn't do anything about. He didn't have it to worry about anymore. His life distant as ball games back in high school, games he'd played and remembered not at all, though his name was printed in box scores in newspaper clippings he saved in one of the striped boxes that once had contained matching cologne and deodorant, the gift his grandmother gave him each Christmas. His life long gone or sometimes just a half step away, tantalizingly close enough so he felt useless as he did in games after he'd partied too late the night before. In those zombie games a pass would be zinging to him and in his mind he'd catch it, launch himself toward the basket for a slam. So easy. A play he could finish in his sleep. As the ball leaves his teammate's hands Wally tastes how good the goal's going to be. His body coils. He reaches out. But the pass buzzes through his sure fingers and flies out of bounds. He can't believe it. Shakes his head as the referee's whistle signals turnover, other team's possession. Why didn't he catch the ball? Why hadn't he rammed it home?

His life could be that close. Play Technicolor on the screen of his imagination, trick him into believing he was participating in the flow, that he retained the power to make things happen. Then a blast of the referee's whistle leaves his hands empty. Always a step behind or a play ahead. Steady fucking up no matter how hard he tried. When the target wiggled, straight shots or crooked shots all the same.

Wally'd taught himself to profit from detachment. Working as a recruiter helped because his job took him places where he wasn't born yet or where he'd been buried and forgotten. Gyms in rural Ohio, Wisconsin, Illinois, Pennsylvania, Iowa. Flat-assed zones time ignored.

Wally watches from the second deck. The best seat for what brings him to those gyms. From where he stations himself the court shrinks, the players are animated counters choreographing the game's inevitable patterns. A kid could be taught a system, x's and o's can be hammered into his brain, he can be made stronger, smarter, by drills and weight training. But basketball has an essence. You need to know how quickly a player runs from base line to base line, his hunger for gobbling space, his anger, his pride, his fear, his willingness to bounce, bounce, bounce even when he has little or no chance for a rebound. Did a player respond to the flow of a fast break? Did he fill the lane, did he take off and fly at the finish, could he skate on the thin ice of the air, maneuver on that invisible plane three feet above the floor where the best ones played the game? That's what Wally calculates, unobtrusive as a spider, perched on second decks, balconies, in the shadows of rafters, if he can ascend that high.

Staring down into these time tunnels he remembered himself as a high school star. The sweet oblivion of nothing mattering but the next basket. Would he *Sink it, Sink it* as cheerleaders pranced in front of the stands, pretty girls almost as naked as he was. If he sinks the free throw, which set of meaty legs could be talked into wrapping themselves around his back? The short,

short cheerleader skirts bobbed. Bare thighs quivered. *Sink it. Sink it.* Ten years ago, but here he was caught up in that moment again. Inside and outside. A dead man, a ghost, a nut like Reuben with lives to spare.

In these rural towns, blacks, if there were any, kept to themselves. People spoke well of them, or not at all. Everybody knew where the colored lived. Could point out over on the far side of the tracks the shabby, skimpy two or three streets where most of them raised their families. Alleys, unpaved, sidewalkless streets, the cluster of shacks behind the Grange, the whitewashed storefront where they worshiped. Black kids silent as their parents. Strong-armed, thick-legged country kids. Yes ma'am and No ma'am and never look you in the eye. They knew their place. Saved their ass-kicking for the football field, the basketball court. Then they could whip whole squadrons of white boys. Single-handedly carry a team to the playoffs, a state championship if the hick officials let a team starring a nigger win. If they didn't start calling fouls soon as he stepped off the visitors' bus. Dynasties of black brothers—Allens, Crumbys, Slaughters, McCoys—would rule districts of a state for decades. Old-timers would spit and remember when the daddy of the clan first came to town, how many years he been at the mill. How they always been your good, hardworking, quiet kind of colored people.

Wally always tried to catch a kid's eye. Let the recruit know that Wally Carter didn't believe all this bullshit he was hearing. Hey man, everybody drinks a little wine on the sly and tries to hump the farmer's big-tittied daughter out behind the barn on full-moon nights. He'd try to let a kid pick up on how much he despised the small-town coaches. Smile when the watery blue eyes were staring at him, then wag his shoulders with disgust when the chump turned to his prize stud, complimenting, appraising the kid pound for pound, attribute by attribute—springs in his legs, big long arms like his daddy, and strong, scares his own teammates in practice. A hard worker too. Jump through a brick wall if I say jump. Bid em in. Bid em in. All that horse-trader, nigger-driver bullshit right in the kid's face, and Wally tries to let the kid know he knows how ugly it is. How crazy it is for this cracker to be chatting with Wally like Wally's a white man and like the kid, big, black, and solid as he is standing between them, doesn't hear, doesn't exist. Wally tries to hint how far away from this little town the kid must flee. I'm on your side, my man. We both know this dude's a clown. He burns us up, but we can laugh at him, too, can't we? His baggy pants with sewn-in creases, his K Mart shirt and shoes. Wally searched for signs, a wink, a nod, a shucking and jiving glint of intelligence in dark eyes that are mirrors of his own. But if the intelligence, the smirk, the anger and hurt are there, they're buried so deep he can't coax them out. He's alone. Detached. Watches the charade in the coach's office from on high, the last row of seats in a huge, domed arena.

Do you take this boy to be your lawful, wedded recruit?

I do.

In spite of darkness and ignorance and hurt so deep he still doesn't know what hit him?

I do.

And the long-suffering of generations. The monotonous fall of the hammer on the skulls of the livestock time out of mind as they pass through the needle's eye on the way to become hamburger?

I do.

To love and to cherish.

Till he perish. I do.

Well then, wrap him and take him with you, brother.

Brother.

Well done.

Wally marvels at the white men who sell him recruits. Runty lots of times, failed jocks, nothing guys you'd never pick out of a crowd except to say this one's what the crowd's all about, featureless, undistinguished, a mediocrity. But these middling white guys had their phone booths. They could make or break the careers of their athletes. Maybe everybody had a phone booth, a button they could push to become a man of steel, a superhero. The men made Wally think of sharks, tigers, lions, dangerous bloodthirsty beasts that seem so benign when you watch them maundering round their habitats at the zoo. Nice animals from bedtime stories, picture books. Worth your life to underestimate the power, the ruthlessness, of these pale coaches and guidance counselors and vice-principals. How safe they seem when Wally and the recruit meet them in a narrow, locker-lined corridor mouthing the nicey-nice and chitchat of the game that's brought them together, the game that's placed them into a tit-for-tat balance of needing something the other has and having something the other needs.

Wally treats his life like a memory so he won't have to worry about what's happening to him. Since the shit was already over, since it had gone down the way it was going to go down, like it or not, he would treat what he was doing as if it was happening to someone else. Stand way back. Be sorry for the sucker. Laugh at him. No sense in worrying. Too late. And since his life was a memory, he could change it next time he played it. He could tell any lie he needed to get by. It's all in your mind. A dream made up as you go along.

But if you're not there, living smack-dab in the middle of your life, then where the fuck are you? Every once in a while the question stings Wally. If your life's not a memory or a tale you concoct at will, playing it fast-forward or reverse, stopping and starting in the middle or end, if your life's more than this mix of yes no and maybe and skipping and losing and somebody else working the dials, then who are you? A fly tracking across the dome of the arena, a spider curled in the rafter's shadow?

Once, seeing himself in a recruit's brown eyes, he wondered if the needle gets stuck, the same dumb sounds hiccuping over and over.

If you were a recruit, life was easy. You shut your eyes, did what you were told. You belonged to somebody else. You got fucked or did the fucking on somebody else's orders. If you were the farmer who raised the stud, you profited from the rules of buying and selling, so that's how you treated everything, everybody. If you were Wally the recruiter, you'd seen it all before, played every role in the transaction, done the bidding, the signing, consummated the deal, signed, sealed, and delivered the merchandise. If you were Wally, you treated the whole business like something that never happened, like a joke, because none of it made a goddamned bit of sense.

Wally. Where are you, Wally? Are you in there? Earth to Wally. Earth to Wally. Do you read me?

Felisha thought that kind of talk was cute. One of her favorite ploys when silence dropped down between them. Felisha pecking at his shell. She was smart and walked around in the kind of lip-smacking-good body Wally dreamed he'd luck up on someday. Trouble was Felisha couldn't stand silence. She needed to be talking or needed Wally talking to her. Riding that perfect body was the only way to shut her up. Then she was quiet as church on Monday. Not a peep out of her. No heavy breathing, no sighs or moans or groans. Stillness perfect as that lean-hipped, pillow-bosomed, every-pubic-hair-in-place body like none he'd ever seen before or since. Quietest, stillest bitch he'd laid. Like the whole time I'm fucking her, man, the chick's lying there listening for a phone to ring in Cleveland. You know. A real important call five hundred miles away so she's steady listening, man. Don't intend to miss that call. Quiet like that. I wanted to hurt the bitch sometimes. You know. See if she'd holler if I pinched her behind or pulled a hair out her pussy. Scared sometimes the bitch was dead. I'm doing my best. Pounding away. One look at that body she's packing and my johnson's ready. Got to get on board. I'm pile driving and sky diving and bitch's dead to the world down there under me. No sooner I unplug, though, there go her mouth. Yakedy-yak. Yakedy-yak. Asking me a question. Bothering me with some off-the-wall mess I ain't hardly in no mood to be hearing. No, man. I'm not lying. That's just the way the chick was. Why don't you ever talk to me, Wally? Only way to shut Felisha up stick your dick in her.

Earth to Wally.

Got tired the bitch disappearing on me. Good as she looked, after while, with her being so damned still and quiet, mize well be fucking my ownself. Felisha strictly for show, not go.

Why are you ignoring me, Wally?

A disappearing act. Felisha had that "now you see me, now

103

you don't" down pat. She left her beautiful body behind for him to play with but nobody home. No fun roaming through it alone. Romance hadn't lasted long. Still amazed Wally that he could walk away from so fine a woman. He remembered her now, standing at the foot of his bed, gloriously naked from navel down, pulling a sweater over her head, unable to stop talking even while the sweater's covering her face. Muffled words while her beautiful arms flail at the ceiling.

Earth to Felisha.

Do you think anyone ever figures it out? How lives begin, when they end? Funny, isn't it, when you come to think of it. The two biggest events, birth and death, yet for all intents and purposes we're not there. Because we have no memory. Either time. No memory, but I think the feeling must be like coming apart, coming apart and being put back together again. Simultaneously going and coming . . . a dream taking shape inside another dream. . . .

While Reuben continued talking, trying to say whatever he had on his mind, Wally thought about those crazy shots that couldn't decide whether to drop through the hoop or spin out. The ball whips around the iron more times than you can count. You sky for the rebound and land again and the ball still hangs on an invisible string, can't make up its mind to go in or out. Laughing at you while you try to time your next jump, whirling like it just might do its thing forever, round and round the rim.

In the middle of the chase Wally would lose track of the kid he was pursuing. In spite of his loose-leaf notebook with colored tabs separating each file, the neatly typed stat sheets, personal data sheets with phone numbers of contacts, in spite of photos paper-clipped to the top right-hand corner of bio sheets, the kids in Wally's book all wore the same face. In the Cincinnati airport, behind the wheel of a rental car ready to embark for 2410 Maple Street, Wally would freeze and ask himself: Who is it this time? What's this one's name? Whose face will be in the doorway? And no matter how many times he'd repeated the name that day, it would not come to him. The face at the recruit's door would be his, starting out all over again.

During plane rides Wally forced himself to study each recruit, construct flesh-and-blood personalities from the bare facts at his disposal. He'd imagine a mother, a father, a tiny living room crowded with trophies, bric-a-brac, miscellaneous furniture, the long legs of an uncomfortable kid who would be willing to sit in this claustrophobic room with his polite, bewildered parents only for as long as Wally lied to him. Recruiters must fake humility, express awe at what the kid has accomplished even though oversized boys like him are duplicating his exploits in hundreds of towns across the country. Even if you knew better, you conned him into believing you believed he'd be the one who'd bust up college games in an undiminished blaze of glory till some NBA owner carried him away in a sweet chariot of gold. After the first recruiter gets to the kid with the first lie, representatives of other distinguished educational institutions, if they wish to obtain the recruit's services, must embellish the original bullshit. Take it and run with it. Because that's what the kid wants. Parents cut their eyes at you, dismiss you as a fool if you offer a vision of the kid's future any less glorious than the one spun by the last salesman who sat in the plastic-wrapped armchair where you sit staring at a worn rug, cracks in the plaster, the decay and ineradicable grit dulling surfaces, weighing down the air, familiar signs telling you nothing about the people who occupy the house, everything about those who keep them tamped down here.

Wally's home again. In his grandmother's kitchen. Food smells, the reek of burnt grease baked into blackened burners of the stove. And above these kitchen odors, blending with them, partaking of them, the smell of his grandmother, the scent of her presence as strong in the little kitchen as it was in her bedroom, the bathroom. She was an old woman so her smell was compounded of things he didn't want to name, things an old woman wore next to her body, the body itself, whatever it became, whatever its parts looked like when a woman hobbled and creaked and wheezed around the house like his grandmother.

Her old breath. Her old legs rubbing together, sweating. Not a stink, not something unpleasant when he entered the kitchen where she sat sipping hot Ovaltine from a mug. He was bothered by her odor no more than he was bothered by his own funk, that envelope of body wrapping the idea of Wally. His grandmother's house didn't stink. It was as if she'd taken a blanket she'd slept under for years, a blanket older than Wally, and stretched it over roof, doors, windows, shutting their three rooms away from the treacherous streets. You couldn't see the blanket, it was thinner than skin but it stayed where she draped it, holding in the warmth, the care, she lavished on him, her love inseparable from the smell of her body soaked into each of the blanket's fibers.

In these far-away places with strange-sounding names—Waukegan, Massillon, Des Moines—in little houses and little rooms crowded with plaques, pictures, souvenirs, with big people he'd cornered at last to deliver his version of the lie, he'd recall how the love smell of that blanket trapped and embarrassed him. Did it follow him into the street? Could people smell it on him? Each house he'd visit had a blanket of its own, a perfume stale to Wally because it was fashioned by the comings and goings, the talk and cooking and touching and movements of strangers, the funk of their strange lives accumulating, betraying them, as he was betrayed by his own cave full of shadows.

These are your people, Wally. What's left of the green hills of Africa. The dream of something better till something worse comes along. This gangly, pimple-faced one with pogo sticks for legs and a deadly jumper from the key is their favorite son. Their pride and joy. Their winning ticket in the lottery. Some recruiter's going to steal this manchild and carry him far from home. Mize well be you. You mize well collect the thirty pieces of silver. Whether it's you or not, he'll meet his flame-haired, freckle-faced Felishas, learn another language, grow a second skin.

Wally should pull out his sword. Let them see the cold glint of steel. Let them touch the razor edge. Maybe even draw a drop of his own blood to show them the blade is real. Because that's

106

the news he brings. He is the cutter of cords. He will split the kid down the middle, from his guzzle to his zorch. Leave some, take some back to the university. Sever this boy and release a ghost that will spend its days floating back and forth between two places, two bodies, never able to call either one home.

Reuben. Reuben. Do you hear what I'm saying? They did unto me. Now I'm doing unto others. Chopping myself into smaller and smaller bits.

Reuben once upon a time told the story of a woman whose son was torn into thousands of pieces and the fleshy fragments tossed into the wind and the winds scattered the body to the earth's four corners. Beset by grief the woman sat down beside a river and wept. Her tears are dark lilies that bloom in stillness at the water's edge. And after she had mourned seven times seven years, she donned a black cloak and set out gathering the remnants of her lost son. Up and down the land. One by one she searched out every quivering morsel. Molded them together like you'd shape in your fingers wet clay from a riverbank. So many tears, so much stopping and crawling and wandering over the hard, cold, white earth, but one day the son was reassembled and she breathed the smoke of life down his lungs and they danced off together. The frown of winter lifted from earth's face. The smile of spring was born. The wheel of the seasons began to turn evermore.

Why had Reuben spun that lie? Why had he listened? A child's story, if you thought about it. Happy ever after. That didn't sound like Reuben. Reuben's tales usually end "all the king's horses and all the king's men couldn't put shit together again." Ended on a downstroke or didn't end at all. Left you hanging. On the edge like that Humpty-Dumpty motherfucker ready to fall again.

You could talk silly with Reuben. Nursery rhymes, serious business, pussy talk, lying, bragging, the blues, any old junk happened to pass through your mind and slop out your mouth was okay with Reuben. And you never knew what was coming next from him. His pointy teeth and pointy beard and pointy stories. He did, swear to God, look like a rat sometimes. Rat bones holding his narrow face together. Bones thin as eggshells. If you wrapped your fingers around his big head, you could crush it like an egg. Make his skull talk like Rice Krispies when you poured on milk.

You could tell Reuben anything because he's liable to say anything back. Like fairy tales. Like he's trying to put a kid to sleep. Like he ain't heard you ask him serious as money, How my gon keep the man off my back, Reuben? He's coming down hard. Breathing his skunk breath down my neck and I need help, Reuben, or they'll lynch me over at the university. You think you got the old nigger's attention, then he come back at you grinning with some off-the-wall mess. In Egypt, when Egypt was Egypt and Pharaoh the Sun King, they had priests could empty your whole brain through your nose hole and never leave a mark on you. One curved needle all they used. It was the touch they had. Delicate, delicate touch like your finest Italian barber or New Orleans cook and knowing exactly what was in there, what they had to deal with. Unravel that gray matter like it was a ball of yarn or a string of spaghetti. Have it laid out beside your head good as new. Not a mark on it. And you look peaceful like you're sleeping. Some say the priests could use the brain again. Plump it up. Sing to it, get the nerves dancing around again and it's good as new. Use it again in another body that ain't worn out or damaged. Stick it in a baboon or a falcon or a leopard. Then they could talk to the parts of God in these animals and yes indeed, the animals could answer.

Yes, Wally. Sometimes I'm back there with those wide-eyed Egyptians. An outsider, of course. Always the outsider. A dwarf stolen from the Land of Spirits, the black land. I know exactly how he felt, a plaything, a curiosity, a slave. Poor little fella can't speak their language and they sure don't speak his. I can hear the queen laughing when he sings his sad, sad song. All the fools around her laughing cause she's cracking up.

Reuben slipping further and further off till you want to scream. Him talking a mile a minute about one thing and you about to pee your pants waiting for him to get back to what you asked in the first place.

Scuse me, Reuben . . . but could you please . . .

Maybe the point wasn't answers. Maybe the point was having somebody to ask. And maybe that's why he'd missed Reuben before he'd met Reuben. Because you needed to know there was someone you could ask, even if you never asked, you needed to know you could if you had to.

When Wally went away to college he trusted no one. His grandmother had died the summer preceding the fall he arrived at the university, and for at least seven years before that, she'd been the child, Wally the guardian. To say he hated everyone at the university would not be fair to him. He did, however, strongly dislike being thrown into the midst of lots of white people he didn't know. Walking across campus he often felt like one of those huge, ugly pimples that sprouted regularly on his face. Sore to the touch, begging to be busted. His secret life throbbing plain as day in the center of his forehead. Anybody looked at him knew he was full of white, nasty pus.

In those days he'd prayed for trouble. Hoped one of the smooth-faced gray boys would say the word, give Wally an excuse to waste him. His first autumn in Philadelphia was hot. Late November before the weather turned. No one had told him to pack summer clothes. In the department-store windows at home the going-back-to-school crowd wore wool and corduroy, bulky sweaters with shawl collars, plaid flannel shirts. So that's what was in his trunk to fight the heat wave. No one had told him scheduling a free hour before and after each class was unnecessary, in fact stupid since you tended to piss away this dead time in the student lounge, or else your days became continuous commutes back and forth from the oven of your room to class. Since Wally made no friends, he spent lots of his days sulking along the blistering Philadelphia streets no one had warned him about either. He yo-yoed up and down Spruce, from the dorm gate on Thirty-seventh nearest his room to the complex of classroom buildings behind College Hall. He could have stayed behind the four-storied wall of dormitories separating campus from city, Joe College strolling across the quadrangles on his way to higher learning. He preferred the sound of tires and horns, corners where you had to wait for traffic lights to change, wading through the press of people certain times of day in and out of the university hospital when shifts changed, the blank eyes of strangers, the freckles of sun reflected off the pavement. Better to suck up dogshit fumes of PTC buses filled with black people headed home down South Street than pass through a gauntlet of bare white bodies sprawled like they're dead, sunning themselves or sailing Frisbees over his head, students who had enough sense to organize their classes in blocks so they could enjoy free time, students smart enough to be born a color they could change if they chose.

He talked to no one. Ached for basketball practice to begin so he could look forward to a daily, three-hour drain of the pent-up forces that bayed like a panicked crowd in his body. All the folks off Homewood Avenue piggybacked on his shoulders, arguing, fussing, trying to get over. They rode him up and down Spruce, wearied him, but they were his only company, a song he didn't like that kept sneaking inside his head. A jingle, a commercial, a herky-jerky, paddyboy, top-ten tune you heard in spite of yourself, fifty times a day on the radios up and down the dorm halls.

Wally needed Reuben that first year at the university. So many questions he wanted to ask someone like Reuben. Someone who'd been there before, someone like Reuben who'd survived it once, a witness, someone, some ways like him.

He'd decided to give up school. Run home tail between his legs. In the underground bus depot names of cities topped wide glass ports where buses docked. Did it matter, one city or another. No bus could carry him home again home again, jiggedy-jig.

What difference would it make? Wally could stay or he could go, he could haunt bus stations or haunt the streets of Homewood or pass like a ghost through the university. He remembered a pretty, sleepy-eyed girl in the never-closed snack bar on the lowest level of the bus station spearing hot dogs on the spokes of a rotisserie. Someone would buy them, eat them, the wheel would stay empty, be filled again. If he escaped Philadelphia, he knew that he'd soon be craving green lawns, slim, tanned legs, the vision of himself as a gunfighter against the odds, bad-assing it down the middle of Spruce.

He put in his four years. Was working up on four more. He'd learned to treat what was happening as a memory, a film he watched on a screen. But if he could see himself that way, if the only life he knew was not his own, then whose was it?

During those years at the university Reuben could have been a big help. Talking to Reuben could have been like talking to himself that first year at college when a guy pulled him aside and said, Ah . . . say, Wally . . . how come you tie your tie that way? So it hangs down past your belt. People don't tie ties like that.

First question he would have asked Reuben, or somebody like Reuben, was why should people make other people change their ways, adjust the lengths of rags they wore round their necks, especially if such changes signified nothing. That's one he would have asked Reuben if Reuben had been around on campus the first year Wally attended the university. And why was small stuff connected to big stuff in such treacherous ways. If the game was set up so you could never win—short rag, long rag, no rag, ten rags—if you'd never be one of them, why play?

If those social occasions sponsored by the student activities board were mixers, what was being mixed? Wally's drop of blackness in an ocean of whiteness. Whose color was spozed to change?

See, Reuben, what bothered me most at the time, what I spent so much energy on, what hurt me most was the ticky-tack little shit that made me feel like a fool. Things like the tie. Yeah, a goddamned tie. Shit. By the time I graduated most people I hung with wasn't wearing no ties. Nowhere. No time. But my first year I sweated the tie. Doing it their way in front of the mirror, going along to get along. Every time since then, when I turn up my collar and start sliding a tie round my neck, I remember that guy's voice. The whole bunch of them must have talked it over. You know. My teammates. What should we do about

Wally and that silly nigger hoodlum way he wears his ties? One guy volunteered to do the dirty work. The others lined up behind him. Shaking their heads, smiling. Nothing personal, Wall. Nobody in this life had ever called me *Wall* till those white boys got hold to my name. Wall. Hey. Now that's better, Wall. That's cool, man.

You never know exactly what's at stake when you give up on some little point and go along with the suckers. You never know if they mean to hurt you as much as they do or if they're just dumb. Dumb, and treat each other bad as they treat you. One thing sure they accomplished. I learned to hate the face in the mirror. My own face. Hate it for giving in, hate it for not being the right one, hate it for hating itself.

Those days were sure enough trifling, Wally says to himself as he crosses campus. Is that what Reuben meant when he said all black men have their Philadelphias? Was Wally's Philadelphia Philadelphia? Stifling heat, crazy bus rides to find a corner like Frankstown and Homewood? His heart crying like a baby as he hides for hours in the Greyhound station reading the same sign over and over. HARRISBURG, PITTSBURGH, AND WEST. Reuben said all black men had a Philadelphia. What about white men? What about women? Was Philadelphia a limbo stick everybody had to crawl under? Why had they left her . . . left Flora tied to the bed?

Wally checks out the coeds lounging in the sun. Could be the same ones made his jaws tight freshman year. Only these ladies more bold. Halters, bikinis. Wide-legged short shorts hiding nothing when a chick sitting on the grass with her knees cocked up. Used to be women had a way of knowing lots of things they don't seem to know or care about now. Like in the old days women could tell if you were fucking regular. Just one look and they'd know. If you were getting it regular, they couldn't wait to jump out they drawers. If it been awhile and your dick hard as a telly pole, forget it. Women could smell how bad you need it. Treat you like disease. Don't know how they knew, but they always did. Girls nowdays don't give a shit one way or the other. Ain't no pearl of great price no more. Easy come, easy go, bargain-basement pussy. You don't even have to be a cocksman to get over regular as rain. Nothing to brag about. These little wimpy dudes, man, lame cats like that get a piece ass in a minute. All you got to do is open your mouth and ask. Don't have to ask sometimes. Just put a jam on the box, one of Bimbo's heavy-breathin raps. Serve the bitch a couple drinks and down come them panties, if she's wearing panties. Chicks be grabbing you, man. Trying to carry you home to they crib. White, black, yellow, red. Don't hardly make no nevermind these days. But like the song says, partner, the thrill is gone.

Reason he asked Reuben how long he stayed in Philly was because there are times, now, looking back, when Wally has memories of those school years that don't make sense without Reuben around. If not Reuben, somebody like Reuben talking to Wally. Or maybe it was more a matter of missing Reuben, the way you miss your water after the well runs dry. But you got to have the water first, don't you? Like wouldn't he have to know Reuben *before* he could miss him. You had to have a thing at least once or you couldn't miss it, could you? So he had asked the old man, How long did you stay in Philly? A dumb question, Wally knew when he asked it, because Wally was out of school four years, which meant he'd first trucked to Philly eight years before and hadn't he been seeing Reuben, hearing about Reuben in Homewood, long before that? Reuben's trailer's older than Wally and God only knows how long it's raggedy ass been planted over there behind Hamilton Avenue. When Wally deserted Homewood for college and all that knowledge, he'd left Reuben behind so how could the old man be in both places. He hadn't been. No way. Just a dumb question. Wally had never spoken to Reuben till he returned from the university so he couldn't have carried Reuben's conversations to Philadelphia. Couldn't have missed him because he didn't know him yet. He'd asked a dumb question. Even though some memories of college, about the way Wally had felt, required Reuben's presence to make sense. Or maybe they required Reuben not being around,

113

Reuben missing . . . sorely missed, so his absence part of the memories. Part of Philadelphia. The rain. The emptiness of the wide gray sky.

Had Philadelphia been Wally's Philadelphia? Had he lost something precious in Philly? Is that what Reuben meant? Or did he mean pain. Pain that changed you, seasoned you for your next city, and the next, for the rest of your life.

Or had he been listening too long to Reuben run off at the mouth? Was he remembering Reuben's story and tangling himself up in it? Wally imagines Philadelphia as it appeared in a book of old photos, brown-tinted, weightless. You could poke your finger through rows of wooden houses. Blow them down. They existed only in a picture. Streets he's never walked on but remembers as soon as he turns a page.

Wally wondered about the man in Chicago. Had Wally treated him to his Philadelphia? How long did the treatment have to last? Could it continue for years? Could you enter as a freshman, become a senior three years later. Play ball then work three more years in another city and still have miles to go? Did you have to survive your Philadelphia? Was it like a jail sentence? Hard time. A state of mind. Could you be in the middle of your Philadelphia, pain stretching backward and forward as far as you can see and not even recognize your fatal city, your cross?

Reuben might have a few words to say about the incident in Chicago. Sooner or later Wally would bring it up. Not confess exactly, but put it to Reuben in a way that would allow them to talk about what happened as if it had happened to someone else. Like I met this crazy guy once, Reuben. We were on a plane between Chicago and Pittsburgh. Business, you know. Been seeing the dude here and there ever since I been on the road. Black dude. Bout five or six years older than me. A former player like me. Doing the same bit I do. You know. Bring em back alive. Recruiting for a New England school, I think. Or Big Five. Doesn't matter. Point was we're working the same turf. He'd turn up every now and then in a spot I'd be. See, there's a regular circuit. Certain players everyone is after. You'll have

114

coffee or a drink with another recruiter going or coming from the house you just visited. Funny sometimes. Sometimes you try to duck the other guy because you've been telling such nasty, barefaced lies about his school, its basketball program, maybe even the recruiter himself you see checking in at the ticket counter. Anyway, this dude's familiar. We'd spoken before. Hey, hiya doing? Leave some for me, boss. Stuff like that. Time of day, the weather, and so forth so we wind up sitting together on the plane.

We ain't buckled up good before he starts in on this weird tale. He's tired as I am. Has that bleary on-the-road look about him. Drinking too much, staying up too late. Tough time falling asleep in jive motel rooms. Early rise to catch a plane. We're both whipped. I was figuring on nodding between Chicago and Pittsburgh but this brother gets going a mile a minute. I recline my seat, lays back cool, my head on one them peanut-size pillows. He don't need me saying a word. Once he starts it's all gon come out. No doubt about it. And after I catch the drift of what he's saying, you better believe I pays attention.

He had this theory, dig. About killing people. Killing them and getting away clean. But that ain't what he started talking about. The theory came later. First he told me about his daddy being lynched by the Ku Klux Klan. Then they raped his mama and she went stone insane. One morning she woke up and killed his brother and two little sisters. Stabbed them while they was sleep. Woulda killed my man too, but he woke up. Just barely managed to escape. Mama's in the loony bin now. She ain't spoke nor winked an eye at nobody in twenty years. Like talking to a rock, he says. He tells this part real quiet and I'm thinking this man sure caught hell. And thinking to myself life is a bitch. Here's this brother, a nice-looking dude, well dressed, working for a college, sitting like a prince on this flying carpet just like me. You know what I mean. Then he begins talking. A pit opens up. A goddamned horror show. He been through shit like I read about in history books. Stuff I thought didn't happen no more. At least not that way. Lynch mobs and shit. Then the mama killing her own kids. Damn. I'm wondering how the cat sur-

115

vived. Wondering if I could. How anybody could and look so normal, so everyday.

The recruiter lights up a cigarette. We're in the no smoking but he lights it anyway and nobody bothers the two burly niggers in 12C and D who probably can't read. Plane just about empty anyway. It's not a red-eye special but the few travelers on it all got red eyes. A plane carrying the wounded, too late for the early flight, too early for the late. Not a good day's work in anybody. We're out of O'Hare maybe ten, fifteen minutes and this recruiter slides into the second part, his theory.

No doubt about the first part. White people did in his whole family. Mama, daddy. Mize well say they the one holding the knife killed his brother and sisters. So ain't no surprise he hates white people. He called it abstract hate. I remember because abstract hate sounded like the way you talk about things sometimes. Tell the truth, I thought of you, Reuben, as he explained hisself. Abstract hate means you don't got nothing against any particular person. You may even like or respect a particular individual but at the same time there's something about that person, "the white part" you can't ever forgive, never forget. So deep inside you you don't know you're rooting against them. Sometimes you even think you're in their corner. Till they fall. Then you're laughing inside and realize all this time you been thinking you like them, grinning in their faces, grinning at yourself, you've been waiting for the fall. It's a deep hate you can't get over no matter what happens. You can live among them, thrive, love one or two, but you never move beyond the abstract part. It's in your gut and there's righteous cause for it to be there, so it stays there, like a sickness, a cancer, unless you root it out.

Rooting it out's the hardest part. Next to impossible, according to the gospel my man the recruiter is laying down. Trouble is the hate's bad for you. Takes something away. Fucks with your insides. Spoils what you try to do, how you feel about what you've done. Whether you're dealing with black people or white people or yourself in the mirror. He'd thought about this shit for years, he said. The white men who lynched his father might be

116

dead and gone yet he let them keep on hurting him. Seeing them in the emptiness of his mother's eyes caused him to desert her, leave her to rot in the asylum because he couldn't stand feeling what he felt when he visited. Knew he must cure himself or become one more victim of crimes that had occurred when he was not much more than a baby.

A cure. He had studied and talked and prayed to whatever a cat like him prays. Racked his brain for years trying to figure a cure. Just thinking hard about the shit was sort of a help. I mean, he kept his mind occupied. Left Indiana, where the killing had gone down, and moved east. Lived with an aunt and uncle who took good care of him. Went to decent schools, played a lot of ball, won himself a scholarship. Was doing okay it seemed. I mean, if you stood outside and looked at his outside, he seemed to be climbing up the ladder. Inside, the hate still eating away. Abstract. He couldn't put his finger on it. Like gas. Invisible but strong enough to choke you to death.

Finally he works out this theory. Explaining it he sounds like you again, Reuben. If the hate, the anger, is abstract, if it's a matter of principle, then you have to fight it on the same terms. Take your revenge in the abstract, on principle. If you're a recruiter, your job keeps you hopping from city to city. You pop in and out, touch down a few hours, at most a day or two before you're off again, hitting that everlasting road again. Which makes you kind of abstract in the first place, if you dig what I'm saying. In the second place, you got no ties. You ain't part of where you land, you ain't really no part of what you left behind. You float. You're a floater. People begin to see you that way. Which amounts to not seeing you at all. Invisible. Prince of the air. Nobody expects you to stick around. In the third place, being on the road alone, out of touch except for a minute here or there with strangers, gives you plenty time to think. You talk to yourself and ain't nobody answering but you. Now that's about as abstract as you can get. Put it all together and what you have is a situation where you can be whoever you want to be whenever you turn up in a new place. You are an abstract person so you can test your abstract feelings. Release the abstract hate through an abstract crime. Murder one of the motherfuckers you wanted to kill ever since they killed a piece of you. Nothing personal, you dig. Letting off steam in a way. You free yourself from the burden of what they've done to you. Free one of them, too. And what you're really doing is working on the biggest problem: the abstract hate. That's what you're really killing.

Yeah. I listened to every word. Something in his tone of voice hipped me to the fact he wasn't just theorizing to hear himself talk. This wasn't no abstract bullshit for the sake of abstract bullshit. Meat on them bones, mister. I could smell it, taste it, Reuben. Cat was up to something. I was on his trail and it definitely was leading to some strange places.

You watch the old man for a reaction. You are so slick you're at least three places at once. Watching Reuben. Listening to the recruiter rap. Making it all up as you tell the story. Eyes and mouth where they usually are, stuck on the front of your skull. Other sets of features in reserve behind your bones, ready to work just as hard, talking, seeing, hearing, hiding. How many faces do you own as you construct an imaginary dialogue for an imaginary conversation you aren't conducting with anyone but yourself? Who was the person next to you in 12D? How do you make him real in Reuben's mind?

The recruiter touches my arm. I feel his whole weight a minute. The goddamn airplane tilts. He presses harder on my arm but I don't pull away. He kind of pins me to the armrest like he's afraid I might try to split before he finishes. Either that or he's scared he might fly out his seat so he grips what there is to grip. Like he's rising and gripping at the same time and my poor arm happens to be laying there on the armrest between us so he presses down on it, pins it, almost flips the damned airplane trying to hold on and finish whatever he needs to finish. Which is to begin the third part. The part I knew was coming even though I didn't know exactly what it would be. Tone of his voice hipped me. Brother had a tiger by the tail. Couldn't let go, couldn't reel it in. I'd heard fear in his voice all along and now he was going to put words to it. Let the cat out the bag.

Dude claimed he'd killed a man. Wasted him in a public bathroom. Whamo. Just like stepping on an ant. Killed him a perfect stranger to get rid of the abstract hate poisoning his system.

Should I have believed the guy? Would you have believed him, Reuben? A dude in a sharp, three-piece suit, dap, down. You know. A recruiter like me. College educated. Getting ahead in the white man's world. A ballplayer. An intelligent, smooth-talking, sensible person swearing to me he's just killed a white man in a toilet. On principle. Because he had a theory. Because he'd been hurt so bad he believed he had a perfect right to try anything to make himself well.

What do you think, old man? Would you have believed him? Would it have made sense to you? Would you have changed seats, called the cops, or shook the nigger's hand?

And there's more. He wasn't finished with me and I'm not finished with you yet. The last part was this: he thought he'd proved his damn theory. Felt real good about what he'd done. Intended to do it again and again. Long as it felt good. In the next city and the next till the hate was gone. For all I know the dude's out there today perpetrating his plan. A ghost choking the abstract shit out of some poor soul.

Wally surrenders his claim to the armrest. His companion's quiet. Wally lets his hand drop into his lap. The plane is over Lake Erie. Captain says it, so it must be so. A magic lake slaves crossed fleeing to Canada. On the airline map the Great Lakes like gobs of icing spilled over the humpbacked outline of the US of A. One was Lake Michigan with Chicago like a finger in the dike. Holding back wind, clouds, a million million tons of water. If Chicago wasn't there, the blood would drip down over the rest of the land. The United States standing upright on its stubby legs was like a cartoon animal screeching to a halt, a lopsided, long-necked animal with a Reuben hump on its shoulders. Goo gobs of sweet icing or blood or blue watery tears poised on its back. A ragged crack down its middle. Old Man River splitting east and west, linking north with south, its traffic in slaves and cotton closing the seam, stitching the land back together, rending it, then healing or festering again, dividing again. Wally had learned the dates, memorized acts of Congress, the debates and issues and personalities who had named him, decided his fate, just as he'd taught himself the silhouette of the map. Had he lived in America before he learned the shape of his country? Did he exist before he became acquainted with the tortured logic of his history in this land, the Compromises and Conventions and Supreme Court rulings determining what he was, what his life was worth, where he might live and go to school, how many of him clustered on the head of a pin equaled one white man?

Hmmmmm. This recruiter on the plane . . . Reuben strokes his pointy beard.

Careful now, old man. Don't roll your pop eyes at me. I see what you're signifying, Froggy. But you jumped to the wrong conclusion. This recruiter, he may look some like me, and maybe he is me in some ways, but don't get confused. Don't let them resemblances take you too far. He's older by five or six years. Probably more. The recruiter's reaching that kinda middling, in-between age and he's holding up pretty well for a guy always on the road. People gon look at him and think young man for a while yet. Closer look you'll see he ain't no spring chicken but young man will suit him for a decade maybe, if he keeps wearing at the rate he been wearing. If he don't get fat behind too many pork chops and do. He's not me, Reuben. He's kinda like me in this, that, and the other thing but the differences between us are big. Big as your pop eyes. And don't gimme that all-niggers-look-alike smirk, neither. You know what I mean. The differences. He's the one telling the crazy story. I'm the one laid back in my seat, thirty thousand feet up, listening.

Differences, Reuben. Lots of differences. Start with hair. His is nappy but neat. Shortish and squared off like you clip hedges. Razor line defines his ears, his sideburns that stop a half inch past the bottom lobe of his ears. In other words, the dude visits the barbershop regular. A kind of barber-lotion smell when he

120

leans closer to me rapping. You know. Those sissy-shaped green bottles and pink bottles lined up on a shelf under the mirror. Like whiskey bottles in a bar. Only funny-shaped and more colors. Red, purple, yellow. Barber sprinkles a drop or two in one hand then rubs his palms together, swish, swish. Wipes the stuff on your skin where he's been shaving you and it stings but feels fine too. A clean, sharp tingle. You know your haircut's about over. You look better going out than you did coming in. Barber whirls your chair so you can see yourself all around in the wall mirrors and doubled in the hand mirror he lets you hold so you can scope the back of your head.

That was his hair. His skin was Indian brown. Rust in the brown. Or blood. Seminole, Cherokee, Apache, Comanche, Sioux, drums and fires and the Long March and Wounded Knee and dying in the snow. That color.

Have to admit his eyes a lot like mine. I said a lot. Which leaves some that ain't. Like mine, I mean. But start with mine. Except something crazy in his eyes. That theory, that claim he killed a man, his promise to kill again. What struck me from the front was he could get away with it, if he was careful. Like I said. A recruiter's kind of invisible. Biff—bam—thank you, ma'am. In and out real quick. No reason to be anywhere, stay anywhere, except a couple hours taking care of business with some hot-shit kid or pain-in-the-ass coach. Couple hours of bullshit business then you're on your own. You see people once and you're gone. A rabbit out a hat. Cincinnati one day, Detroit the next. If a white man turns up dead in a city you just split, what's that mess got to do with you? And who's gon connect a murder in Columbus with a murder in San Diego? Unless you turn greedy and dumb and ain't enough space, enough time, between bodies. Who reads the newspapers from all these cities I visit? So how's anybody make connections unless you ignorant enough to leave clues or kill the same way each time? Hey, I read them detective books, man. And watch TV. No apparent motive, no relationship among the victims, just a body turning up here and there. Cops don't never solve them kind of murders.

Less some psycho confesses. Who's gon find a pattern, a reason, if there ain't none. Just a bunch of stiffs, unsolved crimes like lots of others they got filling their books.

So there was crazy in the recruiter's eyes, the kind of crazy that's convincing. Because the dude knew what he was talking about. The abstract hate bit. Tell me you ain't felt it. As for the atrocity story about his family, you can take it or leave it. True as half them lies you tell, old man. Whether his story makes sense or not to you, he believes it. So a door's open. And once he steps through and takes you by the hand with him, you can't argue about what's on the other side. Cause there you are. Through the door. It's real. He's picturing a world both of us, shit, all of us live in. If you take the step, chances are things would work out just like he said. So his eyes had the shine of conviction. Brown like mine, but deep, deep behind the conviction, and a spark in them from the craziness, and a mirror on the back of his eyeballs nobody could see but him. I know the mirror was there cause I'd catch him staring at it as he talked. Like hello, how do you do. Meeting up with his ownself in the mirror. Like he'd be staring off in space but the stare couldn't go no further out his head than those black, taped, one-way mirrors behind his eyeballs.

A nose like . . . well, it wasn't like much except a nose. A good African nose taking up its sizable share of his face. What else can I say? A hill, a pyramid, between his cheeks. Starting at the eyes, then it grows wider, higher. Flares like a woman's skirt. Tunnels for breath. Terminates at a moustache, bushier, darker than his head hair, another thick, curly hedge trimmed neatly with the same clippers gave his head hair that barbered, squarish look.

And mouth. Not a bit like mine. See, mine speaks the truth, Reuben, as you well know. I'm still not sure about what comes out his. It's like yours. I mean, what he said was plausible, possible. He was right on in most of his rap. What I wasn't sure about was the actual killing part. Did he do it? Was an actual white man dead on the floor of an actual public rest room? Didn't know then and don't know now. Probably why I brought it up to you. I need to find out whether or not the dude was lying to me. It's important that I know.

Did looking at another person's lips ever embarrass you, Reuben? You know. Everybody got this hole in their face and the skin around it turned sort of inside out. Like the edges round the hole, the puckered wrinkly different-colored skin is the underside, the inside of skin. Like somebody slit open the bottom of your face and folded back flesh and it dried up withered like a raisin. You see inside a person when they open their mouth. Wet and pink in there. A mouth really like a asshole or a cunt in your face. You ever see it that way? Person wouldn't think of turning his behind up in somebody's face and blowing the lips open, making somebody see up in the pink, juicy inside. Assholes private, right? People hide it under clothes, under their underwear. But we strut around all day with our mouths gaping open. Let people peek down in our guts. Don't look at me that way, man. That ain't how I see mouths all the time. Just occasionally, when I'm in a certain mood. Hell. In another mood a butthole can look pretty good. A matter of privacy. A matter of remembering what belongs to who and whose face you shove yours into.

The jet drones. Vibrations agitate the round edges of transparent ports. Wally forgets the noise, the trembling, unless he reminds himself to remind himself. Yet the edges of the triple-paned windows lining the plane's belly are never still. The plane's engines lull Wally into forgetting he's on a plane. To hear the constant roar he must listen for it. You're either on the bus or off the bus. He must stand aside in freezing, inhuman air to view the plane, the whole plane containing him and a handful of weary survivors. On it you don't see it. Make the effort to see it, you lose your place in the story the man beside you is telling.

Now put all the pieces together. You got you an Identikit, brother. Pull together the hair, eyes, color, nose, mouth I've been describing. It's a face. Have you been paying attention, old man? Is that rat face of yours asleep again at your desk? Don't be so smug. You need me to make you up, too. If my recruiter's full of shit, if I cut him off, shut him down, where's that leave you? Nowhere, Mr. Reuben. In the slum of your catnap. Looking for a dream to wake you up. So pay attention. You heard about his hair, skin, eyes, nose, mouth, color, a whole face if you've been listening. Do you believe him, see him, are you ready for the rest?

Reuben is dead. A white man sprawled on a white floor, bathed in white fluorescent light. Water runs in one of the alabaster sinks. Water laps from the flooded bowl of a toilet. Reuben's head on the hard marble is situated uncomfortably. If he ever awakens, he'll have a stiff neck. He'd be groaning now if there was breath in his body. But life in him is as still as the veins, bluish, gray, off-white, faintly mottling the marble.

Fee Fi Fo Fum
I smell the blood of an Englishman

Say, mon. You got light, mon? Wally flicks his Bic at the dreadlocked man beside him in 12D. The recruiter changes voices, faces, again. He's laughing now. An inscrutable Oriental. Then an Eskimo venerable as Buddha squatting on his fat hams, chewing whale meat, fingering the nether lips of the roly-poly, naked lady squirming on his lap. You vant zum? You a nice boychik. The recruiter's laughter roars louder than the jet engines. Louder than the stallion, hi-ho Silvering as it gallops away into the sunset of Wally's chest. Sleep, sleep *mein Liebster*. *Schlafe*, my sweet prince. Earth to Wally, signing off. Sleep . . . sleep . . .

7

REUBEN

Reuben parks his ancient Buick at one of the meters outside the Mayflower Hotel. Two blocks further down Fifth Avenue the metallic breast of a new skyscraper looms, demanding that Reuben take it seriously. He looks through it, past it, remembering a tacky row of brick office buildings once situated on the corner where the newcomer reigns. Off to the left newly sandblasted stones of the matching courthouse and jail yawn in a midafternoon caress of light. Reuben preferred the scorched look, stones blackened as if they'd survived a fire. The courthouse and jail had earned their crust of grime and smoke and grit, endured sooty rains from mill stacks downriver. He recalled high noons when streetlights sputtered on to fight back clouds of coal dust bringing night prematurely to the city. For years the stones of the jailhouse and court had remembered with him. Blasting them clean was like stealing. If all the witnesses disappeared, who would remember? Nothing caused Reuben to feel more lonely than the thought that he was the only one left who remembered. When he disappeared, what would become of the record he'd kept? Had there really been afternoons when you couldn't see across to the other side of Fifth Avenue? Had there been a Reuben once swimming through motes of black dust. He'd believed the dusky stones of the courthouse and jail would tell the truth long after he was gone. Now, victims of the city's urge to clean itself, they gleamed yellow as tapioca pudding, as absentminded and forgetful as the old man plodding toward them.

Women in long dresses, men in tall hats, derbies, boaters, trolley cars with wicker seats, horse-drawn before powered by cables—had Reuben dreamed it all? Was he remembering pictures he'd seen in books or had he been there, in person, on this corner or corners downtown in other cities, busy streets alive and breathing with that motion Muybridge had dared to capture, the motion everyone saw but nobody believed till the photographer stopped it, froze it, spread out its bones for the doubters. You can't go anywhere, Muybridge screamed, unless you've first been here and here and here. A million *heres* and each one separate, discrete, enduring. So still our eyes cannot slow down enough to see the stillness. What we see very little of what we get. Is Reuben a humpbacked little brown man gimping down the slight incline of Fifth Avenue toward the abstract justice of the county courthouse? Is Reuben an ant seen from the fiftieth-floor window of a gleaming tower he skirts? Is he the big shot who tips Carmine, the janitor and parking-lot attendant who will feed quarters into the meter beside the Buick until Reuben returns from his business and reimburses him because once upon a time Reuben saved Carmine from a charge of indecent exposure and public intoxication when Carmine and his family still lived in Homewood, on Dago Row, too poor, too proud to budge even though a flood of black immigrants from the South islanded their Little Italy? Is motion progress, the fiction of one Reuben making headway toward a particular place on a particular day? Or is it all the Reubens who ever lived or could have lived, plunged into a speed-of-light dance, like the particles that comprise Reuben, break him down, bind him? The thought of Reuben courses through his

126

own mind, through infinite banks of cameras Muybridge has installed along these last few blocks of Fifth Avenue before the city's core starts up like a belch.

No matter how many cameras, a different Reuben in each frame, a slightly altered pose, a separate reality. Amazing, isn't it? How protean the simplest gesture. And each pose real, definitive, if we possessed a means of capturing it. If we could see everything. If we bore God's eye in our foreheads. A paradox, an irony. To slow things down, we must click the shutter faster and faster. Do you see what I mean? Less light. More and more pictures as the time scale shrinks. The shutter blinks a million times an instant yet it's not fast enough. Motion defeats it. Motion slips through the net no matter how fine the weave. Motion the sum of all the tiny inchings forward but something greater, irreducible. Fantastic. Don't you agree, Mr. Reuben?

Too late in the day, too much work to do, no time to agree or disagree. Just behind Reuben, up the hill he's descending, the mostly abandoned storefronts of Jews who'd once owned this end of Fifth Avenue. Best buys in town if you knew how to bargain, to haggle, to shake your head no and put your hands in your pockets and slouch out the door just slowly enough, the bell ringing as you exit, so the shopkeeper can scoot from behind his counter and rush after you with a better deal. Reuben knew his Bible. Called the Fifth Avenue merchants Joseph and his brothers. Not to their faces. It was his private joke, yoking them all, those seven quarrelsome tribes of vendors, wholesalers, hucksters, Joseph and his brothers. Part of the joke was his name, Reuben, which few of them ever asked and he never offered. *Behold, a son.* Reuben was his name, his kinship with the brethren. He had learned their mannerisms, ambitions, the secret language they chattered among themselves, their suspicion, fear, and disdain of outsiders, the games they played, the energy and time they expended maintaining the fence that protected and stigmatized them. A little less busy with their getting and spending they might have recognized Reuben's tribe as the exile's exiles, toting their Egypts on their backs to the earth's four corners. Perhaps they meant no harm when they called him *shvartzer, meshuggener,* baptizing him in the Yiddish he pretended not to understand and they pretended was opaque after twenty centuries of commerce with Hamites seeking bargains. Perhaps those words on their tongues confirmed him, lifted the veil so he could at least stick his foot in their doors.

The wandering minstrels of the Sekou said that their harp, the Ngoni, never forgets. Kings, blacksmiths, slaves, warriors can forget, but the heart of the Ngoni remembers everything. Sekou bards also sang this tune: "All things are tied, and they have been brought together in a fragment of time to make the City or the Kingdom visible." Was the visible city the real one? How many cities had scored their music on his poor old heartstrings?

Below him a wedge of steel and concrete and glass, a bundle of the city's tallest buildings, in whose shadow, on the river side, lay his destination, the stubby, mock-gothic, nineteenth-century courthouse and jail joined navel to navel by an arching Bridge of Sighs. Reuben consults his watch, rubs his brother's pointed crown. For weeks now, it's been ten-thirty. When he checked his watch this morning in his office: 10:30. Every time he's checked, the hands of his watch have indicated that hopelessly depressing, ambiguous hour. A day already half gone or gone already. Ten bells. Sea rocks the cradle. Mist wet as rain, heavy as dough, melts the sound. Ten times the bell oozes, the ship plows and bellies and tosses, dropping sounds like a turtle depositing eggs in the gloomy sea. *Deep in the hold thy father lies . . . those were pearls that were his eyes.* A poem written over and over again on the same raw parchment. Cracked, blackened as the hide of a slave's corpse left to rot in the desert. The caravan swims on, *As Salaam Alaikum . . . As Salaam Alaikum,* disintegrating, dancing in waves of heat, undulating toward the horizon, camel bells dinging, camel dung dropping dry as a mummy's hand in its wake.

This city built on hills, its heart, its downtown crisscrossed by rivers. Blood in, blood out, a silent systole and diastole accented by trains of tugs and barges plying the brown channels. Bridges everywhere. Everywhere hills to climb over or tunnel through. They called the delta formed by the confluence of three

128

rivers the Golden Triangle, which Reuben on his good days visualized as a pubic mound fleeced with a silky, shimmering nimbus. He liked that image but it seldom fit this downtown. *Dahn Tahn* the natives pronounced it, their peculiar accent defining them, revealing them, setting them apart like the Yiddish of the merchants up on the hill. Dahn Tahn was dark and red, a crude pump sucking the city's juices, expelling them, a muscle grown rude and thick from the exercise of its power.

Beside the Kramer Building, long extinct, was where once upon a time Reuben set his shoebox down each morning. At dawn, always first on the corner, claiming his spot. He savored the street's early morning privacy, its crisp, quiet emptiness would brace him for the rest of his long workday. From his quiet corner he would watch downtown stagger to life. The first feeble surges, his dark tribe of janitors, elevator boys, cooks, waiters, doormen, cleaning ladies trickling in on trolleys, buses, or trudging on bad feet down off the Hill. The first white men in suits and ties carry sandwiches in their briefcases, huge rings of keys somewhere inside their clothes. Reuben could have started it up himself. He knew the routines. Which doors to unlock when. Which steel gates to fold. When lights should be snapped on up and down the block. Who sent out for coffee, who needed a belt first thing in the tavern underneath the Kramer Building, one door down from where Reuben set up shop each morning. A city was a simple thing to bring to life. You squeeze in enough people and it takes off on its own. It's their blood surging through it, feeding it, their bones it grinds to make its bread. You know this if you watch the faces arrive in the morning, then watch the same ones departing in the final waves emptying the chambers each evening.

How many pairs of shoes had he shined on that corner? How many lies had he listened to and told? When there was nothing but a log fort down at the point and hostile Indians lurking in the woods, Reuben had been shining shoes. Officers' boots, sabots of tongue-tied immigrants, the beaded moccasins you could wheedle from redskins in exchange for tobacco or whiskey. He'd done it all. Shined the silver horseshoes of a

129

redcoat general who'd pranced in with his entourage to inspect the garrison. Polished brass cannon, bayonets, belt buckles. Ladies brought him their glass slippers in velvet bags. He polished fingernails and toenails. He could spit-shine anything. He could rub and buff this whole dingy city with his talking rags till it sparkled and crackled like a mirror.

Right here on this corner he'd shined shoes till all the wounds from Philadelphia were healed. He'd watch Flora's face materialize again and again in the looking glasses he spit-shined atop the toes of white men's shoes. Her face drowning in that dark water, then his own, then nothing but the hard glaze of saliva and polish turning leather to stone.

From this corner he'd seen a double rainbow, a pair of giant horseshoes intersecting, shivering with color as the sky cooled and cleared after a sudden summer storm.

He'd prospered on this corner. Began with the homemade shoeshine box fashioned so it slung over his shoulder and he was like Brer Turtle, his whole livelihood, home, and hearth on his back, roaming the city till he found the steps of the Kramer Building with their busy traffic in and out. He learned the corner was a gateway, that he could catch tons of folks entering and leaving Dahn Tahn with his smile, his nod, a pop of his shoeshine rag, the jingles he'd chant to his customers, to the thin air if no one sat on his cloth spread over the stone steps, if no one's foot was mounted on the iron lasts, inverted, nailed to his box. After years of shines and fetching coffee they'd allowed him to set up in the Kramer lobby. Three borrowed wooden chairs on a platform, a fixture for years, an institution after a while nobody could remember ever doing without. Pity at first, the little crippled nigger, wet as a drowned rat, shivering in icy wind off the river. When the weather was bad, they began to let him stand in the basement, the furnace room with Old Bill. Once in, he and the favors he performed became indispensable. Once the Kramer people learned they needed him, could use him, they told him all their secrets. They believed, because he never said otherwise, that they had pried loose all of his. His clients discovered what they'd always

130

known, that he possessed no secrets, that his head and heart were empty of any desire besides the willingness to scurry off on their errands, their dirty work. Once they'd figured out this accommodation, Reuben was afforded the opportunity to prosper, if prosper he could on pennies, nickels, and rare dimes people dropped in his shine box.

So in winter or inclement weather he did his thing indoors, in the marbled Kramer lobby, which was gone, gone, gone now. Outdoors was what he preferred. Quiet dawns, the parade of pedestrians featuring creatures more varied, more exotic, than the Highland Park Zoo. Melancholy would cloy him as the year wound down. He'd smell ashes in the October air. Down the block the scorched stones of the courthouse and jail would bleed when it rained. Snow was the color of bone. When winter finally settled in, he'd hide out in the Kramer lobby. Snow the color of bone. Then snow heaped along curbs would turn the gray, dingy color of courthouse stones or churn to slush or freeze again in dull, slick patches on streets and sidewalks. In the hissing, dry, radiator warmth of the Kramer lobby Reuben would ply his trade, shine and fetch and carry and chant, weeping inside for his lost Flora, knowing she'd never return, knowing he'd never stop waiting. Spring lifted his spirits: he would take up his accustomed spot outdoors. In the sunshine under the vast canopy of open air, quickened motion eddying around him, he'd sense again what was left of Flora, the mites of her released, scattered, breathing in these immensities.

He'd lost his Flora. Yet slowly he'd prospered in this iron-hard city, his fortunes rising in spite of his loss, in spite of his days of feeling sorry, sorry for himself, the urge to go Lawdy, Lawdy, Lawdy Miss Claudy. Go down to the Allegheny River and jump overboard and drown. In spite of these urges, he'd hung on, hung out, and let himself get better. His next move was to the tavern, shoeshine box far behind him then. A vested suit and tie every day God sends. A gold link chain girding his belly. The comfortable presence of that other lost one, his brother, next to his heart. Reuben's Flora had been snatched from him. She lived in the sky now.

Meet me, Jesus, meet me,
Meet me in the middle of the air,
And if my wings won't hold me,
Make me another pair.

He'd rescued the tiny statue and his twin had saved him. Passing, passing strange. That love could be so easy. Could pass through the needle's eye of pain and in a thousand years be born again, whole again, real again in a shape he'd never dreamed of finding it. This cold idol dangling from his watch. Flora inside it. His own hot, beating heart. One bright morning whole again.

Who was Reuben, what was he? What work did he do? Some old-timers remembered the hunchbacked little spook who used to shine shoes in the Kramer lobby. But that was years ago. Building's gone now. He must be dead by now. Or not worth a good goddamn, like me. This little guy reminds me of that shoeshine boy. They all look alike, though. This Reuben, or pack of Reubens, who's always in here, who everybody knows, who seems so busy, who does nothing, who hangs around from can to cain't, indispensable again, too crippled to move, a streak who makes a million lightning shuttles a day from courthouse to tavern and back again, messenger, factotum, busybody, moron, spy, gossip, hustler, old dog tray, cuckold, cocksman, nothing, everyman, flunky, fool, mountebank, wizard, storyteller, mute. Yeah, that's him all right. That's who he is. Everybody knows Reuben. You can trust him, talk to him, ignore him for years but he'll crop up smiling if you need him. Damned courthouse would crumble if it wasn't for Reuben. Little monkey. Knows everybody. Knows the law inside out. Knows nothing, sees nothing and tells less. That's him. Our boy.

Reuben's shingle is his presence, all day, every day, whenever he's needed. Reuben's practice is being Reuben, taking care of business being Reuben brings. He's explained it to himself on many occasions. His success. His prospering. Like Topsy—he just grew. Like the law. A matter of precedents. Nothing ordained, divinely sanctioned. Certain things were decided in a particular way for particular reasons and the fact that they were recorded in that configuration gives them a force, an authority. This record then governs the outcome of other matters; its authority is strengthened because it becomes a precedent for matters both similar and dissimilar to the original situation. Point is it's better to have something to go on. To establish a beginning so middles and ends will take care of themselves. Models, guidelines, standards of some sort, arbitrary, even capricious, are deemed better than starting all over again each time a decision must be rendered, a course taken. Reuben fashions a career for himself, propagates a role based upon the same loosely unfolding, backward-looking logic of the law. On sand he builds, with foundations no deeper than his fingernails are long.

Philadelphia had taught him the law. This city cuddled in the lap of three rivers had proved the law's tenacity. And Flora proved . . .

He was still waiting. Still wondering about the answer to that question as he crossed over to Grant Street, the lying, scrubbed stones.

Amen sayers. Witnesses. Where are they now? The crowd has dwindled so. Loneliness is standing and testifying and no echo, no one bearing witness. Where are they? The lost ones who shouted: Oh, yes. We were there. On the banks of Jordan, beside the pyramids, the rivers of Babylon, singing down the walls, crying up the City of Refuge. We were there too. Tell it. Tell the truth, brother.

When they tore down the Kramer, the law crowd moved to Stanley's. Lock, stock, and barrel. Of course, Reuben migrated with them. Some say he led the exodus. Little Moses with the multitude in tow. Who else better than Reuben would know the next best place after Kramer's Tavern for judges, lawyers, clerks, politicians, magistrates, bailiffs, tipstaffs, flunkies, cops, and bail bondsmen to congregate? Reuben certainly among the pilgrims that first day when as if by plan the law crowd began to turn up at Stanley's Bar and Grill. Perhaps it was just the nearest watering hole available after Kramer's Tavern closed. Perhaps the old crowd had discussed and debated and argued, called witnesses, filed briefs, affidavits, depositions, rendered a collective judgment. Fact of the matter is Stanley's became headquarters and Reuben among the first, if not the very first, to arrive, a fixture the moment he gimped through the door, an instant legend, the guy who always hung around Stanley's just like Stanley's was the place where the law people had always gathered, time out of mind.

Heaven presses down on us.

Reuben had said that to someone lately. Or someone said it to him. Why on earth? To whom would he say something like that? What did the words mean anyway? Damned if he knew. Damned if he could recall the person, the occasion. Reuben withdraws his neatly shod hoof from the first step of the courthouse. Heaven presses. More action in Stanley's than in the halls of justice this hour of the day. His spit-shined shoe returns to the sidewalk. It gleams impersonally. No face in its depths stares back at him. If the shoe fits . . . if it doesn't touch the floor when you scoot back into a chair . . . you are Reuben. You wear it. You hobble off toward Stanley's Bar and Grill.

Heaven presses down.

8

BIG MAMA

Nowhere to go. She'd started out too early. Not a soul in the streets yet, none of the Homewood doors open. If someone had been out in the street at dawn beside her, they might have seen the gray sky, a crazy-quilt patchwork silhouette of roofs, dull windows, empty stoops, damp, broken pavement reflected in Kwansa Parker's eyes as she slowly surveyed the dismal stillness that returned not a clue to the whereabouts of her son, Cudjoe. She did not ask herself, Why am I out here? She didn't wish for Toodles's warm bed. She was doing what she had to do. She would not be denied this morning. Even if the air tasted like metal, even if her head pounded as bad as she knew she looked, nothing would turn her around this morning. If the sun, wherever it was hiding in the soggy grayness of sky, if it stood still in its tracks a thousand years, she'd be waiting here when it started peeling the lid off Homewood.

I got time. Time's all I got. I can wait. She spoke the words aloud, to no one in particular, to anyone who knew what she was talking about. Like she'd told the world last night about Toodles. Spoke to nobody and anybody who wanted to hear because she was telling the truth. She was the one who knew. She was the one it was happening to. She was telling it like it is. Never mind you heard it before. Heard it different. She'd heard all about it too. But hearing was one thing. Being there another thing. And now she's been there and now she's telling it the way it really is and if you have ears it pay you to listen. You might learn something about Toodles's bed. About this empty corner and how long, how long I'm gon beat these hard streets till I find my son.

The first hour she walks past all the places he might be, the places she tried last night in the rainstorm, the places she visits again and again in her mind, on her way from one to the other, telling herself he might be there, what signs she should look for, convincing herself she'll be able to see through drawn shades, locked doors, dark rooms, through brick, wood, and plaster into the sealed fastness of whatever's keeping her son from her. She never stops calling his name. Listening, sniffing, searching the sidewalk for his tracks. The second hour she patrols every station again, asks the same silent questions, beats the same path up one street and down the next, pausing where there might be a sign, pacing back and forth because she might hear a voice, catch a glimmer of light under a blind's edge. The third hour she sits on a bench in Homewood Park, listening to her feet, which throb and whine at her, Give the other end a chance. Think a little bit about the best place to go and we'll carry you there, but sit down and think a little bit first.

But it hurt too much. Bad as her feet ached she couldn't sit still in Homewood Park. The grass is wet. Looks like a dark ring of blood round the edges of her flat shoes. Damp seeping through her clothes again. She'd be down with walking pneumonia before this was over. But she could not sit long on the bench because while she sat the streets were being scoured of every trace of Cudjoe, somebody was grabbing up all the bits of him, grabbing them and flinging them away. She must find him. Save him. It's too bittersweet in the park, watching his shadow bob across the green grass, listening to him pump the rusty swing by the track, holding her breath while he rolls like a log down the hollow's steep sides. He's here and not here, like the cries of kids playing, which echo from the hollow even when it's empty as her heart this morning.

The park was Cudjoe's favorite place. Bringing him here to play, it had become her favorite, too. Even though it was in the park Waddell lied to her. That Sunday in spring when he told her he loved her and would take care of her. In the park on the cement-and-wood benches by the basketball court was where junkies—Waddell grinning among them—took care of their business. In the park at night a man had ripped down the front of her dress before she got her knee up in his nuts and left him and his vomit by that big tree she'd thought was the most beautiful tree in the world, a tree that had always been standing in Homewood, always just about touching heaven, especially that day Waddell had lied to her, promising to love her. White buds beginning to open, leaves were that palish lighter green on one side the way they are till they get ripe in summer. Trees and grass and quiet paths you could walk. Benches to sit on, flat places for spreading your blanket, shady spots, clear spaces for catching the new heat of those first fine spring days, the deep scooped-out field at one end of the park with sides you could roll down or run down, wind in your ears, under your dress. Bells on Sunday morning when the park is deeper, stiller than church. She had memories as sad as these tall, rustling trees when the wind strips them, leaves falling like rain, and the chill gets in your bones, even though you're wearing a sweater and it's still an October afternoon, the sun bright, but wind catches you, rattles the big old trees, chases you away. Memories like that and stuff that made her mad. Boys laughing at her big belly. Junkies nodding, dead to the world and little kids got to pass by them on their way to the swings. The shit junkies leave behind. Cudjoe with one those plastic syringes in his hand. What's this, Mom? Her blood boiled. Her anger drowns out the sweet rumbling bongos and conga drums, the ceremony for calling forth the stars and dancing them you heard some summer nights from Homewood Park.

Cudjoe loved the park. So she learned it over again. Forgot. Remembered someone holding her small hand and listened for laughter echoing up from the hollow this morning. Which was empty now. Like her empty hand.

Cudjoe, she said to nobody.

Nobody answered. And the answer jerked her to her feet, set them pounding for a third time through the empty Homewood streets.

Now the emptiness broken by early birds, early worms. Some people up and out already at the bus stops, headed for work. Others moving because night's a rock they crawl under and every morning someone turns the rock over and they got to slip away, hide till the sun sets again. Every now and then the sun beats down and one of the night people stays where he been laying, in an alley, the filth, till some kid chasing a ball back there or delivering the morning paper takes a shortcut and stumbles over a lump of old army surplus coats and socks and Sunday funnies in color wrapped around his chest. Some die bundled that way. Curled up like flies on the windowsill the first cold night. Just last week two boys found a woman in the alley. Piece of sweater all she had on. Laid out naked to the world behind some garbage cans, her mouth open, her thighs open, alley dirt and alley filth and she's stretched out in it dead as a stick. A young woman, they said. Kwansa heard the story like everybody else and clucked her tongue and wondered about the children who found the dead girl, wondered why some mother had struggled to give the girl life, carried her, nursed her, squeezed her bleeding into the world and what would that mother think if she saw her daughter like those boys found her? A baby once. A little sweet baby once. Like us all. And here she is naked to the world, nothing but a ratty sweater strangled round her neck, that baby, my child. Who would have believed it comes to this? These streets and alleys,

138

these trifling chicken-coop houses close in on you like a rat in a trap.

They say it was pretty once. All in through here. Big trees like in Homewood Park. White people tripping over one another trying to buy these nice houses and wide streets. They say a fancy racetrack used to run here. That's why it's Race Street now. They say once upon a time was a different world here, even after white folks left it be and colored come in and took over. Nicest place in the whole city to live. Old people tell you that today. They could remember. Kwansa's heard them say those very words *nicest place,* but under this gray, swollen sky and dead bodies in the alleys and junkies blinking and looking for someplace to hide and people stealing other people's children, she finds it hard to believe, hard as it is to believe those same old folks sitting around now half dead, gumming lies, used to dance and sing and make love like bandits, hard as it is to believe she was young once, like Cudjoe galloping through Homewood Park, hard as it is to think she kept her son safe beside her, within reach of her touch, her voice, and that was just yesterday and look at her now, Cudjoe nowhere in sight, she could yell his name till her throat dropped out and he won't answer, even though she kissed him and left him at Miss Bracey's just a day ago. Now kisses don't count and all the days at her side don't matter one bit. She's no closer now than she was three hours ago, nothing she ever did, no night she sat up beside him watching the wings of his chest rise and fall, the room so full of Vicks VapoRub smell she was dizzy, no days in line at the clinic spending her hours to get Cudjoe's minute with the doctor, none the good times Cudjoe bouncing on her lap, laughing, tickled, playing horse and higgledy-pig rider, the Waddell in him lit up, high, shining in those sleepy bedroom eyes, none the bad times doing what she had to do to put meat on the table, keep a roof over their heads, all that matters not one bit, brings Cudjoe not one inch closer now that she's let him get away.

Kwansa can hear the sky. A heavy, gray voice telling her the ugly about herself she does not want to hear. When she looks up it stops, like Cudjoe into something he knows he shouldn't be into, and she stares at him and he sees her and stops on a dime but she knows as soon as she turns away he'll start up again. A gray sky still soggy from last night's rain. Nothing has dried out good yet. Sidewalks, benches, the grass had soaked up rain from last night. She'd seen some of it early, steam rising, a faint mist bleeding back into the sky. Most of the rain had seeped down, making rivers beneath her feet, and they spoke now, taking their turn, reminding her she'd messed up every time. And here it is another time, this child you say you love, and you're messing up again, losing again.

The hardest thing of all to believe was the dream she'd carried of a better Kwansa, the Kwansa she'd find one day and throw her arms around and they'd cry and laugh like long-lost sisters, like fools in the middle of Homewood Avenue don't care who's watching, don't care what anybody got to say. Look at you, girl. You look so good. You're the one, you're a sight for sore eyes. Thought I'd never see you again. My, my. Let me look at you. How you been, child? Where you been hiding? Don't you dare get lost again.

Hard as it was to believe, she could still feel it sometimes. Look down in a puddle and the shadow moving in there is her. Her other, better self alive in a place like that, a slick, green-black puddle on these nasty streets and *suffers no corruption there*. Kwansa on her way somewhere, probably into something she knows ain't right and she just about trips over the shadow, drowns in the puddle where there's a face like hers, but better than hers, sleeping in the hole under the street all the way to China. Kwansa too busy. Never takes time to stop. Her sister gliding like the chip cross the Ouija board. Don't have to touch it. Circle of old ladies move it with their minds. One day she'll bust right out the ground. Steamy, shining like the shine in Cudjoe's eyes. Two sisters meeting again, after all the years, all the distance, meeting and weeping like fools in each other's arms. Kwansa can still feel how good it would be. Her body warming to the other's touch. She just doesn't believe it will happen. She'd lost the chance as she flitted from one wrong

140

thing to another. Busy, ugly. Taking what she could get. Losing everything.

First she hears him whistling, then the broom scratching at the sidewalk. Clement's real job, if he had one, was down the street, around the corner at the Velvet Slipper. No one knew why he swept the corner of Homewood and Bruston, the wide apron of pavement on two sides of the Homewood AME Zion Church. Never in church on Sunday but Clement kept the ground spotless as anything could be in Homewood, sweeping it four or five times a day some days so it was cleaner outside the church, one smart-mouth said, than inside. So clean another somebody asked Clement, What you trying to do, boy? Sweep all the black out the pavement? Nobody knew. Everybody counted on it. Clement regular as rain, whipping his broom back and forth till the sidewalk, in the minds of everybody who'd watched Clement work, shone like a pearl. Lots of people would cross the street rather than mark Clement's floor. Not that Clement would ever know. Soon's as he's finished, he's gone. Swallowed up again by the Velvet Slipper, doing whatever he does all day inside the bar when he's not running errands or sweeping the church sidewalks.

Maybe if he got it clean enough, bright enough, you could see the church's reflection in it. Maybe Clement understood that upside-down world, the mountain she saw under her feet stretching down, down, as far as the mountain towering over her she must climb every day. Perhaps Clement shares her secret. The day it got too hard to lift her foot, too hard to start the struggle that never raised her an inch higher than she'd been the day before, on that day when up or down didn't matter no more, she'd shut her eyes and let herself slip down, sink into the murky, easy darkness at her feet. Two churches on the corner of Homewood and Bennett. Twins. The big brick one with stained-glass windows and a bell steeple abandoned by white people when they fled Homewood and the other one Clement was scratching away at the stones to find. The red brick one people passing by the corner saw, the other one floating up to greet them when she and Clement let everybody know their secret.

Clement's hair was turning white. Frizzy popcorned white as an old man's. Clement couldn't be no more than twenty-five, thirty. Probably a whole lot younger. Nobody claimed him, so nobody could say. Couldn't say his ownself. He was feeble-minded. Living in the street, off the street, long as anybody remembered. The barber, Mr. What's-his-name, who died of cancer and had one the nicest funerals Homewood ever seen, blocks and blocks of cars, a sunny day, people dressed so neat and sad, the big yellow man cancer took so quick, he let Clement stay behind his shop. Clement swept out the barbershop, the Velvet Slipper, anywhere they'd let him, to keep a little change in his pockets. He might sleep in the bar now, or the alley, or the church basement for all Kwansa knew. Always used to be somewhere to hang your hat, hang your head, in Homewood. Some porch to crawl under, a garage to keep the rain off. In winter they'd take you in for the night at the Salvation Army. Better than carting away the dead ones in the morning like they did now. Every winter fires burn down these shacks old people and mothers with a string of babies trying to keep warm. Every summer old folks disappear, nobody see them for a week till they start to stink boarded up in these shacks no self-respecting roach call home. Wasn't even news no more finding bodies. Elephants spozed to have some secret place they all slink off to to die. This must be the graveyard where niggers spozed to come.

Clement ought to keep going. Sweep on down Homewood Avenue. Sweep it all away. Clean it up, Clement. Sweep, boy. Whiter than snow. Downtown to the river. Sweep it all away so I can find my Cudjoe. So he can walk these streets and stay clean as God spit him out.

If she laid naked in the street and Clement whipped the broom back and forth across her bare back, could he change her? Could he strip the skin away? Get down to the clean parts? Were there any clean parts? Was there a better Kwansa buried under her dirty skin? Could Clement peel her skin with the needles of his broom. Would it hurt enough, would she scream loud enough to be heard wherever Cudjoe's been taken?

When she'd neared the AME Zion Church earlier this morning, she had crossed the street, like lots of people do, so's not to spoil Clement's clean floor. She crossed again, over to the side of Homewood Avenue where two movies used to sit, just two storefronts away from each other. One cost a quarter on Saturday morning, the other fifteen cents. Many times as she'd gone, many times as she'd cried because she couldn't scrape together a quarter for the better picture, the nicer kids who went where it cost more, she couldn't recall now which movie house was which. One show, the Belmar, one the Highland. One a quarter, the other fifteen cents. She crossed over to the empty sidewalk where everybody used to stand in line, where she'd read and reread what she could of the big posters and the little bright scenes when the movie was in Technicolor. Like she was making up her mind. Like she could fool people into believing she was choosing one movie or the other. Pretending she had a quarter. As if somebody was watching. As if anybody cared whether the little ashy-legged black girl with bad hair went in one show or the other. As if either show could change the ugly. Kwansa can hear kids yelling at each other, at the screen. The cheap show was the noisy one. Couldn't listen to the movie half the time. Big kids throwing stuff. Her ear sore for a week something hard, a stone, a piece of old candy, ripped into the side of her head while Woody Woodpecker squawking his fool noise. The walls gone. The noisy darkness the walls once enclosed still ringing in her ears and she wonders if she'd kept to the other side of Homewood Avenue, would she have seen her face, the doubled gleam of church in Clement's polished stones?

You gon wear it out, Clement.

You gon wear it out, girl. Shaking your booty like that.

In her grandma's house no music except the gospels on the radio. Kwansa didn't know how to dance when she met Waddell. This easy, he said. Slow drag. Anybody can slow drag. Singing "Bad Girl," like Smokey in her ear. You don't need to know nothing, sweet thing, just hold tight to me. Wrap your arms round me and hold on. I'll be the music. You just listen and hold on we be slow dragging. Yeah. Best kind of dancing. You'll learn real quick.

143

If her grandma was right you'd burn in hell. On fire forever. Dancing, drinking, taking the Lord's name in vain. A straight, hot path to hell, and the flames eat you forever. Screaming and crying and begging for another chance. Fire climbing all down in your throat. Oh, please. Please. I won't do it no more. But it's too late. You should of thought of acting right when you had the chance to act right. Too late now. You was happy as a clam, wasn't you? Crossing your feet and uncrossing your legs fast as you could. Shaking your booty. I know just what you were doing. Don't you think I didn't, miss. Out all night in the street. Drinking and smoking like a man. Going with any sinner would have you. Waddell. Waddell. My Big Mama cursed me. Turned me out her house. I had to tell her the truth. Truth be showing soon. Prayed to God she'd understand. I ain't no tramp. Ain't none the things she called me. You the first and only, you know that. And we getting married. I told her all that, told her you looking for a job, but she just sat with her eyes closed, shaking her fist. Calling down the curse of God on my head. What am I gon do, Waddell?

They were in the park. One of those first bright spring days when you believe the weather might be turning. By the end of summer a watermelon under her dress, next spring a baby in her arms, like those other girls, the moms used to be in her class at school, already carting two or three little ones round the paths, up and down Homewood Avenue shopping. Tiny kids looking after kids even tinier while Mama holds the newest one over her shoulder, dark eyes poking out its cute sunbonnet. Mama wearing kids like a blanket, can't see her for babies wiggling, babies climbing, babies rocking in her arms. No Daddy in sight. Daddy playing ball or nodding on those benches over by the court or in the street hustling up a pocket of change so he can jingle it five minutes before he throws it away like he's God. The men weren't all that way. She had watched how the good ones fall. One or two young men out with the early birds this morning. Whistle-clean and neat. Strong as stallions. Sharp whatever they be wearing. If it ain't nothing but a T-shirt and chinos. Just kids they ownselves but they got kids so they's up at the crack of dawn to meet the man. You see in they eyes they stone serious. Gon do this thing right. Standing tall and straight like soldiers beside old mamas with shopping bags, old men in suits ride the bus downtown and change to coveralls cause they the janitor in one those big buildings down there, got lunch and a change of clothes in a briefcase. The young boys serious about work. Some walk miles to save bus fare. Kwansa's seen plenty good ones start out. Stone serious. Walk an hour each way to work and home cause they got to find a way to feed them crumb crushers, them little ones come out every spring in Homewood like buds on the trees. Kwansa's seen the young men rise in the morning, shaved, hair combed, a pressed company shirt, rise with that serious look and go down the hill like clockwork when she was living with her Big Mama on Tokay and people walked past to catch the downtown bus at the bottom of the hill on Bennett. When she was up two hours before school to cook and clean so it's spotless when she leaves, she'd study the few young ones out there humping down the cobbled hillside. For months rain or shine you could set your clock by them passing Big Mama's window on their way to meet the man. Then they'd fall. Start missing days. Falter and fall. Their eyes went first. Fall in their eyes before the rest starts to go. They be looking round. Why they out on the goddamned corner waiting for a bus while everybody else sleeping? Why they got to be the one scuffling every morning like they going somewhere when ain't nowhere to go? Ain't nobody going nowhere so why they got to pull this long-ass day? Same old shit whether you do or don't. Babies, bills, can't make no headway. Shit flung in they face every step. Forget it, man. Not me, man. No way.

Waddell too hip to try. She knew he'd never be out there at dawn, cleaned and pressed, rained on, snowed on, with a bunch of Aunt Jemimas and Uncle Toms. That would never be his way. She didn't expect that. What did she expect? What was she asking for all those times he said no?

Okay. Okay. Cool now. You don need to be doing all this

crying and carrying on, girl. Waddell's here. Lissen up, now. This Waddell talking. You my girl. Ain't gon let nothin happen to my sweet thing.

Kwansa tries to recall the exact words. Not what she heard, but what Waddell had said. She'd heard squirrels chitter-chattering, kids romping, the noise from the basketball court that kind of slid down off the edge of the park, down to the deep, graveled bed of the railroad tracks where iron rails hummed the sound so it was thicker, quieter when it floated back over the bench Waddell made her sit on.

Look here, woman. You my woman, ain't you, woman? Looky here. Wipe them tears out your pretty eyes. Waddell ain't no chump. Ain't one those dime-a-dozen creeps you see hanging in the poolroom. It's hard out in this world, sugar. But Waddell gon squeeze the rock, babe. Squeeze it till it bleeds. I'ma have something. I'ma get me the things I want. All of it. Like them slick white boys grinning on TV. Waddell gon take care business. Take care his woman.

She knew he was lying. Knew he was just talk. He'd run away first chance he got. Too pretty to work, too pretty to stay with ugly Kwansa, getting fatter every day, a watermelon under her dress, her nose runny and eyes red out here in broad daylight in Homewood Park. Everybody sees, everybody knows what's happening. She got caught. Got Waddell's baby in her. He's telling the lies they all tell. They all believe.

You and me, babe.

Are those the words he said? If the giant trees could listen, could tell the stories they heard, would they say it in those words? *You and me, babe.* Or had she heard through her snotty snuffles and sobs, through his arms smothering her, drawing her back from the edge, had she heard what she wanted to hear, the lies she needed to tell herself, needed to believe, whether he promised or not?

Bring me the belt. Bring it here and bring your miserable behind so I can tear it up.

Big Mama, I didn't do nothing.

Don't sass me. I said bring it here.

146

When I say bring me the belt you bring it and don't you sass me.

Between words the strokes laid on Kwansa's bare backside. Bloomers down round her ankles. The wheezes, the old woman gasping to catch her breath, almost dying between blows, worse than the stinging blows themselves. Like an animal behind her back. A terrible animal breathing its terrible breath on her naked skin. It huffed and puffed like a train, it was dying and coming to life each time it wheezed and grunted and found the strength to strike Kwansa again.

Kwansa had no eyes in the back of her head so she couldn't see what was behind her. She couldn't believe it was her Big Mama hurting her like that. Making those terrible noises. Her Big Mama all she had. Big Mama fed her. When she was a little girl and no one else would have her, Big Mama took her in, washed her and combed her nappy hair and dressed her for school and walked her hand in hand to the sanctified church on Tioga.

Too old for this. Past this raising chilren mess. Big Mama would fuss and wag her netted head and be mean sometime. But not all the time. And the belt sometime when Kwansa too little, too dumb to know better and she'd run till Big Mama, who wasn't big, who could barely hold down a squirmy little girl, would finally catch her, half sit on her, scuffling to pin down the squirmy thing and swing the belt so it meant business. Two or three good licks in those days enough. Kwansa bawling. Big Mama breathing hard, wore out, belt limp in her hand, her face broke up bad as Kwansa's. Like Big Mama done wrong and she's sitting on the side the bed, her old monkey face scrunched up like its gon be her turn next to get a beating.

Too old for this. Too old to be starting with chilren again.

Now she's sick and old and short-breathed worse and Kwansa knows better than to run. She brings the patent-leather belt, drops her slacks and drawers round her ankles, tightens the muscles of her buttocks, wondering why she stands and takes it, wondering what wild beast is biting into the tender meat of her grown woman's thighs.

Shaming me. She's shaming me. Like a child bare-assed with her underpants around her ankles. It's also love, Kwansa tells herself. A little tiny, tiny bit of love, all the love left in Big Mama. The tiniest scrap of love in those blows making them weigh as heavy as they do, making her stand still for them. And the sad thing, the worst thing standing butt-naked while somebody she can't see whips her ass, is that if she doesn't find love here, if there's no tiny burden of love, no drop of love anywhere in the pain, she knows nowhere else to look. Let the old, dying witch tear me up. Let her choke on beating me. It's as close to love a ugly, evil child ever needs to get.

Funny how when Waddell finally stuck his hands in her panties and slides them down her thighs, he was in such a hurry he never pulled them off and her too petrified to kick them off so when he sticks his self in her the first time, her panties are still stretched between her ankles. Her knees wide open as they could spread and Waddell's bony hips between them but her ankles chained, the sweet pain of him sawing away at her pussy but her ankles locked together so Big Mama is there like Kwansa knew she'd be, cursing her to God, laying on blows.

I'll take care you, baby.

The trees heard it all before. They'll hear it again, another spring. She knew Waddell was lying. The way he'd promised was not the way he'd be. His words said one thing and her mind knew that's not the way it's gon be. Her mind had studied the words, stored them. For the season when she'd have only words and Waddell long gone. Waddell spoke the words. Her heart needed them. Her mind saved them so she could repeat the words to herself today. Little dried-up, weightless things, like you crack a peanut shell and nothing inside but dust.

She'd never believed the words. But she stopped crying, nestled into his shoulder. Felt the heat of him all up and down her body, everywhere they touched sitting on the bench, the gritty stone still chilly from rain, from night, from winter. There's love in it somewhere. The heat. Lies. Big Mama's fist pounding the arm of her rocker. Kwansa believed it was there. If she stood long enough, bit her lips hard enough and suffered the blows, she'd find it. No place else to turn, to look.

Waddell's way might work. Maybe he could do it his way and make both of them happy. Waddell full of shit. Still, maybe he knew something the others didn't. A way to sit on his ass and fill his veins with dope and keep her happy and Cudjoe happy and everybody safe forever afterafter.

That was spring and Cudjoe not born yet. Not a boy or a girl. No name yet that brought her smile just saying it. The smile she couldn't help letting slip out even when he did something bad and she needed to be mad at him and smack him and she'd yell, Cudjoe, get over here, boy, and raise her hand but he'd peep the smile in her anger and that would be that. Before he was Cudjoe, she called him Mr. Baby, the character in her belly with his funny ways, his all-night moves, a mind of his own that didn't care if she was sleeping or busy at the stove or exhausted trying to catch a moment's peace. When he wanted her, he'd snatch her away, swimming with his toes tickling her backbone, his shoulder ramming her bladder so she thinks she has to pee, but it's just him saying, Hello. How are you at four A.M.? *Mr. Baby* cause he was a boy. No doubt about it. The busy weight of him. His poking round. His contrariness. Mr. Baby. Her little man in her belly. One she could love even if Waddell never came home. One who would love her. One she'd never lose.

If she had kept him in her belly, safe inside, happy inside, she wouldn't be out here this morning, calling his name in the street. She should have stayed on the church side of Homewood Avenue. Busted through the church's red front door, crawled on her knees down the purple carpet, kneeled and prayed at the mourners' bench. Begged forgiveness, prayed for her son back. Would anyone answer if she called. Homewood AME Zion used to belong to a white congregation. When they'd packed up and sold the niggers this church maybe they left the ghost of their white Jesus behind. Maybe he still lurked in the aisles, pews, behind the pulpit. Big Mama's church was little and yellow, a storefront. On Sunday you could hear it all up and down Tioga.

Rocking, shaking like Big Mama beat her fist when Kwansa had tried to explain. Folding chairs so close people leaning on each other and your knees stuffed up in somebody's back and somebody's knees stuffing you. Tambourines. Stomping feet. That's all they needed to make music. Praise God's name to high Heaven. Each voice trying to climb the golden stairs before the others. Sing His praises. Shout His name. You rock when the chains get to whipping back and forth across the room. You roll one way and roll back the other cause that's how the chain is pulling and the saint next to you be in your lap if you don't. Church rocking and reeling. Ship of Zion in a troubled sea, the preacher hollered above the singing. Yes, Lawd. I'm troubled this morning. My Sweet Lord. My Jesus Savior. Where's His Precious Love, His Almighty Voice this morning? I need to hear it. Father. Father, calm these waves rocking my soul. Take me home this morning on your sweet Zion Ship. Zi . . . on. Two words. A long space between like Big Mama behind her, slowing words down so she can breathe, so she can hit.

Some sister would start it. Hum a phrase. Another take up the burden. Humming little bits at a time. Like the sound will scorch their lips if they're not careful. Like tasting hot broth. Like it hurts to squeeze it out. Here it comes anyway. You know humming will turn to song. This is how they find the song they need. No words. No hymnbook. Like a train a long, long way down the track. You hear it before you know what it is. Then you know what it is as you listen to it thunder closer and closer. Know it's gon tear you up when it gets here. On time. Right on time. Rattling the whole wide world the way it always does. A bullet coming for your soul. A dot. A speck of sound. One sister closes her eyes and hums that sweet light she finds in the dark. Ready to fly on home. Eyes closed, lips tasting that stinging light. She moans and another sister moans back because she knows, on this gray morning, in this room full of wandering souls, in this dark sea of familiar faces, of strangers, in this boat rocking on Jordan water, this Zi . . . on ship like a wafer in the river's lips, there is no song louder than the troubles in your heart so you hum till the hum is echoed by another and another

150

and rather than die, rather than split apart on these squealing folding chairs advertising funeral parlors, you let the other voices take you, ease your burden, let them carry your cry because you are lifting theirs in the chorus of some old anthem everybody knows.

The first time Kwansa saw the inside of Homewood AME Zion she believed there might be room in Heaven for every saint. Pressed together in the narrow storefront room of Big Mama's church, the saints seemed to be squabbling and fussing and fighting each other, like Heaven wasn't no bigger than this hot box they worshiped in, like couldn't but one or two squeeze through the needle's eye when their singing, shouting, and chairs romping back and forth finally tore the old building down. Roaches in Big Mama's stove. You clean it by lighting the oven in the morning. You wait with a bedroom slipper and out they come flying, climbing over each other's backs. That fire wakes em up good all right and you get good at smashing every one think they going someplace. Nastiness but you do it enough mornings you don't see the squishy white mess, don't hear the hard shells crack. Kwansa wants to smash them all, every single scurrying panicked black bug. Every one that ever lived, all the ones not born yet waiting their turn to crawl in Big Mama's stove soon's the kitchen light's out.

Homewood AME Zion was bigger, higher, the seats in curving rows fastened to the floor. If it was God's house on earth and people weren't packed in like roaches, surely His heavenly mansion had a dome like this only more distance and clean, and walls whitewashed, and polished benches in arcs like a rainbow even longer than those she saw first time she entered Homewood AME Zion.

Little church, big church. Did God love one better than the other? Did He love either one? Did He pack up with the white folks and leave town when they left? Was His eye truly on each sparrow? Did He watch her swat roaches every morning in Big Mama's kitchen? Did He know where Waddell had taken Cudjoe? Did it matter if Heaven was big or small? Why was it a Kingdom? Why did you have to die to get in?

Why? Why? *Why* was Cudjoe's favorite word. When he ran out of questions—she's in the bathtub, soapy, dreamy, and Cudjoe dips his hand in the bubbles, wipes suds from her breasts: Why you got big muscles here, Mama? Why you got hair down there? Why I ain't got none—when he was finished with a string of questions and she's still working on the answer to the first one, he'll look her full in the eye and ask one more. *Why?* Just *why?* Like all the questions he's been pestering her with not really questions. Only one question. And nobody could answer it. *Why?* And he ain't growed past her waist yet but his big eyes knew how to ask it.

Why is he Cudjoe? Why is he gone?

If she'd turn down Hamilton she could ask Reuben. His trailer pinned there, like a rusty old nail somebody pounded in the ground. She wondered if he slept in the trailer. The inside smelled like sleep. Like funky socks and a room people pee in and never open the window. Stale, dry, old-people smell. She'd never heard of him living nowhere else. Did Reuben work in the trailer and eat and sleep in there too? One morning he'd be dead in there. Wagon come and haul him away.

Reuben might be sleeping now. He might be dead. He promised they wouldn't take Cudjoe, but her son's gone. Her strength seeping away this morning. Like if she retraced her steps back through the Homewood streets there'd be a trail, plain as blood, on the sidewalk. Not even Clement could scrub it away. Anybody walk those same streets behind her would know she been there, they could see the trail, smell it, taste it. What leaks when your son's stolen, what drains out you and marks the pavement plain as kids scratching hopscotch with stones.

Kwansa didn't want to wake Reuben. She didn't want to yell at him: You lied, old man. You was wrong, wrong, wrong old rat face, slick-mouthed man. My son is gone. They took him away. She didn't turn down Hamilton Avenue because he might be sleeping and because it wasn't the law stole Cudjoe, it was Waddell had him. Waddell thinking he his own law. Do whatever he want to do and nobody better not get in his way. Those yellow sisters of his. They the ones put him up to this. They

152

think they better than everybody. They sit high and pass judgment. Like they the law. Waddell ain't the one wants Cudjoe. What it is, his sisters don't want me to have him. That's all's to it. Don't want me to have nothing they think belongs to them. Even if they don't really want it. Even if I ain't got nothing but this child they don't love, they gon try to take him from me. Why?

Her fist is balled up. Like Big Mama when Kwansa told her, I'ma have his baby. I'ma marry him.

She could bram on the trailer door. Wake up. Wake up in there. Maybe he could help. Maybe he knew. Beat on it like a drum. Wake up all Homewood. Cave in the tinny walls. Come out, Mr. Reuben. Bring your pointy head on out here. You said they wouldn't take my Cudjoe and now he's gone. I been out here since dawn combing these streets and he's nowhere, he's gone.

But Waddell is not the law. Waddell's nothing. He's lower than her. She knows that. Knew in her heart he was lying. Truth wasn't in him. He always lied. To get her pussy. To get his dope. Don't care who he hurt. Waddell gon get over. Lie. Steal. Grab Cudjoe away from Miss Bracey's the minute Kwansa turn her back. He's evil. That's why. Why he hurt her. Why he tried to kill hisself. Why he thinks he's better than other people now. Why he got two evil bitches for sisters telling him steal her son. If she had a gun she'd shoot him. Find the nigger and blow out his brains.

Big Mama looking down from Heaven saying, I told you so. I told you so. Big Mama didn't live to see Cudjoe. She said, You killed me. Killed me dead. Too old for these things you putting on me. Plum past the time for suffering this kind of mess all over again. She said, Gwan away from here. Out my face, out my house. You been gone since you been his whore. Leave my house this minute. Get your rags and don't set foot through my door again. This a Christian house and I'm a Christian woman. Didn't raise no whores. Ain't keeping one under my roof. Let the one shamed you, feed you. And feed your bastard.

Too old for this. Past the time. My daughter's daughter so I

153

took you in. Knew better but I took you in. Raised you up. To fear God and follow His ways. Raised up a whore to shame me, run me to my grave. You killed me. I'm dead. Don't want to see your brazen face again in this world or the next.

Kwansa won't see her in Heaven. Heaven's not where she's going but she can feel Big Mama's eyes peeping down on her. I told you so. I . . . told . . . you . . . so. . . .

People on the street now. Walking round like it's just another day. Stores opening. Sons of Love setting up their long tables outside the plate-glass window used to be Footer's Same Day Dry Cleaning. Long tables with trays on top. They sell the jewelry they make. Sell clothes with designer labels some say is just trash with good labels sewn in, some say you getting a sure enough bargain if you don't mind the heat. Sons of Love fronting for a gang of boosters, junkies ride the busway downtown every morning like they going to work, pick a store clean in five minutes. Get it while it's hot up on Homewood Avenue. Always a crowd. Sifting through stuff on the tables, the racks of clothes lined up on the sidewalk. Sons of Love in their white robes. Women in long dresses, hair wrapped in turbans. Some wear gold rings in their noseholes. Sky don't bother them. Gray as it is they setting up for the day. People say they fuck one another like alley cats. Men can have any the women he wants. They setting up like it's just another day for them. Just another day for everybody else. Don't care who died last night, whose child gone.

Kwansa heard from one the saints, Miss Lawson, who wears her white nurse's uniform inside the church and out. Heard the news right here on Homewood Avenue. Miss Taylor passed last night, dearheart.

Miss Lawson calls everybody dearheart. Another one of Miss Lawson's strange ways. Dearheart. That white uniform she always wears, her little tippytoe walk like she's afraid she might step on something precious if she's not real careful. Like she's sneaking up on something instead of going ahead and getting where she's going like everybody else. Scare you sometimes. She could creep up on you. Be there walking alongside

154

your elbow and that whispery voice of hers, like somebody blowing out birthday candles, make you jump out your shoes. *Miss Taylor passed last night, dearheart.*

Kwansa hadn't heard her coming. So she jumped a little. But she been knowing Miss Lawson all her life and dealing with Miss Lawson's funny ways so they don't even seem that peculiar no more. So she don't leap quite out of her skin, just snapped to attention real quick, recognizing the breathy whisper, the *dearheart,* knowing just where to half turn and find the tiny lady under her white net cap. What Kwansa didn't know till after she repeated the name Miss Taylor to herself, two or three times that morning six years ago on Homewood Avenue, was who Miss Taylor was.

Before Kwansa understood it was her Big Mama dead, dead as the baby was alive and kicking in her belly, she said, Thank you, Miss Lawson. *Thank you,* because that's what you always said to Miss Lawson. Because Miss Lawson's job was sneaking around Homewood delivering *bless yous* straight from Jesus. Hand-delivered blessings, and if you were somebody she remembered as a child from the Tioga Street Sanctified Church of the Precious Redeemer's Blood, she'd say, My, my, you've certainly grown up beautiful. *Thank you* the polite thing to reply to Miss Lawson. Don't ask, How are you, Miss Lawson, or try to start a conversation. You wasting your breath. She's through with you soon's she deliver her message. She's long gone. Got another message to deal.

Kwansa had said, *Thank you,* and Miss Lawson tiptoed off like there was somebody asleep under the sidewalk she didn't want to wake. Thank you.

Miss Taylor passed . . . Miss Taylor . . .

Then Kwansa figured it out. Why her knees shook, her mouth hung open. Big Mama was Big Mama and Kwansa had forgotten her Big Mama's other names, the Miss Taylor her grandmother would be called by other people. Had anybody overheard Kwansa say, Thank you? Would they understand her half smile, that little smile of gratefulness you couldn't help smiling even if you'd heard Miss Lawson say her little piece a thousand times before. She meant well, Miss Lawson did. Blessing people. Pretending people beautiful. Sure didn't hurt to hear that. And maybe you were pretty in her old, fuddled eyes. A baby still, a beautiful child. Maybe she could bless, maybe she could make you better than you were. So Kwansa had a grateful kind of smile for Miss Lawson. She hoped nobody had seen the simpleminded grin, heard her say *Thank you* that day the simpering, mince-footed little ghost delivered the news of Big Mama's passing.

Passed. Big Mama had passed. Passed was what you did with gas. Passed was something you did when you were white enough to pass for a white person. Passing was a way of having another life, a better life than if you stayed black, stayed a poor black nigger. Passing was also no life at all. The end. Past it all. Past the time in life for this kind of mess. You killed me. Killed me dead.

People passed you on the street. One said your grandmother's dead. You grinned and said thank you. It was just another morning in Homewood. Just another day warming up, being what it's going to be, with you or without you. One monkey don't stop no show. Your grandmother dead. Nobody skips a beat. Miss Lawson off to bless somebody else. Turn another sorry soul beautiful one half a second. Nobody listens. Nobody skips a beat. Doors open along the Avenue. Iron gates rattle back. The first white face peeks out a barred window. Somebody jingles keys. The same crack opens up under your feet that opens each time you pass the bank. Your last blood relative you know about is gone. Passed. The string stops with you unless you find your son.

No thunder, no wails from the women, none of the men bowing their heads in shame. Business as usual.

Why?

Cudjoe could ask you why about the damnedest things. Why you eating that? Why it blue? The sky sitting up there minding its own business blue like it's always been when it ain't something else and here come Cudjoe want to know why it's blue. Sometime she'd be mad with herself because she should know

156

more answers and doesn't. Mostly she got tired because before she could open her mouth to answer one question, Cudjoe puckering up, raising his pie eyes to hers, ready with another *why*. She'd kiss him sometimes. Her best answer. Mama don't know, baby. Been that way always, baby. She almost said once, God made it that way, but she'd stopped herself. She wasn't sure why she stopped. Had Big Mama shamed her so bad that she believed the old woman's curse, God's name a sin in your mouth. His name a sin in your filthy mouth. Kwansa didn't blame her grandmother for trying to cut her off from God's grace. Kwansa had no right. She feared standing before Him, His fiery eyes boring clean through her, all her secrets crashing down like the walls of a evil city, like the walls of the steeple you make with your fingers tumbling down and out scramble the people naked and afraid. What she hated, what she couldn't forgive, was her Big Mama's curses falling on the head of the innocent child in her belly. If Big Mama could talk to God, if He listened and damned Kwansa, did the curse also reach inside her skin, hurt the new life she carried? If it worked that way, if God could sit up on high in the sky on His golden throne and hurt little babies ain't seen the light of day yet, she sure wasn't going to thank Him. And she wasn't going to tell her son God made the world to work that way neither. Cudjoe find out soon enough. With all his whys. Wasn't no good reason to hurt her son. Big Mama ought to known better. God ought to know better.

But maybe He didn't. God so far away babies and roaches look all the same. Somebody on their knees with a slipper in hand ready to smash Cudjoe soon's he show his face. So Kwansa didn't answer his *whys* with God. Cause if He made the trees and the blue and everything else, He made the slipper and wrapped the hand round it and that wasn't no fit answer to nothing.

Passed.

One day, old and sick as Big Mama, one day by and by like they sang in the songs, she might look back, understand the good in it all. Losing Cudjoe, finding him, finding herself, losing him again, and maybe that's how it was, how it's spozed to be. Maybe by and by was sweet as honey and she'd understand and say well done. But not this morning. Not on Homewood Avenue today.

Life in the street went on about its business. Cudjoe was lost, but she'd find him. Or die trying. Finders keepers, losers weepers. No weeping this morning. No time for tears. There had to be a balancing, an opening. Things got worse then better. The rain that had fallen last night was the mist she'd watched this morning, curling like breath from grass in the park. The gray blanket overhead was wearing thin in places. Other colors underneath. Maybe a blue sky by afternoon.

Why didn't Cudjoe answer when she called his name again and again? Her mouth full of rain. Choking. Rain pitting her eyes. Cudjoe had never seen Big Mama. She hadn't lived to see him. Would he recognize his great-grandmother if she walked back down the golden stairs in her angel robes and took his hand. If she could curse him, toss his tender body to the demons in hell, could she also be the one to save him. Chant a prayer for him to Jesus. In Jesus' name. Lead him home. Have mercy.

Her mountain like a tree planted in the water. Two trees joined at their black roots. When the water's perfectly still she can see them both, two trees, the way up and the way down, a dark opening in the stillness through which Cudjoe must pass if she's going to lose him, if he's going to return.

9

BIMBO

Shore Road, separated from the water by about two miles of woods, ran parallel to the line of the sea. Wally found Shore Road on one of his visits to Bimbo, lost, too much vodka or grass or both, circling back the way he'd come, his head no longer spinning, lost because he'd needed air, needed to escape Bimbo's pleasure palace, the dope and incense, the stereo pumping Bims's sugary voice to every corner of the sunken living room, the giggling women who waited on Bimbo hand and foot, hovering around the cologned ruin of his body, rubbing, touching, snorting a line of coke tapped from the silver spoon dangling from Bimbo's neck, all winking eyes and coos, flashing bare skin, nipple, and curly hairs Wally couldn't tell if he was supposed to notice or not, if the bitches were Bims's private stock or if it was kosher for old pal Wally to jump right in, grab a handful, invite one out to the pool, down into the cavern of Jacuzzis, steam, and saunas. Bimbo dead below the waist and the three women hovering, batting their long eyelashes, scratching him with Fu Manchu nails, licking their Technicolor lips like they intended to make a righteous feast out of what was left of his body. Bims had been Wally's main man, long before fame and wealth, years before the accident chopped him in half. Bimbo didn't need to parade his bitches to impress Wally. Wally hadn't arrived in LA to hang out. He was tired. Dog tired from chasing hard-leg basketball players. Bimbo was his man. Always would be. He dug Bims. Wanted to stay in touch. The slinky women with their shit stuffed in see-through leather and metallic silk, the humping funk of Bimbo's Greatest Hits, the trays of whatever to eat or smoke or pop or snort or shoot, Wally might dream of this kind of setup those nights when he was caught in the middle of nowhere in a motel room, his business done, his joint hard, and a long night in an empty bed all that was shaking, but when he traveled to the West Coast and stopped off to check out Bimbo, this circus was a bum trip. More power to you, Bims, you still the man, Bimbo. You got it all, my man. Wally could keep saying it as long as Bimbo needed to hear it. But the shit got old. Got heavy on Wally's tongue. Weighed on him like the food and booze, the winding snakes of incense and bitches as dead in the head as Bimbo from the waist down.

That's why Wally'd driven off by himself to get some air. Bimbo's private dirt road up from his villa by the sea to another country back road paved but narrow and winding, following twists and turnings, intersections linking one thread of road to the next, high beams on the whole time, dancing up and down dark walls of trees, ending on Shore Road and cranking the rental car to ninety, then slowing, opening a window to let in the cooler night air, noticing the flatness of the terrain, the relaxed bends of the road, a canopy of trees, realizing he'd lost track of how far he'd driven, the turns he'd taken. Wally pulled off on the shoulder. The half hour he sat there not a car passed in either direction. Just black night and Wally clearing his head, thinking about everything and nothing in the stillness. Shedding weight. Pounds rolling off his shoulders palpable as sweat. This is your life, Wally. A silly voice trying to break in on his thoughts, force him to pay attention. His life melting, forming a

160

puddle at his feet. He let it thicken, widen, refused to look down. A U-turn on what he later learned was Shore, some bad guesses, a slight panic of ten or twelve minutes when he'd given up on finding Bimbo's and searched for signs to the interstate, the airport, a town, any way out of the maze and back to the world, before Wally blundered again right back where he'd started on Bimbo's turnoff.

Sheba in a crimson leather halter and matching hot pants with an orange leotard underneath had opened Bimbo's door when Wally returned, smiled at him as if he were a stranger, as if he hadn't been knocking around with her and the others for hours in Bims's playpen just a short while before, a clean-slate smile that also said whoever you are is fine with me, all right by me, so let's get it on, whoever. When Wally informed her he'd been out for a drive and had discovered a good place to run, she said, *Wow,* and led him by the hand back into the step-down living room pit where the party was still going strong.

In the morning while the others slept—where they slept, whom they slept with, mysteries still to Wally, a puzzle he had an urge to solve till he shuffled his joint into a bathroom and talked it out of its curiosity, squeezing till it softened enough to let him pee—Wally pulled on jock, socks, sweats, and took off for a run. Finding Shore was easy in daylight. He kept the sea to his back as he drove. A few little jogs left were all it took. He parked the rental car. Headed on foot back the way he'd driven the previous night.

That first morning on Shore started chilly. Shreds of fog in the trees. Wally remembers a fence of mist shivering low along the sides of the road. Four or five miles all he'd ventured that morning, guessing distance by time spent running out Shore then back to the car. Far enough to confirm the suitability of Shore as a good road to run. A good place to stay in touch with Wally while he waited for Bimbo to get hip to the reason Wally popped in on him when business brought Wally west.

Now Wally knew Shore's landmarks. With a car's odometer he'd measured routes of five, eight, ten, and twelve miles down and back from the starting point at the intersection of Shore and the nameless track angling in fits and starts up from Bimbo's. Shore unraveled with no steep grades, no surprises, little traffic, trees shading a good portion of its length. Wally's stretch of Shore Road grew familiar. In three years he'd run it various times of day, of year, could traverse it almost step by step now in his mind, a catalogue of details he could rehearse three thousand miles away lolling on his waterbed, recalling it stride by stride, turning his legs loose on Shore Road since they wouldn't turn him loose, let him sleep in peace.

The sun has risen. Only the tallest trees throw shadows blackly on the road, a mottled, lacy pattern scalloping one edge of Shore. Wally's grateful for puddles of shade. In this heat they're like a breeze, a drink of cool water. He needs all the help he can get. Running alone is hard for him. He's made it a habit, but running alone still's not easy. He associates running with punishment. Dues you pay whipping yourself into shape for hoop, a penalty for goofing off in practice, for drinking too much beer in the off-season. Running had always been like calisthenics. Preparation for something else. Becoming a runner is for Wally slumming, a cop-out, a confession that he's not a real jock anymore. Running was for losers who couldn't do any other sport well. Running was foreplay, and no matter how tired, how hot and whipped he was after a long run, Wally felt cheated. Close, but he never got his rocks off.

He needed action. Needed to go against some other body. That's who he was. That's what being a jock all these years had done. He needed to beat on somebody, have somebody lean on him, try to kick his ass. Then Wally could get it on. One-on-one. *Mano a mano* contact. His pride at stake. His life at stake. For real.

Running was one-on-one against himself. Wally'd never been good at that. Too easy to lie to himself, fool himself. The pressure had to come from outside. Somebody on his case. Something to prove. Then Wally could rise, take up the challenge. An opponent's hand in his face, somebody bigger sneering down at him, somebody smaller trying to turn him into a clumsy oaf. He

heard voices from the far side of the cyclone fence, voices ringing the court, judging the players, letting the whole world know
who's boss, who's the chump. Monroe picked Wally clean.
Oowhee. Wally comes back. Swats Monroe's dribble away,
steals the pill and jams it at the other end. What you trying to do
to that boy? Don't hurt him, Wally. My, my. Did you see that
shit? Sweet Wally. Good gollee, Mr. Wallee. Don't be so mean.

Running was battling his own self. Two Wallys to tote up
and down Shore Road. One who didn't love running but knew
it was better than nothing now that serious hoop a thing of the
past, the other Wally like one the winos sitting along the tall
cyclone fence at Melon Park, bad-mouthing some brother on
the court like a dog. You know you ain't spozed to be out there.
You cain't even walk right, let alone run. Throwing up bricks,
tripping over the lines. Sheeit. Much Tokay as I drink I could
whip that turkey. Why don't you give it up? Go on home, boy.
Wally one-on-one against Wally. Two bad backs, two big be-
hinds, four gummy knees. A Wally on his shoulders who didn't
enjoy the ride any more than he enjoyed pounding up and down
the damn road like a camel with that hump of fool who won't
let go or shut up.

Wally at his best when he had someone to react against. In
lots of his college games he'd been listless, next to useless because he could single out no opponent to punish. He was best
when the shit got personal. Abstract hate cured by wrapping
your fingers round an actual throat. Days he needed to prove
something, rid himself of a demon, hit back at what had been
smacking him, drew Wally's best games, and every once in a
while his worst. But worse than his worst were the middling,
noninvolved games when he wasn't good or wasn't bad, just out
there on the court putting in time, his eyes slightly glazed, motor
idling. Earth to Wally. Earth to Wally. Are you in there?

Wally likes to jog till he empties out, till he stops fighting
himself, till the signifying voices on the sidelines are still. Ahead,
the blackish surface of Shore Road wiggled in the sun. By this
hour of the day only one side of the road was shaded and only

partially, an oasis of coolness every quarter mile or so, deep pools of shadow dappled by sun streaming like rain through the foliage of overhanging trees.

Wally was running alone now. A canopy of leaves, thick undergrowth sheltered the woods in darkness. Holes in the curtain drew Wally's eyes. He searched for a glimpse of animals or birds whose sudden motion broke the quiet. Sunlight managed to filter into the deepest nooks and crannies of the woods, splashing a tree trunk, a red-berried bush, illuminating the feathery, green branch of a fir tree. He believed he could smell the salt sea. A message tacked on the heavy, piny odor of the woods.

Never easy to run alone. Yet some times better than others. Wally would pretend he was someone else. Train for the Olympics. Decide to become the fastest human on earth. He fiddled with his stride. Pushed his hips backward, settled into a semicrouch. There had to be a perfect alignment, body as close to a machine as it could get. The caboose of the behind balanced so its weight doesn't drag, so it's part of the thrust forward, the lean into the tape beginning not with the last few strides of the race but in every step, start to finish. Running like a slow, slow-motion fall forward. Your legs not hauling the body's baggage but catching it, catapulted forward with it, by it, momentum building, flying faster and faster.

That was one theory he played with, a temporary groove to interrupt his plodding along the lonely road. Another was the odd style of the Indian who taught Papillon in the movie. Straight-backed, arms lax at his sides, running from hips down, like a horse bearing a wooden rider. Stretched-out, ground-eating strides, torso stiff as a board, trucking Indian-style the way Papillon had learned in the forest. Running day and night, leaving his jailers in the dust. Papillon and his Tonto remembered, welcomed, as Wally mimicks them through a straightaway, around a bend.

A frog lay on its back, dead as a man. One short-thighed leg, bent at knee, crosses the other splayed leg to form the numeral four. A skinny arm folds over a bloated white belly, pledging allegiance to the emptiness. Other corpses litter the margins of the road. Wally jogs on. His street buddies had told him how they made jokes out of the bodies of enemy dead in Nam. Stuffing dicks in mouths, legs where arms should be. And gooks returning the favor. On Shore cars stamp living creatures into grotesque, unrecognizable shapes. A hunk of frizzy carpet is a hunk of frizzy carpet until spokes of bone poke through. Dead white of bone the giveaway. First they stink, then the bodies sea-changed to shoes, an open umbrella, a pile of mud. You ran past paying them no mind until the guts melt, pelt rots, the skeleton begins to climb out its cage. Bone caught Wally's eye. Tempted him to look closer or snatch his eyes away to the treetops. Before he was near enough to determine if a mound of something dark and irregular on the sandy shoulder was the scrambled remains of some animal, he'd decide his stomach wasn't ready for a close-up of whatever it might be—the rank wave of decay, blood and guts smeared like tar over the fur, the curled finger of a paw, hard swell of belly ready to burst, mouth open starting a sentence it would never finish. He'd steel himself not to look but he always peeked. Usually the corpse turned out to be crumbs of asphalt scraped from the roadbed, a petrified rag, a strip of tire. Things never alive looking deader than the dead. And the dead could fool you into believing they were stones, hunks of wood.

When you choose a road you learn the intimate history of its wear and tear. How the giant tires of logging trucks pressed instant fossils into the surface. You almost hear the prehistoric farm vehicles clanking out of fields, their mowers and reapers gouging scars that will last as long as the road lasts. Wally read stories in the skin of Shore Road just as he'd read the lines of his grandmother's face. Breathing hard, he scuffs along behind the V-boned track of a reptile two hundred yards in length till it slithers off the margin of Shore Road. Wally hopes the creature is buried deep underground, dead for centuries.

He thinks black lace when he aims a brief sprint at a patch of shade fringing the roadside. Pushes himself. His knees pump higher, his thighs burn as he accelerates. The sun over his shoulder is throwing darts. He'll hide his face in that black lace.

Only lace he's ever touched was white. White lace handkerchief in a box in a paper bag in a drawer in his grandmother's bureau. She'd never used it, a gift from some white lady she'd cleaned for, but Wally would bet his life she knew just where it was in the drawer. Which box in which bag tied with string. She owned the lace handkerchief. It was one of her nice things, the stuff unused, secured in tight bundles wrapped with brown paper and tied with string, the boxes inside of boxes, inside of gift wrapping, inside of brown paper, inside of bags, the spoils of birthdays, weddings, baby showers, holidays, a smattering of this and that, delicate, expensive little gifts his grandmother had saved and stockpiled in two bottom drawers of her chiffonier, valuables she didn't trust to life, keepsakes unused, yellowing, and musty that Wally unearthed after her death and threw away.

Lace was white. He'd tucked it under her ice-cold hands. The only one of her things he'd saved and now it too was gone, wherever his grandmother had gone in her bargain-basement casket.

Or lace could be black as a tunnel. Big-tittied, narrow-assed women modeled slinky black lace underwear in magazines. So fine they make you want to cry. He was panting as he reached a splash of shade blacker than Shore's tarry surface. Blacker than skid marks, blacker than the vertebrae of dinosaurs bruising the road.

Wally pounds on. He writes letters while he runs. Hello. How you doing? Long time no see. People respond immediately, no waiting, no disappointments. No envelopes to lick, address, no stamps to buy. When Wally commences a letter, it's sent while he writes it. A reply on its way before the hot sun dries Wally's ink. Letters zip back and forth. Wally rekindles a friendship, catches up on the news. Receives photographs, gossip about mutual acquaintances. He likes being in touch this way. Learning other lives are as arbitrary, disposable, unlikely as his own. He inserts a person in a city, a job. Gives or takes away a family. The lives he fashions seem right. Letters answering his letters confirm Wally's fictions. If he's wrong, it matters not.

Lives he makes up keep him moving, shrink the space between Shore's landmarks.

Wally wonders whatever happened to Eliot. *Fuck you, Eliot,* is the first line of the letter. Eliot will wag his head and purse his lips but keep reading. Wally. Wally. When will you ever grow up? Wally, you're just like a little kid. Eliot impatient with him as per usual. Scandalized when Wally's too raunchy for Eliot's taste. So Wally loves to gross him out. Fuck you again, Eliot, if you didn't catch my meaning first time. El, baby. You still searching for the world's largest set of tits? You were a trip, my man. Hopeless. If your date wasn't sporting the biggest knockers at the party, you sulked. Ditched the poor thing and sat in a corner by yourself scheming up on where you'd find a chick with a more humungus set. You still that way, Eliot? Did you marry for tit? How come you didn't pass me the ball that time at the end of the Villanova game when I was open on the break? We might of won. Was the basketball tit too? Is that why you had such a hard time giving it up? Remember the time your lady for the evening passed out and we took her in the shower to revive her? Remember those big ones tumbling down, tumbling down . . .

If letters were started properly they finished themselves. Correspondence bounced back and forth building up its own momentum. Sucking wind through his nose, Wally let the image of Eliot move off, allowed part of himself to slip away and continue talking with the ghost he'd summoned. They'd have a good time together. Somewhere. They were a lot alike in some ways. Poor city boys, both pussy-struck, ruthless, cunning, hungry, scared, predatory. Eliot even had that kinky, almost nigger hair. Except it was carrot-red to go with the freckles, the hook nose, the Boston twang.

Hey, Bob. Hey, Dave. Hey, J.D. Eddie. Where are you guys? Ray. Carl. I'm still hanging in. Killing myself on this hot-assed road. Hot as asphalt in summer on the courts back home. Carrying some extra weight. Got to burn off ten or fifteen pounds of ass, thigh, and belly. Then I'll be ready.

Strange how he feels closer to them now, his teammates

scattered, unheard from, unseen for years, closer than when they spent hours a day, every day, together. It's taken so much time to know them. Years of distance and growing apart and losing touch. Now he can enter their lives, change them. The play lives he creates more real than the bullshit they'd collaborated on, fabricated together to get each other through four years of hoop and school.

Did you guys believe that shit back then? Did you bring it home?

Wally considers Bimbo, five miles away, lowered by harness into his purple whirlpool bath. He could tell Bimbo stories for days. His main man. Ace boon-coon. Cut buddy. He wrote Bimbo lots of letters as he ran. Maybe he'd tell Bimbo what was up. They went way back. If Wally had a real friend, Bimbo was it. Maybe he could tell Bimbo about Chicago. Reuben probably knows already, anyway. Fuck you, Reuben.

Bimbo was always big. Not hard big, not exactly soft either, but big and easy. Too many sisters. Bimbo grew up in a houseful of sisters, him the youngest, the only boy, the pet. Didn't make Bimbo a sissy, but there was girl in his walk, his eyes, his hands always patting you, the lilt in his voice. Bimbo was big but you could take his lunch money. He'd rather give it up than fight. Not because he was scared but because he was easy. Gwan, take it if you got to have it, man. Only time Bimbo really got in anybody's ass be if they mess with one his sisters. Those girls fought many a time looking out for their little brother so when he got big you better not say a word against any of them. Bimbo wasn't no devil. Didn't bully nobody or scare nobody but he was big and he'd only fight if he was real mad and once he started you'd have to pull him off or pull somebody off him because Bimbo acted like you had to rumble till you or the other guy was dead.

Bimbo only had a few fights but people remembered them. Beat the shit out of Waddell Foster. Most people let him alone after that. Plus, with all these good-looking sisters you didn't want not liking you, you be dumb to pick at Bimbo. Anyway,

Bimbo didn't hang out that much. I mean, he had it too good at home. Just a easy cat.

He and Wally got along so well because neither one asked for much from the other. Both liked not being bothered when they didn't want to be bothered and both liked knowing they had a buddy around wouldn't ask for much but was somebody they could depend on to be around not asking. They hung out together without getting in each other's way. As close to alone each could be and still be with somebody. Bimbo used to lots of company. Wally to none. Bimbo was easy because his sisters pampered him, spoiled him like a big doll. Bimbo didn't need a fuss made over him when he was outside his house. Wally didn't fuss over nobody. Bimbo good for Wally because Bimbo was easy. Bimbo let Wally lead him. Was patient while Wally made up his mind. Wally invented all kinds of dangerous stuff for the two of them to try. Bimbo knew his sisters might turn him sissy soft if he didn't run with crazy Wally.

Scut. Scut. Scut. Wally's Nikes scutted when he ran on the sandy shoulder of the road. Hard-packed sand and gravel gave his feet a break from the burning asphalt. Wally listened till the sound of his stride was a word. *Scut.* Regular, monotonous, a heartstroke outside his body measuring his progress down Shore Road. If he counted the scuts, there would be so many per mile. A mile would equal x number of scuts. Divide the scuts by y and you would have traveled . . .

The sun had climbed out of the trees. Wally could see a half mile or so ahead. The road shimmering where parallel lines converged. If you could see far enough there'd be a speck, a pinhole, the eye of a funnel into which the earth poured. Wally thought he heard another pair of footsteps rhythmed with his. Almost on the beat but not quite. He looked away from the black hole at the end of the tunnel. Checked out the margins of the road. Who was running beside him? He wished for Bimbo. Whole again, big again, his crushed legs remembering how to motor. They said Bims's Rolls looked like a crushed tin can. Papers said it was a miracle anyone survived. Wally wanted another miracle, yearned for Bims beside him, the whomp, whomp of Bimbo's big flat duck feet on the asphalt. Bims's easy smile floating.

Not Bimbo running beside him today. Not anyone else Wally could see. Yet he'd heard footsteps solid as his own. Someone dogging him, matching him stride for stride. Maybe the sun. Only mad dogs, Englishmen, and crazy splibs running from the devil out in it. In Reuben's riffs there was a brother, a twin the old man sometimes mentioned. Wally had never sorted out the truth. Whether Reuben was one of an actual set of twins or whether Reuben had talked himself into believing a phantom existed somewhere, Reuben's double from Planet X or wherever spooks like that came from.

Reuben always talking about doubles, twins, other lives he might or might not have lived. Wally wondered about his own doubles, the letters he posted to himself as he ran, the disguises in his suitcase, all the lies he'd told or believed. Wally made up a million other Wallys. Kept in touch with some of them. Hey, man. How you doing, man? Maybe they had a way of answering. Maybe he'd just heard one of them out for a run. One who just happened to be on Shore Road at the same minute as Wally so they trotted along side by side a quick minute, almost bumped into each other. And what would happen if they did?

Reuben said your twin didn't have to live in a body exactly like yours. Maybe yes. Maybe no. Things the eye can't see are what makes him your double. The guy in Chicago in the bathroom. It could be him. Maybe his twin is what Wally saw in the mirror as the white man scrubbed his hands. Wally's own eyes staring back at himself in the man's white face. Not scared. Surprised mostly. What's a nice fellow like you doing in a place like this? The white guy's eyes suddenly sorting out the puzzle. Recognizing Wally. After all this time. All this distance. Dead before he can say, Hey bruh.

If you killed your own sure enough double you'd be alone. Alone forever. With a double you had more than one chance. If you fucked up here, always a chance you might be getting over there, wherever the shadow you, the spirit you, hung out. Always a chance. Hearing a clippy-clop, scut, scut echo as close as you're ever spozed to get because accidents do happen. You could crack the glass.

But Reuben full of shit. Did he have a brother in jail or didn't he? And so what if he did. The old dude says anything comes to his mind. Different story every day of the week. Reuben might have a twin, might have twenty-seven brothers and nineteen sisters or be alone as Wally. Wally born once, mama and daddy lost and gone, grandmother dead, a handful of memories that don't fit, don't connect. Be a damned shame if little orphan Wally murdered his long-lost albino brother in Chicago. And funny too.

Bimbo's tunes used to be about falling in love and losing the one you loved. Sad, whiny songs Bimbo could chirp the shit out of cause he was soft, pampered by all those sisters. Then later his songs about fucking, about getting it on. Full-blast, straight-ahead fucking. Forget the tears-on-my-pillow, heartache, and crying-in-the-chapel shit. Bimbo singing about stone getting down. Getting over. Some of his songs, don't know how they let them on the radio. Bimbo grunting and groaning and yelling like he just hit the pussy lottery for ten million dollars. Everybody knows what he's doing in them songs, what he's talking about. Even got sound effects, all that heavy breathing and sighs and the bass stroking right on time. Humping music. That's when Bimbo really got to be a big star. When you start hearing him on white stations. Then a special on pay-TV. Then the networks and a movie. Bimbo the superfly gangster. People getting off listening to old Bims getting off. Wally wondered if Bims ever really did his business in the studio. He'd never asked Bimbo, but he'd intended to. Bimbo whaling away with some chick and a microphone stuck up close to catch all the action.

Bimbo the superstar national cocksman. Can't move a muscle below his waist and he's still turning everybody on with his bedroom songs. Rubbing, squeezing, kissing, licky-face, romp-all-over-the-bedroom songs and Bims ain't ever gon wiggle his toes again. Better at it now, too. Crippled in his wheelchair Bims can make you believe he's superstud. Young girls still squealing.

171

Dudes still sticking Bims on the stereo when they trying to put some lady in the mood. Was Bimbo remembering when he sang his raunchy songs or was he at it again? Twin Bimbos. One pinned in the electric wheelchair. One cut loose, out in the street again setting world records for fucking.

They were alone now, for the first time since Wally'd arrived. Bimbo regal in a blue velvet robe. Wally in a green silk kimono he'd borrowed after his shower. The run down Shore felt good now. Tucked away like a perfect, home-cooked meal in Wally's belly. He wanted to tell Bimbo about how nice the workout had been, but didn't. You had to watch what you said. Bimbo wasn't thick-skinned like little hunched-over Reuben. Reuben never flinched. With Reuben Wally said whatever came into his mind. Reuben would be off somewhere else in a minute. If Reuben was a dwarf, a cripple now, he'd been something different before and would be something else tomorrow. So Wally didn't worry about hurting his feelings, saying something dumb or ugly that would pin Reuben down. Wally and Bimbo both knew Bims wasn't going nowhere. Not today. Not next week. Under all the velvet and cologne and fawning bitches, Bims would wear the same crippled skin. Bimbo was inside his skin and he'd never get out so Wally was careful what he said. Mostly it was old times. Kid stuff, chasing pussy together in high school days, catching up on the years they hadn't seen each other. Bimbo's rise, Wally's ballplaying in college. The surprise of Bims's call one day. Then Wally on the doorstep of Bimbo's palace. Old friends again. Cutting through the crap. Simpatico. Copacetic. Cool again. A nice story. They'd told it to each other lots of times. In their reminiscences the accident hadn't occurred yet. One day they might sneak up on it, but there'd been so much else to rap about. There was time.

Till the day Bimbo said, I want to die.

Once walking home from school Wally and Bimbo had taken a side trip to the day-old bakery near the bridge over the tracks on Ellsworth Avenue. Short, stubby Ellsworth Bridge was framed by rusted girders that rose thirty or forty feet above its steel-plated surface. If you shimmied up the steep side to the beams paralleling the ground, you could walk across the top of the bridge. If you slipped the right way, you'd be busted up bad on the metal walkway and maybe get squished by the traffic; if you slipped the wrong way, you'd surely die on the railroad tracks a hundred feet below. Worst part really was clambering up and inching back down the slanted ends. You needed the welded seams, the studs, to keep your grip. Once on top the going easy. A steel tightrope a foot and a half wide, so even if you lost your balance, room to catch yourself. Room to lay down and cop a nap if you needed one. Wouldn't want to try on a windy day, though. Crouching spoils it. Wally liked to stand tall, staring down on car roofs, the claw marks of the tracks miles below. He'd shame the wobble out of his knees, do a little dippy-do shake dance, then race double-time to the beam's far end.

You did it on a dare. Or just because you felt like it or because you wanted to show off. Or because you wanted to shame somebody else into trying. Wally climbed the side of the bridge that day because the idea of doing it scared him. His heart thumped. He couldn't speak. Part of him knew he could walk the top of the bridge. He'd scampered across it many times. He could see himself up there, grinning, wiggling his ass, the wind under his wings, ready to fly him away if he wanted to fly. He saw himself poised lighter than air waving at the crowd, a halo of sunshine breaking behind his shoulders. That's me. That's old Wally Steel Nerves up there. Up, up, and away. If it was, and it surely was because who else could strut that Wally wise-ass way from end to end, then who was trembling, who was about to pee his pants at the thought of the first step up the steel frame?

Bimbo rolled down the top of a bag of day-old doughnuts. He was on his second jelly one. They both knew the other was keeping track. Half the bag for Bimbo. Half for Wally. All the best kinds shared equally or split down the middle if an odd number of chocolate-icinged or jellied. Bimbo checking him out to see if Wally was checking him out. Their eyes met as Bimbo took the first bite of his last jelly, but Wally not even counting.

He was dancing in the clouds, he was rooted to the ordinary pavement listening to steel plates rattle as a car hit the bridge's surface, the teeth-chattering rumble that seemed so far away when you were on top of the world with the wind whistling and everybody's eyes on you.

Hey, man. Don't gorilla all the goddamned jelly doughnuts. Gimme mine, nigger.

Bimbo opens the greasy brown paper bag. Wally's fingers dig till he finds the lumpy weight of one with no hole in the center. With the powdered jelly doughnut clamped in his teeth, wondering if it's grape or strawberry, he starts his monkey climb up the end of the bridge. Because he's scared. Because today it's Bimbo's turn to follow. Because tomorrow is Wally's fourteenth birthday.

C'mon up, man. It's easy, man. Wally's holding on with one hand, beckoning with the other full of doughnut.

Bimbo finishes chewing. Dips into the spotted sack again. I'm eating, man.

Well, stop a damn minute and come on up. I'm eating too. Stale shit tastes better up here.

Bimbo watches Wally suck jelly out of a half-moon bite. Wally licks the last bit from the doughy end, dangles it between his thumb and finger, and drops the empty to the tracks.

Ain't chicken, is you, Bims? He yells the taunt over his shoulder before he staggers like a wino across the beam.

Nothing to it, once you do it, Wally is thinking as he scoots the last few feet to the ground. As he'd slipped down, face close to the seamed girders, he'd missed Bimbo starting up the other end. When Wally's on his feet again and finds his cut buddy swaying in the dead middle of the horizontal beam, the first thing he thinks is where's the doughnuts?

Bimbo. Where'd you put the goddamn doughnuts?

They ain't up here, nigger. I don't know where the fuck they is.

Hey. You had em, man.

Don't care neither.

What's wrong, man?

Can't go no further.

You home now. You past the worst part. Just keep moving.

Can't take another step. Not one step more.

Shit, man. What's wrong wit you, man?

Can't make it. Not one step further.

Well shit. You got to finish or go back. You got to come down one way or the other.

I can't.

Then what the fuck you gon do?

Help me.

Shit, Bimbo. Stop crying.

Help.

You got to help yourself. What I'm gon do down here? Go for it, man. You past the hard part. You already more'n half-way.

I want down.

Finishing easier than going back.

Bimb drops to his hands and knees, swaying, wailing. A pitiful, blubbery elephant.

I can't . . . I can't.

Wally's disgusted. Where the fuck he put the doughnuts? Why don't he just go on and get down?

Bimbo, man. What's wrong wit you?

Help me.

Shit, nigger. Jump. Go on and jump if you so damned scared. Jump and you won't be scared no more.

Cars shake, rattle, and roll the bridge. People driving by can't see Bimbo. Wonder why Wally's standing in the middle of traffic talking to the sky. People think Wally's crazy when really it's Bimbo acting like a damned fool. Won't go forward. Won't go back. What the fuck I'm spozed to do down here?

I can laugh now but I was mad then. You up there blubbering. *Help, Wally . . . help, Wally . . .* and what I'm spozed to do? It's your ass stuck up there. I ain't got no damned ladder in my pocket. Nobody told you to try if you wasn't gon finish.

You said jump. My main man and I'm in trouble and what he say? Jump, nigger.

Yeah, well . . .

I say *Help* and he says *Jump*.

Hey man. You lucky I didn't grab the iron and shake your pitiful ass down off there. I was mad, boy.

And I was stuck. Wasn't my fault neither. I wasn't crazy like you. Shit, I wanted to live. Knew you didn't really care if you fell or not. All the same to you. But I had better sense. Least it seemed like better sense at the time. Old, dumb Bimbo wanted to stay alive.

Nobody took you by the hand and drug you up there. I had to lead your lame ass down, but nobody made you go up there.

You know you did it to me. You were always doing it to me. Putting me in shit over my head. Sometimes I think you just got tired trying to kill your own damned self and tried to kill me for a change. Just for something to do. My cut buddy, my main man.

Climbed up and talked you down, didn't I?

After you left me up there long enough to think I wasn't never getting off that bridge. After you hollered at me to jump.

But I did rescue your sorry behind, didn't I?

Oh yeah. Prince Charming and the Lone Ranger and John Wayne. Sure you did. After you got tired waiting on me to jump.

Should have left you up there. You was one sorry dude that day. Couldn't go forward. Couldn't go back.

Maybe I should have taken your advice. Maybe jumping would have been the best thing after all.

Wally's eyes meet Bimbo's. He recognizes the same look he saw over the rolled bag of day-old doughnuts. We both been counting. We both know exactly how many are left, how many of each kind the other's eaten.

Wally feels guilty because he knows too much. He meets himself in his friend's eyes. He knows and doesn't want to know what's coming next.

I want to die, Wally.

And again, with Bimbo trembling, weeping in the dead center of the bridge Wally has the urge to yell: *Jump . . . Jump, nigger*. And he knows Bimbo hears him shout the words again

176

even though Wally won't let them leap out his mouth this time, here in Bims's upholstered, mirrored, hi-tech, lush-as-money-can-buy bedroom and Bims with no legs.

What you talking about, man? You want to die. You can't die. You're the king. Bimbo the king. You got it all.

Would you sell me one of your legs, Wally? Just one. Or your dick? Just let me rent it a day. How much would you charge me, old buddy? I wouldn't ask nobody else. We go way back so I can ask you. Name your price. Give you everything I own for one of your legs. Don't even have to give up your dick. Just rent it to me one night. You can have all this shit. All of it.

Bimbo stretches his arms as wide as he can. They flutter, stutter. Bimbo's way of saying I can't say no more. Can't stretch no further. I've said all I can and I ain't even close to saying what needs to be said. So he lets his fingers flutter in the empti-ness as if he's trying to pat it into shape. But there's nothing out there at the ends of his outstretched arms. They play weakly a moment then give up and settle onto the padded armrests of his wheelchair. Since he was a kid, Bimbo's way of giving up, talk-ing with his arms and hands that way ever since he was a kid. Giving his wings a couple shakes; then plop.

I'm offering all the money in the world. And you my best friend. And still it don't do no good, does it? That's why I want to die. I'm in a cage, Wally. I'm locked in this motherfucker forever. Don't matter who comes along and peeks through the bars, I'm stuck in here forever. In my cage. Ain't no room for nobody else. And I want out. Oh Lord, how I want out. I want it over, done for good.

I know what you mean, man. Some days can get you down so goddamned low. Sometimes seem like a whole string of them kind of days come chugging by. Seem like they never end. Feel like whale shit at the bottom of the ocean. Gets so bad can't get no worse. But you start coming back. You got to come back. After a while ain't no more down. Can't fall no further.

You know you're lying. There's always more down. I've been under the bottom since the accident and I'm still falling. The bottom is right now, today. Tomorrow will be worse. I

177

know that. I know I'm never rising out this chair. I keep falling further. I stay under the bottom. Tomorrow and tomorrow and the next day'll bury me deeper under the bottom.

Jump.

Naw, man. You don't really mean that.

Hey. I'm lucky, right? Still got all this shit, right? Still a star. I'm lucky to be alive, right? No way a person spozed to survive a crash like that. That's what they all said. Lucky to be alive. But they ain't me. They ain't the one with all the fucking good luck.

Bimbo—

Let me finish. This ain't a bad day. And I ain't in a bad mood. This is how it is all the time. I don't want to live no more. What's so goddamned strange about that? All I'm asking is for you to help me. Don't care if you understand, just help your old buddy. Can't ask none of these fools around here. Can't trust them. Don't want nothing from them even if I could trust one to do what I ask. If you help me die, it won't be so lonely. You're my friend, Wally. It wouldn't be easy for you. That makes a difference. I'd feel better knowing it was you helping me get it over with. Knowing it might hurt you just a little bit to do it. My old friend to the end. Hardhearted Wally. One last piece of silly business we can take care of together. Set this nigger free. Help me find peace, Wally.

You mean it, don't you?

Much as I ever meant anything I ever said in my whole life. It's time. I know it's time but I need a little help. Little care package from you. Little anonymous donation to the Save Bimbo fund. Got it all figured out, see. I'll even give you the money for the stamp. You send me the pills by mail. You could be a thousand miles away. No reason for nobody to suspect you. Send me the letter from one the cities you stop in for a day. If it's marked a certain way, the letter comes directly to me. Nobody opens my personal mail. I have a number. Like in prison, you dig. A special number only certain people know. You stick the pills in an envelope and I'll have them and we can get this shit over with. I'm begging you, Wally. Couldn't ask nobody else. Do it for your old running buddy Bims.

Wally hasn't sent the poison yet. Bimbo's personal secret zip code always in Wally's wallet. Wally can pull the pin any day. Found a dude sold him the pills. Bimbo's life in Wally's hands but Wally can't snuff it out. It is two or three in the morning. The stations of Shore Road roll by as if on a movie screen. His waterbed encases him like wet cement. This is how it will be when I'm dead. Wally folds his arms over his chest. This is how you mourn yourself, how you lay there forever, a flower in your hand, staring at the roof of your coffin. Wally uncrosses his wrists, reaches down and scratches slow-motion at the hair on his belly. You die and you're a stiff. He hears the city breathing. Night sounds toy with his sleep. Not keeping him awake but teasing, picking at him, raising an edge of the blanket under which he's trying to hide himself, peeking in at him like he's peeked in so many city windows at night. Night noises reminding him they're out there to keep him awake if all else fails. But all else is enough. Thoughts of Bimbo strapped in his wheel-chair, corpses littering Shore Road, the heaviness of his flesh sinking into the waterbed, sinking to the center of the earth. A lump, a speck of dust swirling away through the needle's eye of the funnel. So boring just to lie there while his thoughts race and play like roaches in every corner of the room. To lie with his mind turning, full of crazy words and pictures, or lie with his mind empty forever, still forever, dust on the marquee, letters fallen away, the boring weight of his arms crossed over his chest, cobwebs of skin draping his bones as he melts, stinking away. To be a pile of shit in a rotten box, in a hole nobody remembers they dug. To be stuck like that forever, bored, endlessly still.

Wally couldn't do it to Bimbo. He recalls the old white lady buying arsenic. The clerk asks her what it's for and she says to kill a rat. Wally liked that story. Even had a nigger in it. They'd read it in American lit. She kills the dude because he's doing her wrong. Same ole Frankie and Johnny shit. Goes to the drug-store, cops the poison, feeds it to the trifling dude. Cold. Cold bitch. Then she got the nerve to lay up in the bed wit his dead body. Cold.

Then there was Sarah, who threw Wally's clothes on the stove, turned on the burners, called the fire engines, and took a bath. Locked in the bathroom when Wally smelled smoke, when the firemen busted in the front door. She was in there splashing around in a bubble bath while Wally tried to explain to the firemen why his clothes burning on top the stove. That was cold, too. Would have strangled the bitch if he could have laid his hands on her. He's groggy and half high but firemen or no firemen, he'd have choked her to death in that grubby kitchen if he could have gotten his fingers round her throat. Yeah. She knew that. That's why she locked the door. Yeah. He was half-way living with Sarah and more than halfway fucking her simple sister on the sly but that didn't give Sarah no right to burn his clothes. And to make it so bad, there's the man at the door, busting in the damned door and smoke filling up the apartment. Shit. What could he say to the man? She's crazy. She did it cause I fucked her sister. She's the crazy one locked in the bathroom splashing around like she ain't got a care in the world, singing and soaping her pussy and what the fuck I'm spozed to say to the goddamned fireman?

Bitches will poison you, throw lye in your eyes while you sleep, burn your clothes, turn you inside out and snatch you bald-headed, if you let them. Cold, cold bitches. But he liked the story about the evil old lady and the dead man stinking up the attic. The kind of old lady wears lace collars and lacy cuffs on her wrists. You could tell that from the story even if the story didn't say so in so many words. A funny story, really. The funniest part the old darky Uncle Tom butler splitting the scene when the townspeople finally bust in the house after the lady dead. Old Rastas knows when it's time to get a hat. Ain't nobody seen nor heard of him since. He knew he'd get blamed. Bet he took something nice wit him, too. A diamond necklace, a fifth of good whiskey.

Most the stories in that lit class a pain in the ass to read. You spend too much time fighting through a million busy words crammed up on every page. You finish and then what? So what? The shit ain't about you. Nor nobody like you. So so what?

Reuben always mentioning books Wally should read. Reuben had a library in his pointy head. So what? Wally would rather listen to music anytime.

He tries to think of music that would help now, this very moment. Something to break the monotony, the stony silence of lying dead two thousand years. He scratches lower, fingertips playing in the wrinkly skin holding his balls. Thinks of Sarah laughing in the tub. He's mad at her. But he likes the way her tits jiggle, the wet, soapy sheen of her skin. They had some good times. Wasn't his fault Sarah asleep and Sandra laying butt-naked on the couch when he comes out the bathroom. He was on his way to bed. Even though Sarah drank too much. Even though she wouldn't be worth nothing that night, or the next morning or all the next day for that matter because she didn't know when to stop drinking. Sarah called herself keeping up with him. Shit. She left him in the dust. One more, let's have one more hit before we go home, baby. Her and that one more for the road snoring in the bedroom, dead to the world and it ain't his fault her fine-assed, pea-brain sister lying on the couch with her legs cocked open wearing nothing but a silly grin.

Didn't say yes. But damn sure didn't say no, neither. Wasn't nothing but a piece of ass changing hands. Don't see why Sarah got so upset. Knew as well as I knew, her sister Sandy ain't never been wrapped too tight. Nobody told Sarah to drink too much and knock herself out, nobody told her to pile his clothes on the burners and light the stove.

He hears her standing in the tub. Water dripping off her breasts and arms, dotting her mink-colored skin, dripping off the washrag she's wiping herself with. Maybe it's so loud cause both sisters in there. Behind the locked door, bathing together. Maybe it's Bimbo's swimming-pool tub behind the door and both women scrubbing their fur. Sarah taller, leaner, and Sandra got the bigger ass, but they favor each other, they're surely sisters when you pull their clothes off or one takes her own clothes off her ownself. Like Sandy did that night he was tired and ready for bed but had to sit on the toilet first and when he comes out, there she is in all her glory. Didn't even have to unbuckle his belt, unzip his fly. Come out the bathroom sloppy, pants dragging down round his hips ready for bed. He thought for a minute might be Sarah on the couch. Didn't really believe that lie but they *are* sisters, it *was* dark, they *do* favor one another. Didn't really need that lie when he plopped down on top of her. Bimbo should have been playing in the background. Maybe he was. Wouldn't have mattered one bit to Sarah. Could have been Bimbo live with a fifty-piece band and Sarah wouldn't have heard a note. Not behind all those ones for the road. Bims whaling in the background and we going at it hot and heavy. Didn't take but a minute, really. That's all that was to it. Quick piece ass changing hands. Wasn't sneaky or trying to hide or nothing like that. Too tired to see, but me and Sandy both needing that nut. Biff. Bam. No big thing. Ain't gon lie now. Good while it lasted, but no big thing. Why'd Sarah have to go and act all crazy? Why she . . .

Wally scratching his balls and Sarah flipflops to Sandy and he stops asking questions, watches her chocolate thighs open, the smear of darker icing in the middle waiting for him to slide in. Easy. Easy. Easy. It's Sandy, then Sarah again, then it matters not one iota whose hot thighs wrapping round his back.

Work out, Bimbo.

Killing, killing, killing, killing me baby with your mean love. Mean mean mean love is killing me, baby.

Oowhee, killing me baby.

Your mean love your mean love your mean love love love love.

The phone sneaks in somewhere between the lines. Breaks in somewhere it shouldn't be. No way. Go way. Phone bringing Wally down. Bringing down Bimbo's song.

Wally doesn't relish the thought of visiting the city jail with blood on his hands. A posse of burly cops will sneak up behind him. The cuffs snap down on his wrists. His buns hustled off to a cell under the jail. Where Reuben claimed they keep his twin brother. Rotting down there forever. Or until the bright morning they dig him out. Burn him or hang him or gas or shoot his pitiful ass full of lead, whatever they do when the cat gets tired toying with the mouse.

He mounts the jailhouse steps. Enters through tall, bronze doors. More slabs of stone rise to a narrow door and a window. The entrance to the jail seemed wide from the street. Once inside the first door the space shrinks drastically, side walls pinch in, the wall facing you stares down, trapping you in a tiny ante-room, vestibule you'll never escape unless you whine a magic word to the keepers. If you were shaky in the first place about visiting jail, one step inside the heavy front doors and you're certain you're in trouble. Wally's heels are screaming for him to split. Exit quick the way he came in. Get out fast before the bronze doors click shut behind him. But not so fast you look suspicious. Don't run or they'll chase you. Like dogs, they can smell fear hanging on you. Big Brother got his evil eye dead on your chest. Inside your chest. He sees your rotten heart thumping unnaturally loud, swollen by its secrets, its crimes.

Wally perseveres. States his business at the barred window. I want to see Reuben. Reuben the lawyer.

Then he cracks up. The whole silly, topsy-turvy mess of it tickles him and he almost giggles out loud. Check it out, Big Brother. Check it out, you be laughing too.

Wally should be the one in jail. Like in the movies. Demanding to see his lawyer as thuggy cops bunch round him, turn their cop dirty looks on him. They know his black ass is guilty as sin and think real hard about whipping on his head till he confesses, but Wally's no chump. Wally's been to the university. He demands his rights, his little pointy-head, pointy-chin Reuben of a lawyer. Wally should be the one incarcerated, interrogated, his ass in a dangerous sling, and old man Reuben should be hobbling up the jailhouse steps to rescue him.

I wish to see my client, Wally . . .

But here it was. Ass backward. Somebody got the plot all wrong. Reuben's locked up. Wally's jackleg, half-pint lawyer in the slammer. The law behind bars waiting for the outlaw to set it free.

Sure he'd come down to the jail. Sure I'll bail you out. Hey, old man. I thought you were a law-abiding citizen. I thought you was the law. Hit Reuben with a few little digs. On his case slightly and politely. How you spozed to be representing me while you sitting downtown in the slam? Reuben good at teasing. Wally sure wasn't going to let his chance to tease slip by.

Be down right away, my friend. At your service. But ah . . . you realize this is a professional service. I mean, I can't do it for nothing. You dig? I expect a fee. What you charge for this kind of work, Mr. Reuben?

That was enough. Silence at the other end of the line said that's enough. Whatever was up, Reuben didn't consider it a laughing matter. Besides, they only allowed you a few minutes on the phone. And only one call. Wally shut up, listened. Reuben didn't sound like Reuben.

. . . Nothin too serious, is it? I mean it can't be nothing too much with the bail set so low. Mize well let you go behind a hundred-dollar bail.

Technicality. Humiliation. They extract their pound of flesh.

Downtown, then. Across from the courthouse. Will they take a check?

If your papers are in order.

Hold on, old buddy. Be right down.

I'd appreciate that.

Old Reuben sounded like he's at the bottom of a well. Damn phone buzzing with static when Wally answered it, held it to his ear. A fire crackling on the moon. Was it worry in Reuben's voice that made it sink, seem miles and years away? Worry or was he tired? Up all night in his cell. Not wanting to bother anybody, too embarrassed to call. And why was he in jail? A token payment would release him. Reuben couldn't be in for anything serious. Why didn't they just turn him loose? Maybe they caught the old billy goat with a whore. Wally'd never let him forget it if that was the charge. Whoring again. Philadelphia again. Randy, billy-goat Reuben. Caught with his pants down again.

All of it funny. None of it funny. Him in the jail bailing out Reuben behind some nickel-dime shit. A murdered man somewhere with Wally's name carved in his chest and the dead man's clean hands pointing a finger at Wally, jabbing at him, shouting, Guilty, Guilty, Guilty loud enough for anybody to hear, if they laid an ear to Wally's chest. Reuben in deeper trouble than he imagined if the best he could come up with was Wally to save him.

10

MR. TUCKER

Reuben picks the wet morning paper off the step of his trailer. News rolled like a scroll. He had studied it where it lay until he heard the sound of Wally driving off. He didn't want to turn again and face Wally again. Didn't want Wally hanging around chaperoning him safely inside the trailer door. Like some melt-in-the-rain young girl escorted home from a dance. So he'd hesitated as if caught by a sensational story lying on his door-step. As if he could read the bands of words, starting nowhere, going nowhere. As if they might make sense reading them top to bottom, bottom to top, vertical meaning in horizontal columns of print. Reuben felt betrayed in the pale morning light. Some-body had rolled back his stone. Exposed his hiding place. He needs Wally gone. Only after Wally's motor snarled into gear, then gradually faded down the block and around the corner, the only car on Hamilton, the last thing moving on earth, could Reuben begin to believe his nightmare was over.

Nobody's fault. Certainly not Wally's. Wally had done his

clumsy best to help. The worst things that happened to people seldom anybody's fault, even though someone usually got blamed. A scapegoat to take the weight, to obscure the conspiracy implicating everybody. No one's hands clean, Reuben thought as his fist wrapped around the newspaper, as his other hand leaned on the tin step. No one's innocent. He straightens from a crouch. Weight of his crooked shoulder ached this morning. It was the straw, Reuben the camel. He trudged up the one step to the trailer door. One step wide as a desert of burning coals. He didn't need the hump on his back this morning. He didn't need undersized limbs, child's arms and legs hauling an old man's head through the world. In the cell where they'd deposited him overnight, he'd rattled the bars. Or rather rattled his old bones as he stood wide-legged, a puny Samson in his cage yanking the unmoving cold steel. Then he'd kicked the bars. Then he'd imagined fastening his teeth in them, gnawing his way out. But he wasn't going anywhere. He knew. They knew. The key to his cell was in his keeper's pocket. He could holler bloody murder and rant and kick and bite till his rage turned to dust. The key would stay where it was until his jailers were good and ready to free him. Once in, once locked away and the key in someone else's hands, you're never free again. The memory always there. Haunting you like a hot lump of flesh on your shoulder. If they come and take you once, you are always their prisoner. They move in forever. Locked in a dark room in your mind.

Reuben sighed aloud, *Ahhhhh* as the stale breath of the trailer kissed his face. The pleased, pained sigh of a man long constipated, *ahhh, . . . at last, at last,* welcoming his stink. The night which was never going to end was ending. He was breaking through. Ready to start up again.

We don't want to do this, Mr. Reuben. But we got to. Orders. We got to take you in, sir.

They sent two black cops. Big, burly, Nubian-looking brothers. Reuben would fit in the coat pocket of either one. That's what they used to call it in slavery days. Putting Rastas in their pocket when they sold Rastas down the river. You better behave, boy, else Massa gon put you in his pocket. If you listened to the way they talked about slaves you'd think the poor Africans were silly putty you could stretch every which way. The white man put slaves in his pocket, black men put slaves on the banjo, slaves were tar babies you push and mash and punch and pull like taffy.

Please come along peacefully. God knows we don't like doing this to you. No more than you like having it done. So please come along easy, Mr. Reuben.

That Reuben would disappear in tow or towing two cops raised no eyebrows in Stanley's. Reuben made a thousand trips a day back and forth from bar to courthouse and jail and he kept all kinds of company so no one paid the trio any mind. Little dapper dude squashed nearly invisible between two tank-shouldered, uniformed men in blue patrolling his flanks.

Send a nigger to catch a nigger. Two to catch one if you have spares loitering around. The tactic made perfect sense. There were historical precedents, parallels. Indian scouts leading longhairs to the hiding places of their red brethren. FBI informers, double agents, infiltrators of the sixties. An unsubtle variation of divide and conquer. You can't tell the players without a program. And the man possesses the only program, making it up as he goes along so he's the only one who knows the score. Creating chaos, fear and trembling. You never know whom to trust, whom to turn to, who's on your side. Send Amos and Andy to catch the Kingfish. All in the family.

Reuben kept his ruminations to himself. Stifled a belch. Smiled at his captors. Accommodated each of their long, slow, deliberate strides with two of his light, quick, gimpy ones, the sheen of his spit-shined shoes winking and blinking unnoticed across Stanley's filthy floor, unseen except from a rodent's eye view, flashes of light in a three-inch-high sea of dirt and shadow, lapping feet, table legs and chair legs, the spills, cigarette butts, general unmentionable muck that anchors Stanley's Bar and Grill.

HOMEWOOD MAN ACCUSED AS IMPOSTOR. Reuben's story beat him home. Unrolling the paper, skimming heads in the first section, he discovered two short columns of print about himself. Too much for a tombstone, too little for a page in a book. He was not ready to read his story yet. He closed the *Pittsburgh Post-Gazette*, spread it on his desk, and flattened its curved spine. Curled edges of newspaper scratched feebly like fingernails at the tabletop as Reuben turned away to fix a cup of coffee on his hot plate.

Mr. Tucker had hooked up the trailer years ago. Let there be lectricity. And so it was. With that gnarled half a thumb on his left hand the old man tested plugs and sockets. A lick of spit on the tip and he'd ram the thumb home. Got juice here, Mr. Reuben. We in good shape here. The crackle and sizzle and pop and spark enough to make Reuben jump back, but old man Tucker just stood there, smoke curling from his thumb, reading it like a voltage meter. Tucker with his mauled thumb and one leg shorter than the other so he limped. Hit my thumb with a hammer when I was just a boy. Ain't growed since. But everything else did except that one leg, and it did, but just didn't keep up with the rest. Tucker way over six foot tall. If you thought somebody was big, the best way to be certain was to stand them next to Tucker. Nobody was bigger but if somebody measured up even close to his size, they were *big*. But even Tucker wasn't big enough to walk away with people's houses the way they said he did. That's the crime of which he had stood accused in the *Post-Gazette*. Here comes Tucker on his way to a job, his long toolbox slung over one shoulder like Reuben used to carry his shoeshine stuff, only you could put Reuben and all his paraphernalia in the giant foot locker Tucker toted around. If you didn't know one leg shorter than the other you'd think old man Tucker's shoulder-dipping gait was caused by too much weight, the burden of his tools making him lean at a steep angle, drawing him down close to falling every step he takes through the Homewood streets. Mr. Tucker in his striped, high-water coveralls, the straps pulled tight so the bib rides high under his chin. He'd speak if you spoke but his mind would be on whatever job he's humping to. A workingman, Mr. Reuben. That's all I been long's I can remember. When Tucker said it, it was *woik*. His voice high-pitched and squeaky coming from such a large man. Woik's all I know, Mr. Reuben. Ain't never taken nothing from no man lessen I give a good day's woik in return.

Reuben knew the truth when he heard it and knew how futile it was. Somebody in the business of dismantling abandoned houses and selling the copper, brass, and bricks, everything reusable that could be scavenged from ancient row houses. That somebody had hired Mr. Tucker to strip the brick facing from a partially demolished shell on Shetland Avenue and the old man had been busy there in the rubble, in clouds of choking plaster dust, under a scorching sun, giving an honest day's work when the cops arrived and arrested him. Because the house belonged to the city and the city'd granted nobody permission to tear it down. All Mr. Tucker knew was that a truck would come by at six to load the bricks he'd salvaged and the driver would pay him after the bricks stacked and counted in the truck. Tucker had no chance to tell his story till two mornings after he was arrested so whether the truck came by or not (and it might have and might have harvested the half day's pile Tucker had stripped and cleaned and never would get one penny for now), nobody knew. And Tucker didn't know the name of the white man in the car who'd rolled up to the corner of Frankstown and Homewood where men still wait outside the Velvet Slipper for daywork like they've been waiting since Skippy was a pup, rolled up and rolled down his window and chose the huge man from the crowd on the corner, Tucker didn't know the white man's name, didn't care really long as he was paid at the end of the day, no more than the white man cared who he was hiring long as the work done and the price cheap. So Mr. Tucker was cutting and scraping brick all morning. White grit coating his coveralls, his eyebrows when they brought him in the jail. Brick dirt and plaster dust and not saying a word to anybody and big so it was like they'd carted one of those half-wrecked houses out of Homewood and stuck it in the corner of a cell. Would probably still be sitting there today in that cell, mute, beat, if Reuben hadn't found him and led him home.

Well, somebody was at it again. Houses disappearing again.

Reuben hoped his client had an alibi this time.

City hall officials remain baffled by a band of strip-and-run wreckers who have plundered seven city homes since January, twice making off with whole buildings in a brazen daylight demolition.

Reuben read while he waited for water to boil in his red pot. The pot stood on legs short and gimpy as Reuben's. Once crossing the country, somewhere in the middle, the outskirts of Omaha maybe, he'd seen a coffee pot tall as a skyscraper. At least in that flat land it had jutted up taller than anything around it. The Mr. Tucker of coffee pots, a giant in that flat country. The moment he saw it Reuben knew a tornado would swat down the crazy pot. That's why big things were invented. To fall. To crash down. To keep little people in line. Scare them, make them grateful for watery, too-short legs, for humps that stoop them over.

Disappearing houses made page one. Reuben studied the headline. The red pot behind his shoulder burped tentatively, once, twice, once more.

STRIP-AND-RUN HOME WRECKERS AT IT AGAIN IN CITY.

His own story, buried in the middle pages of the first section, under its modest banner TRIPPED BY LAW, was what he wanted to read yet he wasn't ready to open the paper again. He wasn't ready for his story to be real again—the cops, the cell, the long night listening to dying animals prowling their cages. When he read his story, it would be real again, happen again. His brother's long, straight back, his blazing eyes stuffed for eternity in the dark cocoon. A Reuben chained by words, Reuben locked up forever. So he played for time. Let the words above the house-stealing story float free until they told another tale.

A *home wrecker* was the other woman, the temptress, the siren who got Daddy's attention when she stripped, and Daddy's company when she ran, and then Daddy's whole sweet household tumbling down in a cloud of dust around Mommy and the kids. Reuben could see it plain as day. The lewd bump-and-grind of some fast woman's hips. Shake it, don't break it. Daddy almost breaking his neck hustling down the stairs and out in the street chasing fanny. The creak and rumble of the walls starting to collapse. God frowning or smirking down on the whole corny scene, the city writhing as outbreaks of the disease explode in every neighborhood. STRIP-AND-RUN HOME WRECKERS AT IT AGAIN IN CITY. It's the pot boiling he hears, and his own story he's avoiding by listening to this one he invents and Reuben knows he's stalling but knows he needs time.

Mr. Reuben, I don't know nothing but woik. Been woiking since I was a little child. Ain't never asked nobody to give me nothing. Ain't right for them to be doing me like they doing.

It's a shame, Mr. Tucker. It's a crime. You're absolutely correct.

I done put in all this time and they snatch me up off the street like one these pitiful young boys going round here stealing and shooting that dope. How long a man got to be a man fore they leave him be?

They won't bother you again. We'll make them see their mistake.

Would that he could. Would that he could . . .

The giant old man is twisting something in his hands. He stoops so his bald head doesn't butt the ceiling. Reuben tries to look at the face leaning toward him. It is Mr. Tucker's brown face; he's seen Tucker's face a million times, yet the face refuses to be anyone. Nose, eyes, mouth, the wrinkled skin have no connection with any name. A scar folds into one bushy eyebrow. An old scar, but younger than the weathered skin of the forehead. Finding the scar is like seeing the first star in what you thought was an empty sky. You find one, then you discover a thousand more. The face he's been calling Mr. Tucker all these years is not Mr. Tucker at all. Nothing in the face looming before him is familiar. Reuben is an insect crawling over the cratered, lunar surface of skin. It will take him hours to cross from ear to cheekbone. His life is at stake as he explores the vast grid of this face, its separate domains, its mismatched patching and shading, the promontory of nose, canyons and valleys and slashes unraveling as Reuben drags his eight sensitive pods across it, praying he won't be swatted before he escapes. An alien, hostile country. Reuben wonders how he's managed not to see it all these years. No way to put the parts of this face together. The old, yellowing eye staring down at him belongs to no one. It's embedded in a face Reuben has always called Mr. Tucker's face, the ancient, giant carpenter, electrician, handy, fix-it man you see bent by the weight of his oversize toolbox plodding up Hamilton, down Tioga, across the trolley tracks on Frankstown. You see him everywhere, every day there's *woik*. The eye goes its own way, dances to its own tune, dulling with age, crusted shut in the morning, oozing a teary film, raw and irritated by brick dust as he pounds and scrapes each brick clean again, usable again. An eye with a life of its own. Like the mouth, the ears, the scars that refuse to be part of anything bigger, anything more, scars that are all Reuben sees as he searches for Mr. Tucker's face in Mr. Tucker's face.

See this rag I got in my hand. I wipes sweat wit it. I blows my nose. Carries it now cause water just rolls out my eyes. Be sopping wet by the end of the day. Ain't crying, Mr. Reuben. I ain't crying. I'm mad, not sad, so they ain't tears, Mr. Reuben. Don't know when I last had time for tears. Don't remember ever crying and now I got this water just rolling out my eyes and cain't stop it. Ain't tears, ain't blood. Cain't stop it. Started soon as they turned me loose. I wiped it. Hour or so they wet again. Like some little peeing baby. Sometimes I think maybe I'll just keep this bandanna wrapped round my eyes for good. Swear that's what I'd do if it wasn't for me needing to woik.

He twists and untwists the flowered rag. A big farmer. A hundred-year-old country boy don't know what ails him, what hit him. Here he is in the big city and his mama gone, papa gone, brothers and sisters, cousins and aunts, rice and beans and preacher gone and Reuben can't help him, can't let him go.

Reuben dumps two spoonfuls worth of Taster's Choice in his mug. The coffee grit bursts into foam which climbs and bubbles to the lip of the cup before it sighs, settles, and Reuben tops it with more hot water from his red pot. Each sound registers, each minute hiss and burble and clink of the coffee-making ritual, as does his heartbeat, as does the halting, irregular

193

breathing of the trailer offstage, in corners out of sight, register-
ing although no one is at home to listen. Reuben answers the old
puzzle for himself, smiles at Muybridge because it's the sort of
puzzle the bearded billy-goat photographer likes to play with: If
no one's in the forest when the tree falls, does the tree's dying
make a sound? Reuben is absent and these woods are full, mur-
muring, sputtering, metal and wood and paper and plastic and
glass doing what they do, though he is far away, sealed in the
tight, dark room of his own troubles, his story he turns to now
as he swallows one glob of coffee so hot he shivers.

... may have been an impostor or simply a do-gooder.
In either case, he didn't lack for clients ...
   Most of his clients were poor persons who either could
not afford the fees of a regular attorney or were unsure
about how to engage one ...
   ... readily available and eager to assist, at little
cost ...
   According to many who know him, he has been adept
at mediating disputes, handling paperwork, and untan-
gling problems with government bureaucracies. . . .
   You don't necessarily have to be a lawyer to do such
work ...
   ... his lawyerlike representations either helped or hindered the matters at hand ...
   ... he was finally arrested as a phony and jailed overnight ...
   Unquestionably, he provided considerable assistance—
some of it legal or quasi-legal in nature—to many of his
appreciative neighbors ...
   The possibility that for years he may have provided
misguided advice to many who sought his help, however
well intentioned, cannot be lightly dismissed.

Reuben stares at the ping of light reflected in the tarry pool
of coffee. His hand is too shaky to touch the brimful mug.
Important documents, life-and-death matters, litter the desk

top, hide beneath the newspaper. He waits for the trembling to subside, drums messages to himself with the fingers of one bad hand rat-a-tat-tat against a bare corner of the desk. It's all there in the newspaper. Unbelievably plain and simple. His life story in three hundred words or less staring back at him. The unvarnished truth.

He dips like a bird into a rain puddle. Slurps the coffee he can't raise to his lips. Mohammed to the mountain, because the mountain won't rise up on its hind legs and slouch to him. He sees a shadowy face in the black circle. The whites of bubble eyes. Is it his lost brother staring back? Is it Reuben, ugly as sin, trapped like he's always trapped, inside someone else's wish to be free? Distorted like a face in a spoon. He should own a spoon. He does somewhere. In a box or bag or underneath something. Two or three white plastic spoons and a white plastic fork too, somewhere. The fork wouldn't do him much good. Except he could plunge the tines into his eyes. Pay for his crimes. What crimes? Was it his fault Reuben's head was stuck on a pole at the gates of the city? Was he the one drawing and quartering and dragging the pitifully small corpse through the streets? If they'd lynched him, raped him, ground his bones to make their bread, why should he feel guilty? Who, if he wept in this sardine can of a trailer, on this dull summer morning, would hear? Would care? And if no angel listens, if no angel hears, sly, sly, slick Mr. Muybridge would claim none of it ever happened.

Reuben, you know what you look like sitting up there on that stool . . . a pile of shit. Anybody else ever tell you that's what you look like cause that's just how you look. Like a pile of shit them little shit beetles dragged in crumb by crumb and heaped up on that stool.

Dung beetles, Wally. Dung beetles because they roll balls of dung around their eggs to protect and feed the larvae. The Egyptians believed the beetle was sacred because it seemed to be creating itself when it emerged from the empty earth. A royal scarab pushes along the disk of the sun, brings light, warmth, the possibility of rebirth. Dung beetles. Your profanity's much more effective laced with polite words here and there to give the impression you know something besides the vulgar art of swearing. And no. I've never been called a pile of shit. Someone once pointed out my resemblance to an African termite mound. The pointed crown, the unfortunate, irregular protuberances. I found that comparison intriguingly suggestive. But no. You're the first to call me a dung heap.

Pile of shit, Reuben. Don't care how much your silk suit cost.

[*And before this exchange, leading to it . . .*

Why did you kill him, Wally? (They've met for lunch at Stanley's—Wally seated in a chair, Reuben across from him on his special barstool, legs chopped down so it's shorter than a stool, taller than a chair, so he can see eye to eye.)

What you say?

Why'd you kill him? I know you did. I just don't know why.

How'd you find out?

Maybe you could answer my question first.

How'd you know, Reuben? This is nothing to play with, old man. What the fuck do you know? And keep your damned voice down.

I guessed; you confessed. Comes out to the same thing. A little of both probably. I knew you'd killed someone. I guessed it was a man, not a woman. I guessed it had happened recently. I guessed you needed to talk to somebody about it. You have been talking about it, confessing in your fashion, the last few times we've met. The smell of killing's on you, my friend. The shadow. I know when I'm in its presence.

Back to the above, Reuben speaking again.]

It's not me you're angry at. You didn't hurt me and I certainly intend you no harm. Besides, I'm sworn to secrecy. You're my client. Let's talk. Let's be frank. Name-calling's rather beside the point.

Wally resists a reference to Reuben's pointy head and pointy beard and pointy rat teeth and asks instead, calmly, politely, What is the point?

196

I think you'd better tell me.

Tell me something first. Who are you? What are you? You called me your client. Client of what? What do you call yourself doing, Reuben? Who do you think you are?

The possibility that for years he may have provided misguided advice to many who sought his help . . . cannot be lightly dismissed.

I draw up papers. Route them. Grease palms which need to be greased. Pay one of these fools to sign as attorney of record whatever needs to be signed. My stuff goes through—neat—fast—correct. Most business never proceeds that far. Never becomes official. It's a word here, a promise there, a favor asked or returned, *quid pro quo* barter or bargain, a draft choice for future considerations, that's how things usually work. A few dollars pass from hand to hand, wheels are set in motion, or stopped, or lost or forgotten or stamped, sealed, and delivered. My clients get by, get through. A sort of sleight of hand. This paper, this plea—now you see it, now you don't. Presto chango—the bear goes over the mountain, the mountain comes to Reuben—whatever it takes. I understand how the law works; my clients' business gets done. After a thousand years I've become pretty good at what I do. It's easier than shining shoes. Pays about the same, except I dress better now, project a different image. Deal with a better class of people now. Our people, Wally. Homewood people. The best.

. . . his lawyerlike representations either helped or hindered the matters at hand.

Most of the time I'm here in Stanley's. Eavesdropping, you might say. Keeping up. Refining my trade. Loafing. Doing not a damned thing. Daydreaming. Contemplating the navel of the universe. I put in long hours. Can to cain't, as the old folks used to say. I like to stay busy. Time moves faster that way.

I conduct my downtown business in Stanley's. Seldom enter a courtroom. You might see me on the front steps or in the halls of the courthouse but I can do my people more good right here. When I bring my clients' troubles downtown they usually get handled inside Stanley's four walls. The atmosphere's more congenial. It's more efficient to work things out here. Often just a matter of pondering a problem, thinking it through. By the time a solution presents itself, the problem's taken care of. Almost as if what I sit here and imagine in Stanley's comes true. You might understand what I'm saying better if you turn it around. What happens back in Homewood, in the streets, runs its due course, resolves itself while I dream up a resolution in Stanley's. I guess at what's happening outside. My guesses usually turn out to be on target so there's a sort of coordination, a match between the event and my imagining of the event. Which comes first is immaterial. My clients want their troubles resolved. They bring them to me. In time things straighten out. What's hot gets colder. What's cold, sooner or later warms up again. I get credit. But I also give credit. And I'm cheap in the first place, as you know, Wally.

Turns out I'm a sort of go-between. I stand between my clients and their problems. I intercede, let them step aside awhile. I take the weight. For a while at least ease a bit of their burden. I invite my clients to depend on me, lean on me. When I retire from the picture, things are often better. And if they're not, I'm available to blame. I'm not the agency of change but I'm my clients' bona fide agent. Reuben on the battlefield, in the smoke, on the firing line. People need that. I offer that service.

Mostly I listen. Oftentimes it's enough. More times than not, it's all anyone can do for anybody in real trouble. With full knowledge that I can change little or nothing I do my best. What more could anyone ask?

. . . he was finally arrested as a phony and jailed overnight.

The peace of mind which comes from being assured you have an advocate, someone on your side, seeing to your interests. I try to provide that illusion. I give our people their day in court. And if I may say so myself, my clients receive a species of justice here in Stanley's they seldom receive up the street, around the corner, and down the block in the courthouse. If you know what I mean.

You're full of shit, Reuben. Look like it and now you sound like it, too.

We're back to name-calling, then.

Hey. You're the one snitching on yourself. Charging people for daydreams, illusions, taking people's money then sitting around on your ass doing nothing.

I'm not on trial, Wally. We're here because you wanted to see me. You said you needed help.

Not from you. Not after you done let me peep the kind of help I'm likely to be getting. . . .

If you know a better kind of help for your troubles . . .

Hey. I ain't in trouble yet. Forget that shit about killing somebody. It's the scam over at the university. I don't want my ass in a sling behind that. Thought you might help.

And the man in Chicago?

Dammit, Reuben. How the fuck you know so much about Chicago? Was you hiding in one the toilets?

I know what you've told me.

I told you about the dude on the plane. The one told me the crazy story.

No. You didn't tell me that story.

Well, I meant to tell you.

Tell me now.

Nothing to tell. No point in going back to Chicago either. If a man's dead, he's dead. What good would it do him or me to return to Chicago? Don't even know if I could find the bathroom . . . maybe there ain't no goddamned bathroom. Maybe it's all in my mind.

The worst place for it to be, Wally.

Dead or not. I got away with it. What the fuck I want to go back for. I'm free. . . .

Yes and no.

Always yes and no. I've heard that yes/no shit a thousand times, Reuben. Tired of it. Anyhow, this time it's all yes. If I killed a man, he's dead. Yes. They burn niggers for killing white men. Yes. Ain't nobody in the world connected me with no stiff in Chicago, and never will. Yes. So I got away with murder, if there was a murder. Yes. I'm free and yes that's damned sure how I want to stay: free. Yes. *No* got nothing to do with any of

199

it. Except. Hell no. I ain't traipsing back to Chicago and confessing. Hell no.

Yes. What point would confessing serve.

No point. That's right.

Right.

Suppose I did. Suppose I was fool enough to go back. And suppose they don't have no dead man in a cooler, no unsolved killing they need to pin on a nigger. What they gon do with me confessing? Cops would think I was crazy. Lock me up till they need a fall guy, then put me out there, public enemy number one. We got the nigger did it. Here he is, folks. Had to blow his balls off but here he is. Shit. They'd put me in the bank. Save my ass for a rainy day. And that's what would happen if nothing ain't happened in Chicago. If I dreamed the whole bit. They'd burn me for thinking about murdering a white man.

You wouldn't be the first.

Damned right, I wouldn't. So what I look like returning to the scene of the crime. Maybe there ain't even been a crime.

Would be nice to know, though, one way or the other, wouldn't it?

Who I'm spozed to ask . . . the dead man . . .

If you returned, retraced your steps, followed yourself, it might lead you . . . you might remember.

Lead me in a circle. Lead me right back to what I'm saying here. Chicago's a noose and I'd be putting my neck in it. Why I got to remember? Why I need to know? I got away with it. Whatever *it* was. Killing one. Or dreaming of killing one. They owed me one at least. The thought I might have collected makes me feel real good sometimes.

And other times . . .

Here you go again. Yes and no again.

I didn't say it, Wally. You said it.

No. I don't always feel good. No. My whole life it's been one thing or the other like this that keeps me jumping. Keeps me from being where I want to be. Keeps me awake at night. Keeps me running.

It may be too late.

For what?

To sort it out. What you did. What they did to you. But the past lives in us. There must be ways we can change things. Make them better.

Like sticking my neck in a noose. Like asking the crackers for mercy. Crazy as a bedbug. And they'd be right thinking I was crazy cause nobody but a crazy man would go back to Chicago.

Something might work out.

Yeah. Might. And then again *might* not.

Yes and—

No way. Wally ain't risking his neck on no *might*.

The abstract guilt.

Guilty or not. I wouldn't have a Chinaman's chance. They'd waste me either way. You know I'm talking truth, Reuben.

I know. I know. And the truth seems less than enough. It won't set us free. We need more. Truth just starts the wheels turning. There's more . . . we need more than truth to save us now.

Not my skin. Not this time. I'm staying far away from Chicago. Staying home.

Where we all belong, I suppose. In our bottles with the caps screwed on tight.

What?

Till someday somebody comes along and rubs the glass. The magic touch setting our magic free.

We finished discussing Chicago, ain't we?

I believe we have.

You want another drink, old man.

I could do, Wally.

The band begins playing again. A serenade of the sounds of the bar, the city, the country, the whole eggshell earth. The eye of a funnel closes in on itself, spinning like a whirlpool, lines of force like ribs whirling in its white maw. A device in old movies for dissolving from one scene to the next. The picture on the

201

screen whorls down a drain. Darkness gulps the swirl of actors, actresses, the elaborate set topples too, tumbling, wiped out. Script reads: *Dissolve to . . .*

Reuben makes it a ranch. Home, home on the range. Blue Wyoming sky, gray waves of sage. Stars and Stripes crackle like tinsel in a fabulous sky. Everybody's happy, wherever they are, whatever they're doing. The ranch house, the cookhouse, the bunkhouse, in the saddle riding the range, fishing, singing round a campfire, mending fence, steering the steers, daydreaming, nightdreaming, climbing a ladder of stars and bars to heaven and back. Yippee. I. Oh . . .

Later that night, deeper that night, blood flows from the open wound. The humiliation of jail, the insinuations of the news story, hurt Reuben more than he believed he could be hurt again. But there was something else too. He'd found his brother's hiding place. Joined him down there in the catacombs beneath the city streets, the place legend had it the city buried its mistakes, its incorrigibles, its lies. The statue was warmer tonight. Two's breathing an itch on Reuben's bony chest. Lost and found. Lost again . . . that was the rhythm joining them, keeping them apart. The dream began in a cell. Reuben can hear his feet measuring space, pitty-pat, pitty-pat, quick gimpy steps. Four down, four across, four back, four down again. Each step a nail, from each footfall springs the spear of a dragon's tooth. The prisoner fashions the mouth which swallows him. He verifies its length and width, defines his cell as he measures its limits, makes it real with each set of sixteen steps. The walls grow thicker, higher, each time he stops before them and changes direction. Who built the cell? Who'd dreamed of Reuben caged within it? Who had invited Reuben to be a partner in the enterprise? You, my little buddy, my fine, unfeathered friend, have the responsibility of watering and nursing, keeping my invention alive. Even concrete and steel can't last forever. The finishing touch depends on you. You make the cell last and last when your pitty-pat monkey feet confirm the plans sketched on parchment. Four-by-four always. Or shall we stretch it to five-by-five like the fat, jellyball five-by-five singer, Mr. Jimmy Rushing. *Don't the moon look lonely shining through the bars.* The stars and bars. Mr. Kansas City five-by-five his own fat self can't cheer you up this morning, this dream, this long square night, all corners and pitty-pat and darkness forever.

Whose singing do you hear now? Shuffling chains dragged like a chorus of mourning women by the hair by the feet you trample them to make them sing. Divas, sweet mamas, Malindy, the fallen empress and lost ladies, where are they now? At your feet now, under your feet. African queens the spoils of war, the long train obscured by wailing dust, dust clouds and dust roosters and plumes of dust swirling like a feathered headdress over these captives dragged from the Land of Spirits. Say hi to your mama, your sister, your daughter. Say hi and goody-bye to Flora as wolfhounds bay at their spiked heels and the sun melts the tar of their eyes and the nougat of their hearts and their caramel breasts and those sugary thighs you rode in another country, proud as spit, proud as dust then, enveloping, grinning, her hair braided to your toes, her breath coming in rumbles and pants and the high-pitched squeal of a panther, like chains dragged through sand and over flinty rocks and a bed of shells and flailing open the purple sea.

You hear the captive women. But you see nothing. Blinded by long darkness, the deep darkness of your cell. You smell them on the breeze that lifts off the Nile and fans the delta. Crystalline light burdens the wind, keens like a razor so it flays you before you know you're cut. The ashy perfume of women singing is cool, dry hurt buried in their throats, like seed, like dead men wrapped in swaddling clothes, like the promise you made to Flora, who begs you to hurt them, to save her son, Reuben. You goddamned crackpot.

Deep in the hold. Above you in fading purple dust you hear the bellying of wind in the sail, a single mast, bent like a scimitar, bellying, slicing, scattering the fleet so each boat, the *Niña,* the *Pinta,* the *Santa María,* scoots like a bug over the current, at the whim of the wind. Wildly tacking. Edging toward one shore then leaning to the other. Chips zigzagging on a Ouija board. Opposites attracting, opposites driving the switchblade sails toward home. Not your home. You know, though you are blind as a bat in your cave, that they've stolen you and stolen the women from home and the only way home again is on a beetle's back, a journey like this, as far from home as this, the scattered pieces of you rolled in a ball, the ball rolling as this broad river rolls toward the sea, your gimpy-legged funeral barge inching forward, scratching its mark in sand till wind seals the wound. You know what you've known forever, that the sea carries you till it tires of you and the wind buoys you till it wearies of your weight and then the drowning, the falling through space till there is a last dark corner where you crouch like a seed crumbling, the scales dropping away, the bandages dry as camel dung, the soil you pinch and ball and roll till it covers you and you cover it, six legs, ten fingers, scratching at the shell. Through it, around it. Pushing the egg before you like the golden scarab on the king's necklace, the amulet guarding an empty pit where once his red heart beat.

Come northward to the court immediately; thou shalt bring this dwarf with thee, which thou bringest living, prosperous and healthy from the Land of Spirits, for the dances of the god, to rejoice and gladden the heart of the king of Upper and Lower Egypt, who lives forever. When he goes down with thee into the vessel, appoint excellent people, who shall be beside him on each side of the vessel; take care lest he fall into the water. When he sleeps at night appoint excellent people, who shall sleep beside him in his tent, inspect him ten times a night. My majesty desires to see this dwarf more than the gifts of Sinai and of Punt.

Oars fall in unison like the breathing bones of a rib cage and the sleek craft inches forward a frame at a time, holes in the water rushing closed before the feathering oars dip again. To the black Land of Spirits. Then home again, home again. You are a dwarf scavenged for Queen Hatshepsut's pleasure. Her tale-telling

Moor. Her tribute from the land of the Blacks. Chains binding you do not rattle and bump in the night. They are fragile as a spider's web, delicate as its eggs. You are free to die anytime you choose.

The oars stroke again. The water winces again as fingers poke at its eyes. Low hills along the riverbank chant hymns. An ox is turned to stone in its traces. Cornstalks rub and frisk, their roots braided unseen beneath the loam. Tomorrow the great river will flood its banks. It has already lost all trace of you in the well of its memory. You who partied in the splendid train of corsairs, feluccas, and panoplied barges with silk banners and your tubs of bawling animals, your ivory and gold and spices from the black land of Punt.

Then you awaken with a stiff neck. Home again after all. A real crook in your real neck you rub and squeeze and gingerly wobble your skull on its scrawny stock to trick out the kink. A real ache you earned in another dream you must have attended on the edge of your seat, a dream that insinuates itself one last time before you open your eyes.

One of the boys from Alpha Omega is driving the car. Much too fast. Out of control with you riding shotgun for some unknown reason. But there you are beside him in this big, ugly car at night in a busy city rumbling out of control. Then the inevitable explosion of glass and bright noise. The sea spits you out and you are high and dry and scared to death you're gone. Listening for your heart, holding your breath, afraid to check for damage because you may be busted up beyond repair, mangled into bloody bits and pieces, too numb to feel anything till you're reminded in one glorious spiral of agony that this is how it ends, how it ends. . . .

Reuben rubs and pinches and wonders why his neck hurts when the accident was only a dream. Only a dream. And as his overwrought, clumsy-bolted fingers protest the work he's calling upon them to perform, he wonders if he's covered by dream insurance. And what was the driver's name? And would his brother ever be free?

11

TOODLES

Things have a way . . . Toodles said that. Things have a way of . . . Toodles repeated the words three, maybe four times before she formed the rest of the sentence saying, Things have a way of working themselves out. Kwansa would smack most anyone trying to say something lame like that to her at a time like this. In someone else's mouth the words would make no sense. Coming from Toodles, Kwansa knew what the words meant, so Kwansa had nodded. A yes, a maybe . . . maybe. A nod that gave Toodles the benefit of the doubt because Kwansa understood why Toodles needed to say the words she was saying. And for an instant, quicker than Kwansa believed possible, she understood Toodles and maybe everybody else in the whole wide world was just as bad off as she was. Toodles trying her best to help, trying to find the right words and coming up lame with the wrong ones and saying them anyway because no words were the right words and nothing Toodles nor nobody else can say will help Kwansa and Toodles knows it as well as she knows

206

her own name but must say something anyway. It's like seeing Toodles in the grave. Toodles naked as a baby, naked down to the skin under her skin, the skin under her bones, under her eyelids, and Toodles doing nothing but trying to help, and Kwansa hurts for her, feels how bad Toodles feels. And Kwansa loses for an instant the pain she's carried into the Velvet Slipper. Gives it up for Toodles's pain, which is hot and mean and different, yet a twist of the same knife buried in Kwansa's gut. She hollers for Toodles and forgets her own pain though it flickers in Toodles's eyes, in those bullshit words.

Toodles finds her cigarettes in her bag. Calls them *nails*. Got to have me one these nails, girl. Toodles smells good. Good as money can buy. Something from a tiny bottle nobody could afford unless a junkie boosts it. You dab it on after your bath when your skin is bare and fresh. Pat it on in delicate little doo-dabs like hiding Easter eggs.

The Velvet Slipper's been open an hour. Early shift already punched in, each one taking his/her accustomed place. The world, as a poet said, full already of remarkable things. A small summer rain down doth rain. Dead singers' voices rising through the blinking Christmas-tree lights of the jukebox. Who says so? Who sings so? Who says these words or any words living or dead on this possible morning in the Slipper? Who cares? If it fits, wear it. Two women talking at the bar. No one is meant to overhear. They sit on tall stools. One woman is long and sleek. The other short, big butt, big-tittied, looks like five miles of bad road, nappy-headed, porkchop-lipped, overcooked eyes bout to fall out her face. And funky if you get close. Wearing clothes look fucked in and slept in. How many days she's been wearing them God only knows. And he's the only nose liable to poke up there between her plump thighs, under her frowsy wrinkled, too-tight toreador pants and bedewed, bedappled, BOed drawers to check out exactly where this lady's been and how long and what exactly she's been doing.

From a great distance, longer than the time it's taken all the voices that have ever told stories to tell their stories, in the welcome silence after so much lying, so much wasted breath, the women's voices reach us. Where we sit. Imagining ourselves imagining them.

Baby, you gots to take holt to yourself. Smoke curls from Toodles's mauve lips. Her shit is laid neatly atop the counter, as precise and potent as a chalk drawing on a clay floor inscribed to summon a god. Matches. Cigarette pack. A mauve napkin on which rests her tumbler of gin, a water-and-ice chaser. Some small-denomination bills, next to a sprinkle of silver (change, you dig, from the last drink and change for the next one) which she'll diminish gradually, pushing a coin or two with one purple-tipped finger to the bartender. Play me that sweet B-12, that fine C-9. Toodles holds nothing back. Her shit out front for you to see. Today. Yesterday. Tomorrow. Holds nothing back and gives nothing away either. Because whatever happens it's always Toodles sitting there on her stool. Cool. No more, no less than you saw last time she was sitting there. Contained, together. Toodles's style. What she's trying to teach and preach to Kwansa. Though Toodles knows better. Though she knows the pieces of Kwansa are scattered all over Homewood. And all the king's horses and all the king's men . . . Toodles knows. But what she knows best is being Toodles. And if Kwansa was Toodles she'd never have lost hold of what she needed to keep herself together in the first place. So that's all there is to it . . . all Toodles has to say.

Things have a way of working out.

Will they? For this soft plumpish woman. This long hard one who wiggles out of her softness like a snake shedding its skin fifty times in a day.

Smoke rises. Pads like a fat, lazy cat across a room, a thick-carpeted room full of people but empty as far as the cat's concerned, half stalking, half slinking away, absolutely unconnected. Kwansa studies her hands. They seem as unreal as her night in Toodles's bed, as familiar and distant as that woman's body which turned to her and covered her and wound her in netting of pure inky silk. The idea of loving another woman that way impossible, except last night it was not an idea, it was warmth and turning and her own pulsing woman parts strangely transformed, being themselves and more than themselves, doubled, touchable twice in the dark mirror of Toodles's long, fine limbs, her velvet skin. A skinny rag of a body and white, white nibbling teeth. They'd whispered because they didn't want to wake anybody, didn't want to scare anybody away.

Kwansa had lived in Toodles's bed then died there into a sleep so profound she'd awakened stunned, two hours gone God knows where and stumbling around for her clothes dizzy and weak like it was blood she'd lost not time. Two hours cut out of her, her body grabbing back what her mind was trying to deny it. How far away could you fall from yourself? Into the deep black sleep pit. The room had tilted, shivered, as she blinked back the light. She saw a woman moving slow-motion, quiet as a shadow, down a long street. A Homewood street but the houses peeled back on both sides so it's wide and a smoky kind of light softening the cement and bricks and windows. The woman's taking her time down this street Kwansa's seen a million times but can't name sitting up in Toodles's bed, wrapping her bare arms around her heavy-bosomed self, the softness of those titties which been getting her in trouble since she was eleven. On this broad street with the houses leaning away like they're tired or scared and the fog thin and curling like cigarette smoke, there are no shadows, no place for the woman who keeps coming closer, keeps taking her time, to hide. In the chilly morning air of the room, Kwansa rocks slowly, finds herself again, the saggy, yielding meat, the drifts of goose bumps pitting her bare skin. She sees the woman strolling closer through the haze as if she has all the time in the world. Behind her, the woman doesn't hear the street eating itself, chewing itself and spitting itself out and a cloud of bloody dust rising from the shambles. Not a sound as the street collapses, curls up on itself, inching closer and closer behind the dumb steps of the woman. Who can't or won't move faster because she is Kwansa and Kwansa's too drugged with sleep to warn her, help her. Except to tremble and come apart in a wave of shivers. Except to

209

squash her breasts with her elbows and bury the taut thrust of her nipples, deny the twin ghosts trying to suck her, two Cudjoes blind as the woman the street's about to swallow.

Kwansa remembers but none of it more real than her hands splayed on top of the Velvet Slipper's sloppy, long bar. In the dark her fingers had eyes. Sometimes in bed she could see them hovering under the covers, lightning bugs blinking in the night air. Whether she could see the eyes or not, she knew her fingertips glowed and had the power to picture things. They'd showed her Toodles. And it was like undressing and catching herself in the mirror without meaning to look. Seeing herself the way a man might, a man stretched on her bed in his shorts, desiring, measuring, anticipating. She caught a glimpse of herself and nodded to herself, yes, that ain't bad and yes plenty of that to go round and uh-huh, uh-huh. A flicker in the mirror separating what she sees all the time from what he's seeing for the first time. Separating what's familiar, what bores her, from what makes his dick hard. Stealing herself back again. Her fingertips reporting yes, on this woman's body there are surprises, and yes everything works fine. Turning to each other, all over each other, afraid to breathe, afraid to break the spell. And then all the feelings held in so long busting out. The crazy noiseless explosions of everything exploding at once, panting and screaming, the white teeth grinding on yours.

Touch me there . . . and here . . . put your . . . on my . . . Kwansa doesn't say a word, now or then. Her hands are like the strange, bright fish in the restaurant where Waddell said I'ma treat you tonight, babe. A huge fish tank along one wall, close to the table where they were seated and she'd never been in a place like it before. Or ever again with Waddell. A nice place. Just the two of them gliding in, her on his arm, him nine foot tall, like it wasn't no big thing, like him and his lady hung out in fancy places every day. Big white napkins and gleaming silverware bright as new money, the fish tank bubbling and wavy. Fish like they're wearing Halloween costumes. Capes and fancy gowns and masks with funny eyes and stripes and whiskers. Kwansa wondered why the fish were in a restaurant. Right beside where people eating. Fish eyes and sucking fish mouths. She was sorry for them a minute. Wondered if they ever ended up cooked. But the fish were too little. Too much glitter and fluttery hanging stuff to make a meal. The fish swam on, circling glass walls, circles inside the square, drifting through columns of bubbles, swaying plants, something that looked like the wreck of a building, like the columns holding up the bank on Homewood Avenue, crooked toy columns leaning against the water, some tilted, some in broken piles on the graveled bed. The fish swam on and Kwansa forgot them. Yet in the pauses, the moments Waddell stopped rapping while a waiter dishing out food from his tray like they ain't got the sense to help themselves, in the sinking instants when all she could think of was how quickly this would be over, how long it had taken to happen, how it would never happen again, Waddell her man, white men in white coats fussing over her ugly self, the soft music and soft lights and nice people in nice clothes quiet as mice eating their food, when everything stopped and Kwansa alone she felt her eyes drawn to the fish tank. She wanted to put her fingers through the glass, touch the silver and gold and rainbow shimmer. Touch them, cold and wet as they'd be. Quick as it would be over. The sucking mouths. The water rushing away through the holes her fingers had punched. She didn't say a word to Waddell about how scared she was, she didn't open her mouth now in the Slipper or then in Toodles's bed but inside, where she swam in silent, dogged loops, her eyes popped, her mouth sucking, she said touch me here, touch me there and Toodles's hands, her toes, her lips, had poked through the glass, answered Kwansa like she'd heard every summons.

Hey girl. Cool it, girl. Don't you get too excited, but guess who just walked in.

Toodles is facing the door. She whispers, Don't turn around. He don't see you yet. Don't scare the nigger away. Kwansa watches Toodles's eyes. The whites get bigger. Then the long matted lashes flutter. Toodles's way of saying, I see you nigger but I ain't in the mood to pay you no mind, her usual greeting to the traffic in and out of the Slipper all day. She ain't got the time. Knows you're there but ain't got nothing for you. Toodles's eyes narrow, her mouth is a hard slit, the purplish color darker now, smoldering it seems to Kwansa as she tries without turning around to see what Toodles is seeing. Toodles's eyes like eyes in the back of Kwansa's head and Kwansa is straining to learn how to use them, to read in Toodles's features the mystery of what is invisible, there and not there, behind her back.

Then Kwansa stops struggling. She sighs because it is so easy. Yes. Yes. Yes. Clear as in a crystal ball. She whips around. Swoops off her stool and buries ten fingers in Waddell's face before Toodles can holler stop.

Sheeit. Don't tell me. I was there. Them bitches kicked his ass. First one got him in the eyes and he's hollering, don't know what hit him. He's rolling on the floor and screaming and punching the shit out the bitch but she steady raking his face with them fingernails. Yeah, man. Like razors. Could see em drawing blood. And they rolling round on the floor. Nobody don't try to stop it, neither. Shit. Who wants to get down in that mess? Howling and thumping and biting and scratching. She's like a pack of alley cats on that poor boy's head. Nobody don't want nothing to do wit it. Not even when he finally got up on top her. Got the best of her, you know. Him being a man, you dig. But boy, she give him a go for a while. A hefty mama. You know Kwansa Parker, man. Nothing skinny bout that ho. She rip him up good before he gets on top. Sitting on her, you know, pinning her down. Crying and holding his face with one hand. Splat. Bam. Smacking her with the other. It was pitiful, man. Cause he was punching the bitch. Not no open-handed stuff. Bam. Punching down hard as he could in her titties and face. He's crying and the blood running through his fingers, down his cheeks, cause she ripped him good. She's twisting and groaning. She ain't give up even though she's under him. Taking those blows cause she's twisting side to side grabbing at him and calling him every motherfucker in the book. And a name . . . Must have been a name. *Where is he . . . Where's my Cooty* or some kind of name like that. Yelling it when he ain't got his fist in her mouth. Shit getting real bad. Past time somebody shoulda pulled him off. Pitiful, you know. Ho's mouth must been full of teeth and blood but she's still cursing him, still screaming that name, and I'm finally ready to break it up my ownself when *wham*. Quicker than you can say Up popped the Devil, Toodles grabbed herself a handful of the nigger's hair, jerked back his head, and run her razor cross his throat.

God damn. Ain't never seen nothing like it. Stroked him clean cross his throat like killing a chicken. Waddell start spouting blood like a fountain. Blood flying everywhere. And he's still sitting up spraddling Kwansa Parker, don't know he's dead yet. Grabbing at his throat, choking and spitting and blood flying like rain.

Well, he sit there a second longer like he's making up his mind what to do next. But the nigger dead already. You know what I mean. He's stone dead. Just don't know it yet so he sit up there glassy-eyed, bleeding on Kwansa Parker till she look worse than he do.

I wasn't more than a few feet away. Saw everything, man. He tried to squeeze his neck back together. Hold hisself in. Then he start twitching. Start to tilting. And Toodles. Toodles cold, brother. Slit his throat like she been slitting throats all her life. Then she stands back stock-still like a statue. Watching. Stays out the way of the blood he's shooting around. But then she step right up in his face. Bust him with both her hands. Hard but sorta delicate. Like she didn't really want to touch him and get all messy. She lean over and shove him hard with both hands on his shoulders and over he go. Toodles don't pay him no mind. She's stepped across him like he ain't nothing but a sack of potatoes and kneels down to where she can help Kwansa Parker up off the floor.

AND

Imagine a short, gimpy, immaculately dressed, bearded, brown man in the piss-colored hall of a public building. He stops before one of many identical doors ranged up and down the corridor. A square of pebbled, opaque glass, a number, are the door's only embellishments. If there are human beings behind it, or human beings anywhere else in the oppressive silence of the building, they have learned the trick of invisibility because the sole sign of life is this little, big-headed man pulling a gold watch on a chain from his vest pocket, consulting it like a snapshot of an old, long-unseen friend, hesitating another half second, then pushing through the door, which is the same nasty colorless color of everything the building is, as far as we can see.

He leaves the door ajar behind him. We think we hear the ticking of the timepiece he's replaced in his vest pocket but it's too loud for that, it's his heart or another clock chiming in a tower hidden from our view. Even if the tower were visible, we'd miss it because our eyes are directed by the eyes of the dwarfish man to the face of a boy inside the room. There is no accounting for the power that connects the dwarfish man's bearded face with the young face, half a head shorter. A beam of light fuses them. We are momentarily blinded. We see nothing but a luminous, smoky shaft, as for an instant we are surrounded, drowned by light. The sides and backs of our skulls have dropped away. It's scary, but seemly, doesn't hurt. If others are in the room, they shouldn't be. So we lose them and lose ourselves and ride the wave of light long enough to hear the old man say,

Hello. You're Cudjoe, aren't you? I'm sorry I couldn't get here sooner. Don't be frightened. Your mother sent me. She said she loves you and will see you soon and everything's going to be all right. My name's Reuben. I'm here to take you home.

FOR THE BEST IN PAPERBACKS, LOOK FOR THE

In every corner of the world, on every subject under the sun, Penguin represents quality and variety—the very best in publishing today.

For complete information about books available from Penguin—including Pelicans, Puffins, Peregrines, and Penguin Classics—and how to order them, write to us at the appropriate address below. Please note that for copyright reasons the selection of books varies from country to country.

In the United Kingdom: For a complete list of books available from Penguin in the U.K., please write to *Dept E.P., Penguin Books Ltd, Harmondsworth, Middlesex, UB7 0DA.*

In the United States: For a complete list of books available from Penguin in the U.S., please write to *Dept BA, Penguin, 299 Murray Hill Parkway, East Rutherford, New Jersey 07073.*

In Canada: For a complete list of books available from Penguin in Canada, please write to *Penguin Books Canada Ltd, 2801 John Street, Markham, Ontario L3R 1B4.*

In Australia: For a complete list of books available from Penguin in Australia, please write to the *Marketing Department, Penguin Books Australia Ltd, P.O. Box 257, Ringwood, Victoria 3134.*

In New Zealand: For a complete list of books available from Penguin in New Zealand, please write to the *Marketing Department, Penguin Books (NZ) Ltd, Private Bag, Takapuna, Auckland 9.*

In India: For a complete list of books available from Penguin, please write to *Penguin Overseas Ltd, 706 Eros Apartments, 56 Nehru Place, New Delhi, 110019.*

In Holland: For a complete list of books available from Penguin in Holland, please write to *Penguin Books Nederland B.V., Postbus 195, NL–1380AD Weesp, Netherlands.*

In Germany: For a complete list of books available from Penguin, please write to *Penguin Books Ltd, Friedrichstrasse 10–12, D–6000 Frankfurt Main 1, Federal Republic of Germany.*

In Spain: For a complete list of books available from Penguin in Spain, please write to *Longman Penguin España, Calle San Nicolas 15, E–28013 Madrid, Spain.*